Also by Mark Douglas

Pestus Fantasticus Californius
Countryside, December 1978

Good Catch!
Videomaker, June 1993

USS HOQUIAM PF-5 series

Resurrected
Road to Hungnam
Hocky Maru

USS HOQUIAM PF-5

Knock Off Ship's Work

Mark Douglas

Order this book online at www.trafford.com
or email orders@trafford.com

Most Trafford titles are also available at major online book retailers.

Printed in the United States of America.

ISBN: 978-1-4669-5780-0 (sc)
ISBN: 978-1-4669-5781-7 (e)

Library of Congress Control Number: 2012916812

Trafford rev. 09/14/2012

North America & international
toll-free: 1 888 232 4444 (USA & Canada)
phone: 250 383 6864 • fax: 812 355 4082

PREFACE

Last time, in HOCKY MARU, Lieutenant Marston and Seaman Apprentice Lee Harrison Stewart visited ComNavFE (Commander, Naval Forces, Far East) Legal Office in Yokosuka and made a deposition regarding Lee's former girl friend, Betty Echols' claims, and the Clatsop County, Oregon District Attorney's felony charges.

After a brief yard period in January, Hoquiam departed for Sasebo, the great harbor on the Japanese Island of Kyushu, to take up new duties under Commander, Service Squadron 31 (ComServRon 31).

Things looked up when they were ordered to escort ships to Wonsan, North Korea. While there, the Captain pleaded with Commander Task Group 95.2 (CTG 95.2) to assign them tasks more in keeping with their designation of Patrol Frigate. The task group commander, in an effort to put Captain Brown in his place, assigned him to Task Force 77 in the screen.

Back in Wonsan, the ship came along side the Saint Paul CA-73, with Admiral Smith, Commander Task Force 95 (CTF 95) embarked. Captain Brown asked him for better assignments.

Success! Hoquiam would join the bombardment group but first she would anchor in Wonsan harbor hoping to tease the Chinese Communist Army into bringing their big guns out of hiding to blast the Hoquiam. The Captain would hold Personnel Inspection in front of the Chinese Army in an effort to insult them.

When CTF 95 started sneaking ships into the harbor in the dark of the night to blast communist supply boats, the Hoquiam caught a submarine contact and attempted to board and capture it.

The Hoquiam returned to Sasebo for engine tune up. As a result, the Hoquiam picked up about a half-knot additional speed.

On their first liberty in Sasebo, Lee and his shipmate Charles were shocked to find their Yokosuka girl friends Kimiko and Kiki, waiting for them at the Fleet Landing.

The drone operation got one more chance for use. Upon return to Yokosuka, the drone catapult, baggage and aircrew were removed to the joy of the Hoquiam crew.

In port, half the crew is given Rest and Recuperation leave (R&R) to Nara, the ancient capital of Japan. Lee and Charles got the nod.

The story closed as the ship prepares to leave on its next assignment: return to the bombardment group in Wonsan, North Korea.

APRIL 1951

1545, April 8, 1951
USS Hoquiam PF-5
SRF, Yokosuka, Japan

The 1MC speaker clicked and scratched. A Bosun's pipe shrilled.

"Set the Special Sea and Anchor Detail. All hands not actually on watch, Quarters for getting underway. Uniform of the day for enlisted men is undress blue baker with peacoat and raincoat. The smoking lamp is out throughout the ship." The 1MC clicked off.

Stewart hid his face, sucked in his cheeks, and grinned as the other guys in the Radio Shack pissed and moaned about having to go to Fair Weather Quarters in this weather. Lee was on watch copying fox and wouldn't freeze his ass off as they got underway.

I'll keep my thoughts to myself, otherwise I just might find myself going to to Quarters for getting underway. (He he he he.)

1725, April 8, 1951
USS Hoquiam PF-5
Underway
Yokosuka to Songjin, North Korea

A static hiss issued from the 1MC speaker over Stewart's head. The Boatswain's Mate of the watch drew a deep breath, piped Attention, and announced,

"Secure from Special Sea and Anchor Detail. On deck, Section Two, relieve the watch. Shift to the underway uniform of the day—dungarees for enlisted men; open necked khaki shirt and trousers for chiefs and officers. The smoking lamp is lit throughout the ship." The speaker clicked off.

Stewart was still on fox. Masters manned the CW circuit and Roney had the unclassified message board. They, the duty crew, watched and waited with baited breath as the rest of the gang slammed through the office door to tell them how cold they were.

Muttering, they left, quietly walking through Officers' Country, dropping down the ladder to the Mess Deck and walked forward and down another ladder to their compartment on the Second Deck to change into dungarees.

Stewart braced his legs and raised his knees up under the desk as the ship began rolling in Sugami Nada before the open sea. His typewriter keys continued to clack as he copied each character from the Guam fox broadcast.

Well, we're on our way again.

Stewart glanced under the chair to make sure all four feet were in their anchor sockets. He settled back in his chair to the humdrum detail of copying the CW (Morse code) George Fox broadcast. (CW means Continuous Wave.

Turning a transmitter on and off rapidly forms the dots and dashes that make letters, numbers, and punctuation marks as devised by Samuel Morse. Radiomen referred to Morse code dots and dashes as Morse code, code, or CW.)

For Stewart, code was automatic now: the CW code stream seemed to flow directly from his earphones to his fingers, which mechanically pressed the correct keys or moved the carriage back with the carriage return lever on the typewriter. He stared ahead without seeing what he typed as he worked. Sometimes, Stewart looked down at the page to see what he had just copied.

When he finally crashed in his bunk for a few hours, Stewart continued to copy code in his sleep—it was always with him.

The metal earphones were adjusted tightly to his head to better hear the code, numbing both ears after a while. Separating the one CW signal he was concentrating on from several other CW signals always present was like pulling a single musical instrument from a symphony orchestra—or maybe a jazz band. That built up pressure in his temples causing headaches. When that happened, he would pop two or three APC (strong aspirin humorously known as Radioman candy) into his mouth.

Even so, Lee could completely disengage his mind from the code, as he did now, remembering last night with Kiki. Her soft, warm body snuggled up next to him and wiggled around to see how sleepy he was. He wasn't.

Later, Kiki watched him put his uniform back on. When he leaned over to kiss her goodnight, she got up and hugged him.

"Oh Lee San, I am going to miss you," she cried.

He looked at her puzzled. "Are you going back to see your Mother again?" Lee asked.

She shook her head. "Your ship is leaving tomorrow for Korea." Tucking her face into his neck, she said, "you will be up there for a month, maybe more."

Exasperated, Lee asked "What else do you know? Are we coming back here or going to Sasebo? Tell me, Kiki." She shook her head, gave him a final hug and kiss before dropping back down in her bed.

Kiki knew more, but she was still angry at the questioning she had undergone by the Japanese police and observed by the U.S. Naval Intelligence personnel, about how she knew the Hoquiam would be coming into Sasebo. No one was supposed to know secret military ship movements. No one had told that to the girls in Yokosuka, Sasebo and Kobe. They always seemed to know what was going on. Kiki wouldn't answer any more of his questions about that subject.

The next day began with a windless, steady, cold rain that turned to thick snowflakes before noon—and no word or sign of leaving for Korea. Stewart wondered if this was her idea of a joke, then realized that she would not do that. Not only that, she told him about it last night after they wildly, passionately made love, when he was ready to leave for the Hoquiam. Stewart had laughed it off on the way back to the ship.

"Ding ding—Hoquiam arriving."

The Captain is back earlier than I expected.

Stewart glanced at the clock and closed the filing drawer in the four-drawer cabinet. Picking up the unclassified message board, he opened the door and waited for the Captain to pass. He fell in behind the Captain in march step up the passageway to the Captain's state room.

"Make it fast, Stewart. I have Officer's Call in five minutes. We're getting underway at 1600."

Stewart stared in surprise. Recovering, he thrust the board at the Captain and stuttered.

"C-c-c-c-captain, Kiki told me last night we were leaving today but I didn't believe her."

Captain Brown's head snapped up from the message board and glared at Stewart. "She did what,?" he grated with his head thrust forward at Stewart.

Stewart flinched and moved back a step from the Captain's anger.

Don't kill the messenger, Captain!

"Yessir, she told me we were pulling out today. Sorry, Captain, just telling you what I heard, sir." Stewart said, apprehensively. Captain Brown was furious and threw his bridge coat on his bunk before snatching the message board from Stewart. The Captain scribbled his initials on all his messages and practically threw the message board back to Stewart. No doubt about it, the Captain was pissed.

Stewart came back to earth suddenly aware his chair was bouncing around more than usual. The ship was picking up speed, and as a consequence, sea motion was more pronounced. His receiver began to drift and he reached up to adjust his receiver.

Wonder what the fuck this is all about?

The 1MC clicked open—with the wind distorting the Bosun's Mate's pipe and voice. The ubiquitous Bos'un's Pipe sounded Attention. "Officers' Call—Officers' Call in the Wardroom in five minutes."

Again? Just had one right after the Captain came back.

1820, April 8, 1951
USS Hoquiam PF-5
Underway for Songjin, North Korea

Lieutenant Marston, the Executive Officer, sat in his chair holding his coffee cup against all the bouncing around, waiting. All but the Captain, the Officer of the Deck and the Engineering Watch Officer, arrived.

"Gentlemen, the Captain has asked me to bring you up to date on some intelligence that may affect our operations. First, the Peoples Republic of China has been building up troops and supplies along their coast opposite Taiwan. There are hundreds, literally hundreds of sampans and other small boats moored in every harbor.

"The Joint Chiefs of Staff believes those are meant to carry troops across the Formosa Straits to Taiwan. The Chinese Communist regime thinks we are so busy with Korea we won't protect Chiang Kai Shek and the Nationalist Chinese." He took a drag on his Chesterfield, blew it out slowly, and flicked the ash into his steel ashtray.

He leaned forward. "Second, the Navy has to show the Chinks they have made a miscalculation. With that in mind, JCS ordered Task Force 77 (TF 77) to move South. They are on a course that will lead them through the Korea Straits Western Channel right now, heading for the China Sea.

"Washington believes that showing the Flag will be enough to discourage Peking and their new leader, Mao Tse Dung." He sipped some coffee and looked at the faces around the table. The new, young officers looked a little nervous.

He continued. "On the other hand, Washington also points out this could be a feint to draw Task Force 77 away from making air strikes on North Korea. That scenario gives the Chinks an opportunity to move desperately needed supplies and troops down to their lines.

Mr. Marston looked around the Wardroom table at his officers. "Admiral Smith, Commander, Task Force 95, agrees with United Nations Command, or UNC (he pronounced it "unc", as in uncle), in thinking this is the case. Therefore, Task Force 95 is going to concentrate efforts along the Northeast coast watching for troop and supply movements on their roads and rails."

He paused to take another sip and continued to look at the assembled officers. "New orders from CTF 95 just came in. Hoquiam is to make best possible speed to Songjin. So, instead of conserving fuel and steaming at our efficient 12.7 knots, the Captain has cranked it up to 18.2 knots. The Engineers will be watching the engines very closely and back off if any bearings heat up.

"We are to provide anti-submarine patrols for the destroyers and cruisers while they bombard Targets of Opportunity, harassment and interdiction fire, and respond to Fire Missions." Lt. Marston's emphasis on 'they' sounded like a petulant child complaining that those ships have all the fun.

"The Captain is going to ask to be treated like a destroyer and be assigned in regular rotation except for Task Force 77 Screen." Several chuckles and laughs erupted along both sides of the table, puzzling the two new officers who reported aboard for duty this morning.

THIS IS A F R S TOKYO WITH A BULLETIN DATELINED APRIL TENTH, UNITED NATIONS COMMAND TOKYO. MACARTHUR HAS BEEN RELIEVED. REPEATING, GENERAL DOUGLAS ARTHUR MACARTHUR HAS BEEN RELIEVED. FURTHER REPORTS AS THEY BECOME AVAILABLE. WE NOW RETURN TO THE PROGRAM IN PROGRESS.

There was stunned silence in the Wardroom.

"MacArthur relieved?"

"What the hell for?"

"It's about time someone saw that sonofabitch for what he is! He shuda' been hung by the balls for the Philippines, just like General Short and Admiral Kimmel for Pearl Harbor."

"Who's going to run the show now?"

Feelings were mixed about the general who said everyone would be home for Christmas—last Christmas. Officers and men alike remained unsettled, waiting for the other shoe to drop.

THIS IS A F R S TOKYO WITH THE SIX O'CLOCK NEWS APRIL TENTH NINETEEN FIFTY-ONE, AIRMAN MIKE DILL REPORTING. IN THE MOST RIVETING STORY TO COME OUT OF TOKYO SINCE THE JAPANESE SURRENDER, PRESIDENT HARRY S. TRUMAN HAS RELIEVED GENERAL OF THE ARMY DOUGLAS ARTHUR MACARTHUR. LIEUTENANT GENERAL MATTHEW B. RIDGEWAY, WHO REPLACED MAJOR GENERAL EDWIN H. WALKER A FEW MONTHS AGO, HAS BEEN NAMED AS MACARTHUR'S RELIEF. LIEUTENANT GENERAL WILLOUGHBY, MACARTHUR'S STAFF INTELLIGENCE OFFICER, SAID THERE WAS NO COMMENT AT

THIS TIME. GENERAL RIDGEWAY'S STAFF REPORTED ONLY THAT THE GENERAL WAS STUNNED BY THE ANNOUNCEMENT AND HAD NO COMMENT AT THIS TIME.

Commander Brown lowered his binoculars and beckoned to Chief Swenson, who moved rapidly to his side.

"Yes, Captain?" he asked.

"You can send that message now, Chief."

"Aye aye, Captain," he said as he saluted, which was returned.

The Chief ducked into the Signalmen's Shelter and pulled his message clipboard out.

"Barney, front and center," he called, beckoning to Barney.

"Send this message to the St. Paul, Barney," he growled while shoving the board at him.

"Got it, Chief," he responded as he scanned the message.

Barney stepped to the Port light and in one motion, snapped the power on, swung the light out, and aimed in the direction of the Heavy Cruiser with her nine eight-inch guns. Barney began sending '3'—for CA-73—rapidly. The signal light lever springs squeaked quietly and rapidly. Before he had sent three 3's, the St. Paul Signal Bridge answered. Barney sent the message.

P APRIL 11, 1951
FM PF-5

TO CTF-95
CA-73
BT
REPORTING FORDU X REQPER
COME ALONGSIDE TO DELIVER
PASSENGERS AND MAIL X REQPER
VISIT CTF-95
BT

(Hoquiam reporting for duty. Request permission to come alongside to deliver passengers and mail. Request permission to visit Admiral Smith, CTF 95.)

After the St. Paul rogered for the message, Barney and the Chief waited for the reply.
"They callin', Chief."
"Get 'em, Barney."

R APRIL 11, 1951
FM CTF 95
TO PF-5
BT
PERMISSION GRANTED X MY PORT
QUARTER X DINNER IN FLAG
OFFICERS MESS AT 1800
BT

1930, 11 April 1951
USS Hoquiam PF-5
Alongside U.S.S. St. Paul
Off Yo Do, Wonsan, North Korea

The 1MC opened and the bell sounded.

"Ding ding"

"Hoquiam arriving."

The Captain stopped at the Quarterdeck and spoke with the Officer of the Deck, then proceeded to his stateroom.

The 1MC opened again—Officers' Call—Officers' Call in the Wardroom.

The Boatswain's Mate of the Watch aligned the 1MC switches so that only the weather deck speakers were active. His Bos'un's pipe shrilled "Attention".

"All Hoquiam personnel on the Saint Paul—recall recall—return to the Hoquiam on the double."

On the Saint Paul, the Officer of the Deck heard the Recall and notified the Bugler of the Watch to play that message on their 1MC.

The Bugler played 'Attention' on their 1MC, and then the Boatswain's Mate of the Watch addressed the 1MC: "Now hear this. All Hoquiam personnel Recall Recall. Return to your ship on the double. All Hoquiam personnel Recall Recall. Return to your ship on the double."

The Captain strolled into the Wardroom with a satisfied smile on his face, removing his plastic-covered Scrambled Eggs hat as he did. He did not bother to remove his wet foul weather jacket. Nor did he sit down. He was moving to the Bridge in a moment. The other officers moved restlessly as they waited for the other shoe to drop. Something unusual was about to happen.

Commander Brown pulled his cigarettes and lighter from his jacket and lit up, taking a drag before he began to speak. "Gentlemen, this won't take long," he said with a grin. "We are now classified as", he held his fingers up crooking them to mimic quotation marks, "similar to a destroyer and will be given tasks similar to DD's and DE's, except Task Force 77 because of the speed differential.

"As soon as all stores, mail, and personnel are transferred between us, we depart on Northern Patrol. We go all the way to Sosura, just south of the Temon River mouth, to seek out and destroy enemy shipping—that is, any vessel carrying troops, munitions, or supplies." He unzipped his foul weather jacket and continued.

"The basic rule of engagement is attempt to board and search. If the vessel turns and runs, or shoots at us, shoot. For you new officers, the Temon River is the international border between North Korea and Manchuria. Questions?"

The Captain paused, looking at each of the officers.

"Okay, go count noses," he said and left for the Bridge.

Lt. Marston picked up the handset from its bulkhead clip and punched a buzzer.

"Quarterdeck, Boatswain's Mate of the Watch Barnes speaking, sir."

"Barnes, Quarters for Muster at Foul Weather Parade," he ordered. He did not wait for a response and fastened the handset in its holder.

The 1MC cracked open with its usual background hiss.

"Quarters Quarters for Muster at Foul Weather Parade Quarters for Muster."

C Division stood waiting in a single line backed up against the bulkhead outside the Radio Shack. They didn't wait long. Mr. Forsythe came out of the Wardroom and approached his division.

James saluted, returned by Lieutenant (jg) Forsythe. "All present or accounted for, Mr. Forsythe," and backed against the bulkhead facing Mr. Forsythe.

Mr. Forsythe cleared his throat. "Men, as soon as everybody is back aboard, we leave on patrol to seek out and destroy Chinks and Gooks in the sea lanes. It's very wet, foggy, and cold all the way up to the Manchurian international border." Stewart sucked in his breath with that. The rest of the Gang moved around a bit at that.

Manchuria? Them fucking Ruskies ain't gonna like that.

"Every time we see a ship we can't identify with IFF, we go to GQ. The U.N. has expanded the Naval Blockade to include the whole coast of Korea from the Bombline South of Wonsan, North to the Manchurian border. Any questions?" His eyes flicked left and right as he looked for a response with raised eyebrows.

"Relieve your quarters." Salutes were exchanged. Mr. Forsythe flipped his green curtain and disappeared into his stateroom across from the Radio Shack. The radiomen slipped into the Radio Shack to talk it over.

"Motherfuck," said James. "This is liable to get a little more exciting than I like." There were several growls from the rest of the Gang. However, if all went well there would be no big confrontation with the Soviets. The Chinks didn't have a Navy at this time.

The 1MC came alive without the shrilling Bos'un's pipe. The Officer of the Deck said, "Station the Special Sea Detail. Standby to get underway in ten minutes," and the 1MC clicked off.

Roney was taking most of the unclassified message board duty because he wasn't quite up to speed on George Fox yet. He was good on the CW Task Group Common. James had accused the two Seamen of squalling like a bunch of caterwauling cats yesterday, fighting over who got to work the Task Group Common CW circuit.

"This is the way it's going to be," growled James. "Stewart, you take fox, a little bit of circuit time, and a little bit of Board time." Stewart shrugged in disgust.

"Roney, you take the Task Group Common CW circuit, a lot of Board time, and keep getting some fox practice except when you're sleeping.

"But James," Stewart had protested, "getting to sit on the CW circuit is kinda like dessert after having to ride fox for a few hours."

"No shit, Dick Tracy, what gave you the first clue?" glared James. "The rest of us like to work the circuit, too. That's the way it's going to be—or would you rather run the Board all the time?"

"Well, let's not be too hasty, boss." Stewart put on his foul weather jacket, grabbed the Board, and slid out the door to make the rounds. He glared at the board.

Okay Message Board, let's hit the Bridge first.

Stewart cracked the starboard thwartship watertight door and pushed, hunched and pushed again against the gusty rain. He had to squint to see through the driving rain. In an optical illusion, the Saint Paul appeared to be moving backwards; Stewart knew they were moving forward. He stepped out and pirouetted on the wet deck, slammed and secured the watertight door with the quick release handle.

He tucked the board under his foul weather jacket and made his way up to the Bridge. He stopped off at the Signal Shelter to harass Barney and Red because the Captain and Officer of the Deck were busy clearing the near presence of the heavy cruiser.

Barney was singing something that sounded like 'My Darlin' Clementine', but wasn't. Red was grinning and shaking his head.

"You got a sore belly, Barney?" Stewart asked solicitously. "Is that why you're groaning? You ought to go see Porky," he suggested.

Red looked disgusted. "Now you done it, Stew. You encouraged him to sing it some more. We've been hearing it ever since we left Yokosuka," said Red shaking his head disgustedly. Barney took a deep breath.

"Cigaretto, chacoletto,
chewing gum for twenty yen.
Sukahochi?
Never hoppen,
sayonara,
cum again!"

Barney laughed, "I heard that at my favorite place in Yokosuka." Then he looked sour. Hunching deeper into his foul weather jacket, he said, "This is miserable shit, you know that, Stew? I could do without this weather all day long. By dinner time, I am going to be so fuckin' cold again, I won't be able to eat," he said, sounding off, gruffly. He reached over, ran a fingertip down the glistening bulkhead. And inspected the tip. It was full of salt. Barney made a sound of disgust and stomped off to the other side of the bridge.

Stewart, shivering in the cold, wet wind stared after him in surprise. Barney was the quietest of his friends and seldom complained out loud. As Barney stomped back, Barney yanked the hood drawstrings of the oilskin jacket tight around his face; and rainwater dribbled down his face, already blotchy with cold. His foul weather jacket was minimally effective.

"I just measured the air temp at 37 degrees; the anemometer is averaging 20 knots with gusts up to 30 knots out of the North, and we're heading right into this shit. Isn't it ever going to get warm up here again?"

His shoulders slumped for a moment, and then Barney laughed and began humming Clementine again. Red threw his hands up in despair and headed forward of the Sonar Shack to get away from Barney's singing. Stewart shook his head, chuckled and moved to deliver the weather report to the Captain and Officer of the Deck.

"Weather report for you, Captain." Commander Brown took the board, scanned the message, scribbled his initials, and passed the board to the Officer of the Deck, Lieutenant Morgan. After scribbling his initials, he said, "Put a copy in the cubby, Stewart."

"Aye aye, sir."

One quick glance around and he returned to the Radio Shack.

12 April 1951
USS Hoquiam PF-5
On Station, patrolling in vicinity
Songjin, North Korea

The driving rain had stopped for the moment but the wind whipped the sea, blasting the wave tops into a stinging mist. Wind moaned and whistled in the rigging and safety lines, pushing people and the ship around.

The ship rolled, pitched, corkscrewed, and occasionally bucked as the dark green seas bunched, peaked, and slammed into the shuddering ship as it drove northward through the heavy seas. It was like jamming on the brakes in a car. Some waves were higher than the 01 deck. Bits of harsh salt spray stung their faces, sometimes sea water.

Stewart, Red, and Barney were standing in their favorite evening hangout, hunched over on the 01 deck between Secondary Conn and the Stack, watching the seas. Knees and hips automatically adjusted to the ship's motion like skiers on a downhill slalom. They were silent, watching the waves roll by.

The Engineers began to clean the stack, running steam thru the tubes, causing hissing and strange noises, as the boilers were cleaned. Stewart, Red, Barney checked the wind direction to see if all the stack junk would fall on them or out to the sea alongside. They were safe.

Their foul weather jackets were zipped all the way up, collars up, white hats were reversed pulled down over their ears, hands jammed in jacket pockets. Cigarettes in their mouths were smoldering of their own accord, driven by the wind. Flecks of glowing cigarette paper tore off and flashed away.

The Colors above them flying at the Truck on the Mainmast—very large and easy to identify as the American Flag—rumbled and snapped constantly. Sharp but not completely unpleasant smelling smoke whipped across their faces. The young men had nothing to say. Wonsan was far behind them. The Sea of Japan was talking now, loud and clear.

Stewart looked at his buddies. "Did you remember that today is the sixth anniversary of President Roosevelt's death? He was at Warm Springs, Georgia for the medicinal baths."

Barney looked at him sourly. "Rumors say he was there with his girl friend. And, this means President Truman has been in office six years, pounding out the Missouri Waltz on his piano. Big deal!"

Red looked at both of them and shook his head in exasperation.

Shitbirds!

He raised his arm to look at his new self-winding Swiss watch, motioned with his arm and led the way across to the midships scuttle above Sickbay and the Laundry. In this weather, the hatch was secured but the round scuttle could be opened to get in and out.

They held their hats on their heads against the air rushing up out of the scuttle. They each squeezed down through the scuttle and walked forward to the chow line for Dinner. Barney, humming Clementine, was the last through the scuttle. He reached up and pulled the scuttle hatch down, twisting the round handle to secure it.

0230, 13 April 1951
USS Hoquiam PF-5
On Station, patrolling in vicinity
Songjin, North Korea

Stewart was on the midwatch listening to the Task Group CW Common and reading an Armed Forces Issue soft cover book, Zane Grey's Light of the Western Stars western novel.

Most of the time, no one sent anything on this net. But every five minutes, if he didn't hear any of the Task Group ships' signals, he typed "NO SIGNALS" in his circuit log. He ignored the presence of Russian, Chinese, Korean, and Japanese CW signals. This low frequency radio band was crowded with many different CW signals.

Stewart only had to pick up 'his' Task Group Common ships by sound, an operator's hand sending style—called fist—and call sign. It helped having the off frequency signals constantly sending messages. That told him by inference he was on frequency and the receiver was working properly.

Crack

The Hoquiam quivered and shook at the shock. Stewart reached up and tuned the RBA receiver slightly to bring that false off-frequency signal back to its same sounding tone. That way, he knew the signal from the Task Group commander would be right where he wanted it. He noted the time and entered the fact that Mount Thirty-three had fired.

Stewart waited with his fingers on the dial. He suspected that would not be the only shot fired. He was right.

Crack crack crack crack crack crack crack

Both Mount Thirty-one and Thirty-three opened up, firing as fast as they could. He lost count after forty-seven shots when his Task Group circuit got busy. He concentrated and copied everything as he continually adjusted the RBA receiver, shocked out of tune by the firing.

Coyle, saying unkind things, was having even more trouble with the unstable RBS receiver, while he copied George Fox.

Roney was sitting on the deck in the corner, knees up to his chin, with life jacket strings fastened and helmet strap under his chin. His eyes got larger with the increased firing. Stewart nudged Coyle and pointed with his nose.

Coyle curled his lips in acknowledgment but didn't offer any comment. They were not at General Quarters. They were firing at a Target of Opportunity; probably another of those little pot-bellied steam engines pulling supplies and troops south.

Stewart was of mixed emotions. It was fun to watch from the Bridge when the Main Batteries were blazing away. If he asked Roney to take over so he could run to the Bridge with the Board, Roney might use that as an excuse to ask for more circuit time.

Screw it. I got to see this!

"Coyle, is it okay if Roney takes the circuit while I run the Board?" Stewart asked.

Coyle nodded as he continued to pound the keyboard in rhythm with the code coming in.

"Hey, Roney, take the circuit and give me the Board." Stewart watched Roney chew on the idea and begin a strange smile.

I knew it. He's gonna ask James for more time.

"Sure, Stew."

Roney removed his helmut and lifejacket and stood up, stretching from sitting on the deck so long. He stepped behind Stewart with a broad grin, taking the phones from Stewart's head, while Stewart typed in the log entry signing off to Roney, then rolling the paper forward to actually sign off, and leaning over to scribble his name on the log sheet with a pen. He rolled the paper back to the line below his signature and stood up so Roney could sit down.

Stewart grabbed his foul weather jacket, hat, and the Board and ran out. Mounts 31 and 33, the two 3-inch, .50 caliber guns continued with as rapid fire as possible. (The Loader waited for the Hot Shell man to capture the expended brass shell as it was ejected and the Loader inserted the next round into the breech.)

Stewart was breathing heavily from pounding up the ladder by the time he got to the flag bags behind the Open Bridge. Chief Swenson was there in his baseball cap looking through the Bridge binoculars. He glanced at Stewart and looked back down again.

"Stew, the Captain's going to have you for dinner one of these fine nights. Better stay back here by the bags."

"Roger, Chief. Couldn't sleep, huh?" Stewart asked with a solicitous tone, a grin on his face.

"Wiseass. With Thirty-one firing right over my head, what else was I going to do? Besides, I outrank a dumb Regular piece of shit like you, and am in charge of the Bridge."

"Yessah, Chief."

Chief Swenson is in very good humor. He eats this shit up. So do I.

"What's the target, Chief?" Stewart whispered, afraid he'd attract the Captain's attention.

"Another one of those Chink narrow gauge trains with a big load of supplies. Rangefinder caught a glow of the engine's firebox where they were hiding in a tunnel. Combat and Rangefinder zeroed in on the next tunnel about 3,000 yards down the line."

"Mr. Morgan and Chief Billons kept Mounts Thirty-one and Thirty-three on their toes, cocked and ready to fire, aiming at the track just before the second tunnel. When the train crew decided it was safe, they really fired up their boiler. We guessed that 'cause the glow got brighter and brighter. Then out they came, balls to the wall."

"Mount Thirty-three was right on target when the Captain gave the order to open fire. We could see sparks where the Common (a 3" inch explosive), hit the tracks by the second tunnel. The train tried to stop and back up. Too late! The Captain used mount Thirty-one with three or four shots to close the first tunnel's exit. Now, we're killing the entire train, car by car."

Chief Swensen and Stewart turned to watch their guns take out the train. Mounts Thirty-one and Thirty-three continued firing as rapidly as the crews could load Common and High Explosive projectiles to cut the rail and destroy the train.

Stewart could see the fires spotted along the length of the train. As Mr. Morgan directed their fire, dark areas of the train began burning. Two of the cars exploded like the Fourth of July.

"Cease fire, Mike. That's all of them."

"Aye aye, Captain." Pressing his microphone button, he spoke further to Mounts Thirty-one and Thirty-three.

"Captain, permission to clear Thirty-three on target, sir? Thirty-one is clear." Asked Lieutenant Morgan.

"Permission granted."

"Thirty-three—fire the round on target to clear your gun."

Crack

The Captain had a big smile on his face as he looked around the Bridge. Spotting Stewart, he beckoned to him. Flipping through the messages, he saw nothing for him or the Officer of the Deck.

"Enjoy the show, Stewart?"

He's still smiling.

"Yes sir, I sure did," he responded and waited, holding his breath.

The Captain handed him the Board and moved over to the Bridge binoculars to admire their handiwork.

Well, how about that?

Stewart looked forward at Thirty-one, then looked sharply. The barrel was glowing orange.

Wow, that fucker's really hot!

The Chief snapped his fingers to attract Stewart;s attention and motioned with his thumb; Stewart took the hint. As he descended the ladder, the ship turned away and headed to sea. He later found out that fifteen cars, the engine and over a mile of track had been torn up by their shelling. The two guns had fired 127 rounds of HE and COM at this target.

1540, 15 April 1951
USS Hoquiam PF-5
On Station, patrolling in vicinity of
Chongjin, North Korea

Fire Controlman Striker Jonas Evans stepped from behind his Rangefinder optics and looked down at the Open Bridge.

"Mr. Morgan?" He called.

Lieutenant Morgan, Officer of the Deck, studying a suspicious movement on the beach, frowned at the interruption, lowered his binoculars, twisted around and looked up at the Fire Controlman on duty at the Rangefinder.

"Sir, there's smoke coming out of one of the train tunnels. Is that a train waiting for us to leave, sir?"

Lt. Morgan rubbed his eyes in a vain attempt to remove the sting of the salt-laden air, checked the rangefinder bearing angle and lifted his glasses. He studied the shore for a brief interval, lowered his glasses, and stared emptily at the sea as he considered what they might be able to do.

Son of a bitch, I think we got us another Toonerville Trolley! (A reference to a Comic strip of the '30s and '40s.)

He looked up and said, "I think you're right, Evans. Good work."

Evens grinned, feeling pretty good about his finding.

Mr. Morgan reached down, pulled the phone from its spring clip and pushed the rubber-sealed button for the Wardroom.

"Wardroom, Jones speaking, sir."

"Captain, please," he said.

"Aye aye, sir." Jones twisted around and held out the handset to the Captain sitting in his chair, eating a late lunch.

The Captain, irritated and still chewing, place his knife and fork crossways on his plate and reached over his shoulder for the handset.

"This is the Captain."

"Captain, Evans on the Rangefinder has spotted smoke rising from a train tunnel. We suspect they are waiting for us to leave the area before they make a dash to the next tunnel.

"I see," swallowing his last bite.

"I'd like to propose a plan, Captain, if you don't already have one in mind."

The Captain leaned over, placing his elbows on the table, sighed to himself and said, "Let's hear it, Mike"

"We head seaward, making smoke and going slowly. Let them get the idea we're going as fast as we can to a new target. I think they'll wait until we're over the horizon before taking off down the track. The next tunnel is five miles away. If we get out of sight, wait for a few minutes, then pour on the coal without smoke, we ought to catch them in the open." Lieutenant Morgan fell silent, waiting.

"Yes, okay." The Captain considered Mike's plan for a moment and mixed a little more devilment into the brew.

"Good plan. Let's add some mischief to it. Come about to the north track without change in speed. Just before you complete the north track, go to flank with lots of smoke, then come about on the south track until even with the train. Then turn at right angles to the train and head to sea.

"By this time, they will have seen our tremendous speed," he said wryly. "After you've lined up away from them, go two thousand yards, cut back to standard, another thousand yards, cut to two-thirds, after another thousand, cut back to one-third, gradually making less smoke. Okay?"

"Aye aye, Captain."

Lieutenant Morgan replaced the phone and followed the Captain's orders.

Just before time to come about, he leaned over the Wheelhouse voice tube.

"All ahead flank. Make one six five turns."

"All ahead flank—engine room answers all ahead flank, sir. Make one six five turns, sir."

"Tell the engine room to make smoke on purpose—we're going to be sneaky devils."

"Engine room answers make smoke on purpose, sir? They are a little curious about that."

"Just tell them we are trying to trick the Chinks so we can bust another train."

"Thank you, sir."

Lieutenant Morgan looked around the horizon for other ships, then leaned over the gyro compass repeater and took a bearing on the beach. When he was satisfied with their northerly position, he pivoted to the Wheelhouse voice tube and spoke.

"Hard right rudder, steady up on reverse course one niner five true. Boatswain's Mate of the Watch—pass the word—standby for high speed turn to starboard."

"Hard right rudder, aye aye, sir. Steady up on one niner five true—rudder answers the helm, sir."

"Pass the word, standby for high speed turn to starboard, aye aye, sir."

The 1MC cracked open with a shrill Bos'un's Pipe call to 'Attention'.

"Standby for high speed turn to starboard."

Lieutenant Morgan leaned back against the forward windshield and looked aft at their wake.

Look at that wake; it's really boiling.

The ship trembled as it heeled—leaned over—to the left. (In a high speed turn, the ship always leans opposite the direction of the turn.)

The Captain appeared, coming up the ladder with a mug of coffee.

"Captain on the Bridge." Called out Lieutenant Morgan on the voice tube.

"Quartermaster, aye. Captain on the Bridge."

The Quartermaster-of-the-Watch leaned over his Rough Log and entered the fact the Captain was on the Open Bridge.

A lazy smile spread on the Captain's face. He sauntered five steps to the windshield alongside Lieutenant Morgan and settled back in his favorite corner. He admired the foaming blue broth behind the fantail.

"Beautiful, isn't it."

"Not bad, Captain, not bad at all. But just look around to port at that storm we're going to run into when we turn seaward. How's that for a smoke screen."

"Bridge Combat—we're coming up on the tunnel in about three minutes." Lieutenant Morgan leaned over to the 21MC and pressed the talk switch rapidly, twice.

Click click

The ship had been pitching and rolling on seas moving in from the southeast. Motion was much more violent in this high-speed maneuver. Once in a great while, solid water came over the bow. Fortunately, this was not one of the stronger storms.

"Bridge Combat—Mark! Abeam of the tunnel."

Click click

Lieutenant Morgan leaned over the Wheelhouse voice tube.

"Left standard rudder. Come to course one zero five true. Boatswain's Mate of the Watch pass the word to standby for a high speed turn to port"

"Left standard rudder, aye aye, sir. Rudder answers the helm. Coming to course one zero five true, sir.

"Boatswain Mate, aye aye, sir"

The 1MC opened and the pipe sounded 'Attention'.

"Standby for high speed turn to port."

"Talker, tell the engine room they are not making enough smoke," advised the Captain.

The phone talker nodded to the Captain as he pushed in his mike button and spoke.

"Steady on new course one zero five, Mr. Morgan."

"Very well, thank you."

"Combat Bridge—advise when we have increased our distance from the beach by two thousand yards."

Click click

The seas were really rough now. The wind lifted sea spray over the starboard bow, blowing it clear up to the bridge and above. More solid water came onto the foredeck as the bow dipped below a few of the waves. There was a crash as some kind of crockery fell to the deck and smashed.

"Bridge Combat—two thousand yards, Mr. Morgan."

Click click

"All ahead standard. Make one four zero turns. Tell the engine room to make just a little less smoke. We're trying to fool the Chinks with an optical illusion."

"All ahead standard, aye aye, sir. Make one four zero turns. Engine room answers all ahead standard, one four zero turns, sir."

"Engine room understands about the smoke, Mr. Morgan. Do you want them to automatically reduce smoke or would you rather call it—that's from Mr. Hansen, sir."

"Thank you. We will call it."

"Bridge Combat—three thousand yards."

Click click

"All ahead two-thirds. Make one one eight turns. A little less smoke now."

"All ahead two-thirds, aye aye, sir. Make one one eight turns. Engine room answers all ahead two-thirds, one one eight turns, less smoke."

"Very well."

Bridge Combat—we believe the storm front is about one thousand yards or less in front of us."

Click click

The Captain and Mr. Morgan pivoted as one to look at the storm front.

"Wow, Captain, that is really heavy rain!"

The Captain nodded and smiled in appreciation.

The Hoquiam continued to reduce forward motion but the violence of the sea increased, improving the illusion they were still running at high speed. The train crew should be marking how long it took them to disappear into the storm. If they fell for it, the Hoquiam would have two trains under its belt in three days.

"Bridge Combat—Four thousand yards."

Click click

"All ahead one-third. Make eight zero turns. Maintain this smoke."

"All ahead one-third, aye aye, sir. Make eight zero turns. Engine room answers all ahead one-third, eight zero turns. Maintain this smoke."

"Very well, thank you."

The Captain turned to the phone talker.

"Talker—tell the rangefinder to let us know the instant he can no longer see the stretch of cliff where the tunnel is located." The phone talker nodded and passed the instructions. The Captain waited a moment, then continued, "Talker—pass to Mr. Hansen to be prepared to go to flank and stay there for less than an hour."

"Mike—I have the Conn now. You'd better get Thirty-one and Thirty-three ready for action." Lieutenant Morgan nodded agreement.

"Aye aye, Captain. I think that Thirty-one deck crew ought to wait until after we make the turn and head in."

The Captain nodded as he watched the distant shore. "Permission granted."

Lieutenant Morgan called down to the Boatswains Mate of the Watch, "Call away Mount Thirty-one and Thirty-three to the Mess deck for a meeting in five minutes."

"Aye aye, sir," and the 1MC clicked open

"Gun crews for Mounts Thirty-one and Thirty-three meet with Lieutenant Morgan on the Mess deck in five minutes."

Lieutenant Morgan leaned over the 21MC and said, "Wheelhouse Combat Sonar—the Captain has the Conn."

"Quartermaster, aye aye, sir." He leaned over his small desk and entered that fact in his Rough Log, noting the time.

"Combat aye"

"Sonar aye aye, sir"

Then the rain came down, harsh and warm, out of the south. In a moment, the Captain could not see the fantail less than two hundred feet away.

"Bridge aye—roger rangefinder I'll pass the word." The phone talker turned to the Captain. "Rangefinder reports he can no longer make out any part of the shore line, sir."

"Very well."

The Captain leaned over the voice tube.

"Right standard rudder. Come to new course one niner five true."

"Right standard rudder, aye aye, Captain. Coming to new course one niner five true, sir."

"Very well. All ahead flank. Make one six five turns. No smoke."

"All ahead flank, aye aye, Captain. Make one six five turns. No smoke. Engine room answers all ahead flank, one six five turns and no smoke, Captain."

"Very well."

The turn placed the wind on the ship's port bow, which would be rough on Mount Thirty-one's deck gun crew. Everyone in the Magazine and Ammunition Handling room would be snug and dry.

Mr. Morgan will probably hold the deck crew in the Mess Deck until just before ready for action.

The ship trembled from the driving force of the engines and punched through the high seas with better grace.

"Combat Bridge—Let me know when we are opposite the next tunnel. I plan to make another right turn and charge in. Hopefully we'll catch that train with its pants down."

Click click

Commander Brown looked aft at the stack. Just a pure brownish gray haze was all that showed now. When they turned toward the beach, the Hoquiam would be pointing straight into the shoreline against a gray background of the storm. Their gray ship would be difficult to see. Just the white bow wave would be visible over very wind-blown waves.

“Bridge Combat—five hundred yards to point abeam of the next tunnel, Captain.”

Click click

“Boatswain’s Mate—announce standby for high speed turn to starboard”

“Boatswain’s Mate aye aye, sir.”

“Right standard rudder. Come to new course two eight five true”

“Right standard rudder, aye aye, Captain. New course two eight five true. Rudder answers the helm, sir.”

“Very well.”

The 1MC clicked open

“Standby for high speed turn to starboard.”

Gradually the ship moved around in the storm until the wind and seas were approaching from the port quarter. The apparent wind was only four or five knots now because of their building speed through the water.

The Captain heard footsteps on the ladder. He looked over his shoulder as Lieutenant Morgan appeared next to him. They studied Mount Thirty-one for sea spray, none apparent now.

"Man your guns, Mike. Let's bust another train."

"With pleasure, Captain."

"Boatswains Mate—pass the word for Mount Thirty-one and Thirty-three gun crews to man their guns."

"Aye aye, sir"

The 1MC opened.

"Mount Thirty-one and Thirty-three gun crews, man your guns."

The Captain turned to the 1MC behind him on the Sonar Shack bulkhead and flipped all zones on. Then he pressed the microphone lever.

"This is the Captain. We have not gone completely mad up here. These strange maneuvers are in the hope of tricking the Chinks into believing we have been called away on an important mission. They have been hiding a train in a tunnel, which was discovered by sharp Fire Controlman Evans on the rangefinder a little while ago."

Evans beamed a big smile at the Captain below him.

"Mr. Morgan, one of our trickier deceivers, decided on this plan to draw them down to the next tunnel five miles away. We think the Chinks have just about come bold enough to leave that tunnel and head for the next. It is—"

"Bridge, Combat—Contact. Train is leaving the tunnel at this time. Out."

"You heard that. The train is on the way. Thirty-one and Thirty-three, it's up to you men. Let's go get 'em."

The Hoquiam burst out of the storm pointing for the beach about five miles distant.

Thirty-one crew dashed forward below the Bridge and pulled the canvas covers off and barrel plug out. The Second Loader carried a 3 inch round to the First Loader who waited for the Gun Captain to open the Breech.

"Bridge, Rangefinder—I can see the train. It's completely clear of the tunnel. Standby for a count: engine and tender, four flat cars with heavy artillery—real long barrels, seven boxcars, three tank cars, and two troop cars. Air is hazy; range is about nine thousand yards."

"Very well, thank you," rep;ied the Captain as he leaned over the voice tube.

"Ring up one seven zero turns. Then tell the engine room that won't be for long."

"One seven zero turns, aye aye, Captain. Engine answers one seven zero turns and Mr. Hansen says he hopes it won't be for too long, also."

"Very well."

The Captain turned to the 1MC again, and hesitated thinking about what he wanted to say: "This is the Captain. We are not going to General Quarters. All hands not actually on watch who wish to observe may do so. Stay well forward of Mount Thirty-three on the oh-one deck. Stay off the fantail. Stay well aft of Mount Thirty-one. You may go on the oh-two level. This is what we are here for. One more thing, as you watch, plug your ears and leave your mouth open."

The 1MC clicked off and back on. The Captain had a chuckle in his voice. "Stewart, you may bring the message board up now."

Click

Stewart choked on his coffee and looked at the speaker in astonishment. He and Red were eating late watchstanders lunch. His neck and face flushed red as embarrassment spread through his face. Red, his buddy, and others, laughed at his discomfort. He grabbed his nearly empty tray and headed for the Scullery.

"Stewart, you didn't finish your meal," charged the Mess Deck Master-At-Arms, pointing at his tray.

Stewart looked at him in astonishment. He was still poking food in his mouth as he twisted around to go up the ladder to the Radio Shack. He shrugged helplessly and dashed up the ladder.

Comments followed him up the ladder. Stomping into the shack, he picked up the board and turned to leave.

James walked in with a growl on his face.

"What the fuck was that all about, Stewart?"

"Dunno, Jimmy Bob—"

"Don't Jimmy Bob me, I ast you a question." When Jimmy Bob James got angry, he tended to slip into a Deep South accent, and shake his head rapidly.

Lloyd and Roney were grinning at him.

Lee's eyes darted around the room. "Boss, I swear I have no idea what that was all about. But I got the board and I am heading for the Bridge, even if I just got off watch."

James glared at him but didn't know what it was all about, either. He stepped aside and let Stewart pass.

The Captain reached for the board with amusement on his face. Stewart's face beamed with pleasure of being on the Bridge during action and fear of what the Captain wanted.

Maybe this will keep Stewart off the Bridge every time something happens.

"Bridge Combat—Range to Tunnel Two is thirty-five hundred yards."

Click click

"Mr. Morgan, it is my intention to continue straight in until we reach one thousand yards. If we are not fired upon by then, I will continue in until we run out of water. At some point, I will turn so both batteries can bear on the target. Clear?"

"Yes sir."

"Commence firing on Tunnel Two with Thirty-one."

Where the hell is Mount Thirty-two when you need it?

"Aye aye, Captain."

That evening after the Hoquiam turned seaward, the encrypted daily battle report carried the cheering story of a second train busted, two tunnels closed, four sections of the rail breached along its five mile length with Mounts Thirty-one and Thirty-three, and a train trestle and vehicle bridge fired by Mounts Forty-one and Forty-two—firing in anger for the first time.

FM USS MASSEY DD778
TO CTE 95.22
INFO USS HOQUIAM
BT
PERFORMANCE OF LASHING PETER ON NORTH PATROL IN ZERO VISIBILITY CONSIDERED ESPECIALLY PRAISE WORTHY X WITH HIS LIMITED EQUIPMENT HE TURNED IN A PERFORMANCE WHICH WOULD HAVE DONE CREDIT TO A MUCH LARGER AND BETTER EQUIPPED SHIP
BT

April 16, 1951
U.S. Naval Station, Anacostia, Md.
Bureau of Ships

The Mail Orderly checked the BuShips Routing Slip and Office Memo to determine where the Hoquiam letter should be dropped. The slip showed Mailstop 24.

At Mailstop 24, the lady looked at the letter and sighed.

I don't even know what the hell a Patrol Frigate is. Looks like a trip to the Archives will take the rest of the day.

She returned to her desk two hours later, signed off the routing slip and sent it back to her department head noting:

Hoquiam ltrser 95: 3 volume allowance list ordered.

THIS IS A F R S TOKYO WITH THE MORNING NEWS APRIL SIXTEENTH NINETEEN FIFTY-ONE, PETTY OFFICER JOHN ELLSWORTH REPORTING. IN THE NEWS, THE UNITED NATIONS COMMAND IN KOREA REPORTS THAT BRITISH COMMANDOS RAIDED AND DESTROYED EXPOSED COASTAL RAIL LINE 8 MI SOUTH OF CHONGJIN, TWO NEARBY TUNNELS AND A RAIL EMBANKMENT, YESTERDAY. THE BRITISH COMMANDOS, 250 MEN OF 41ST INDEPENDENT ROYAL MARINES, WERE SUPPORTED BY ST. PAUL CA73, W.L. LIND DD703, MASSEY DD778, HOQUIAM PF5, FT. MARION LSD22, BEGOR APD127, MINESWEEPERS INCREDIBLE, OSPREY, CHATTERER, MERGANSER AND GRASP ARS24."

April 16, 1951
U.S. Naval Station, Anacostia, Md.
Bureau of Ships

BuShips Routing Slip and Office Memo
Hoquiam ltrser 95: Allowance List. One N/R PF394, 99102 Vol I of III mailed this date.

0800, 17 April 1951
USS Hoquiam PF-5
On Station, patrolling in vicinity of
Chongjin, North Korea

"C Division, Aaaa tennn shun." James saluted Lieutenant (jg) Forsythe and reported, "All men present or accounted for, sir."

Mr. Forsythe returned his salute, responding "Very well."

He looked at the men in front of him. They looked tense and tired.

Well, of course they are tense and tired. So am I!

He reached up on his tippy toes, raised his eyebrows and said,

"Men, I have some interesting news for you." He paused for effect. "Rotation has finally been established. All personnel are eligible for rotation after two years of being aboard any PF for duty." His eyes flicked in both directions. "Any questions?" he asked as he braced himself.

"Sir, does the time before commissioning count?

"No."

"Mr. Forsythe, does that rotation include reservists?"

"I don't know."

"Mr. Forsythe, does that rotation specifically mean back to the States?"

"Good question!"

Silence.

"Any other questions?" He looked left and right at the disgusted or puzzled look on their faces. "Relieve your quarters," he ordered and returned their salute.

It was the Hoquiam's turn for OPERATION FLYCATCHER again. Before Hungnam, most of the little boats had been North Korean refugees fleeing to the South. It was different now. The Hoquiam stopped and boarded every junk and sampan they spotted. A few of the junks were faster but not as fast as radio signals.

In practice, they would trail a faster junk after notifying the nearest destroyer, who could easily make more than 30 knots, to pick up the junk on their own radar. Most of the junks the Hoquiam stopped and searched, were passed to the South Korean Navy ships near Wonsan who escorted them to Pusan.

Others? When they found mines or other weapons of war aboard any junk or sampan, the ROKN Liaison Officer had the Hoquiam back off and blaze away until the vessel was kindling, along with its crew. Memory of other Navy crews blasted by mines were strong and brooked no sympathy.

April was a tough time to be off the North Korean coast. It was always stormy, either from high winds and cold drenching rains of the Siberian chill express or had tropical storms up from typhoon alley with warm drenching rains and high winds kept the crew wet and cold.

Chief Billons was heard to remark there was so much rain his crew didn't need to freshwater wash down the bulkheads and decks—just exposed overheads. Roney and Stewart were grateful for that. The Radio Shack's section of deck, bulkhead, and overhead just outside the shack didn't need much attention and the overhead was tough on shoulders. The high seas were most wearing of all, day after day without relief.

1505, April 17, 1951
East of Sosura, North Korea
USS Hoquiam on patrol

The General Quarters gong stopped sounding just as the Captain entered Combat blowing on his hands to warm them up and rubbing them. He glanced around and nodded to Parks with an approving smile.

"All stations manned and ready, Captain."

"Very well."

Two men were on the vertical status board. Red grease pencil marks on the status board showed the unidentified ships track.

"Hey Parks!" called the SC Radar operator. "Those ships are changing course toward us."

Intent on his 'scope, the operator was unaware the Captain was in Combat, until he stood next to him. The Captain peered over the operator's shoulder to see the targets.

"Can you see their radar trace on us?"

"Don't know, Captain. They are not on this frequency band. Range is now seventeen thousand, one hundred yards and closing, sir. Bearing is constant at three four eight degrees true."

"Very well."

The Captain reached up and pulled down the 21MC lever.

"Bridge Combat—Mr. Herbert, how is the visibility now?"

"Terrible, Captain. Can't see Mount thirty-one. Should I commence sounding the foghorn, sir?"

"No. Maintain silence. We are supposed to be the only ship in the area."

Click click

Captain Brown sat down on the barstool in front of the Plotter, hunched over the DRT (Dead Reckoning Tracer,) and watching the plot develop on both the vertical board and DRT. A Radarman behind the plot board rubbed off the last position of the target and relabeled them as t1, T2, and t3. The Captain looked over his shoulder at the SC Radar operator and asked, "T2—a heavy?—What do you make of that formation?" (Small caps and Large caps designated the relative size of targets.)

Ensign Hitchcock and Parks RD1 P.O.-in-Charge of the Combat Information Center, huddled next to the

SC Radar operator and whispered amongst themselves. Ensign Hitchcock straightened up and looked at his Captain.

"Captain, those signatures are similar to two destroyers escorting a heavy vessel into our Replenishment Area." His eyebrows bunched up. "Except, they're coming from the wrong direction!"

Is the Soviet Navy coming out to challenge us?

Captain Brown leaned back in his chair, hands holding his chin on the Plotter, and considered what might develolp. Reaching a decision, he reached up to the 21MC. "Wheelhouse Combat—All ahead standard."

"Wheelhouse, aye. All ahead standard—Engine room answers all ahead standard, Captain."

Click click

"Bridge Combat—Mr. Herbert, shift your watch to the Wheelhouse,."

"Bridge aye aye, Captain. Shifting to the Wheelhouse. Captain, if anything, the fog is thicker."

Click click

The Hoquiam trembled and began tossing around in the high seas as it increased speed. The Captain pulled a message blank to him and began writing. Completing the message and re-reading it, he reached for the 21MC, and pulled Radio's lever down.

"Radio Combat"

"Radio Aye"

"Send the Classified Messenger immediately to Combat for a message to encrypt."

"Radio, aye aye."

A few minutes later, Mr. Forsythe undogged the hatch and walked in, dogging it behind him. He was puffing from climbing the long ladder.

The Captain gave Lieutenant (jg) Forsythe time to catch his breath from racing on the two-level ladder. "Roger, encrypt this message and send it out operational immediate, as soon as possible."

He glanced at it, studied it carefully, and glanced at his Commanding Officer.

Mother of God, he's not going to take on a cruiser and two destroyers with this, is he?

"Aye aye, Captain. Will take about fifteen minutes to encrypt, confirm decrypt, and send the message."

"Very well. Go do it, Roger."

Lieutenant (jg) Forsythe pivoted, broke the hatch, and dropped down two levels to the Radio shack. He beckoned to James, and backed into his stateroom.

"What's up, Mr. Forsythe?"

Forsythe handed him the message. "Encrypt this and get it out right away, James."

James studied the message and turned pale. "Is this for real, Mr. Forsythe? Is he really going to attack that Ruskie cruiser? We ain't got a Chinaman's chance in hell."

"Just do it, James."

Mother Fuck!

Jimmy Bob James whirled around and headed down to the Crypto Room.

James entered the Radio shack and walked up behind Masters and tapped him on the shoulder.

"Send this right away on Task Group Common, Masters."

"What is it?"

"An encrypted message, asshole. Just send it."

Masters stared at him in surprise as he pressed the transmitter power key.

What the fuck is eatin' him?

G4G4 DE P3U9 G1X9 OP K

P3U9 G1X9 DE G4G4 K
DE P3U9 G1X9
OP
FM P3U9 G1X9
TO G4G4
INFO P3U9
GR80
BT

There followed an encrypted message stating the Hoquiam had 3 radar targets at 17000 yards bearing 344 degrees true believed to be a Soviet formation consisting of a cruiser and two destroyers. Hoquiam intentions were meet them head on and order them to leave the blockaded North Korean coast or suffer the consequences.

P3U9 G1X9 DE G4G4 R OP AR

James's fingernails rattled on Mr. Forsythe's doorway. He pulled his green curtain aside and looked up at James.

"It's gone, sir."

Forsythe nodded. "Use the 21MC to notify the Captain in Combat."

"Aye aye, sir."

James pulled down the lever.

"Combat Radio—that message was just received by the Task Group commander, Captain."

"Very well, thank you."

"Wheelhouse Combat—Boatswain's Mate of the Watch. Pass the word there will be a meeting of all Department Heads in the Wardroom immediately."

"Aye aye, Captain."

The Captain looked at Ensign Hitchcock, and Parks. "I'll be back shortly and explain what we are doing. Let me know immediately if the Soviets change course or speed."

"Aye aye, Captain," chorused the two. The Captain left for the Wardroom.

The Captain waited until they all sat down, then he stood up.

"In 1947, Egypt nationalized the Suez Canal and upset the Brits and French. The combined British and French fleet decided to attack and take back the Canal.

We, that is the United States government, opposed their plan. Orders went out to the Sixth Fleet in the Med to stop them." Captain Brown lit a cigarette and continued. Lieutenant Marston's eyes got big as he realized what the Captain was going to do.

"The Sixth Fleet Commander sailed his battle group in front of the British and French warships, giving them a choice: fire on the United States Navy or turn aside. It was touch and go for a few seconds but the British commander ordered the task force to turn aside."

"We're going to tackle the same maneuver with the Soviets. I shall sail across the bow, forcing them to turn aside or run us down. It is draw poker, gentlemen. They don't know we need five cards!"

Lieutenant Marston was on his feet. "Captain, one salvo from the cruiser and we turn turtle."

"Mr. Marston, there will not be any salvo." Captain Brown looked at his department heads. "I'll be in Combat. We're already in range of their guns." Mashing out his cigarette, he donned his helmet and left the Wardroom.

Lieutenant Dixon, looked at Lieutenant Morgan.

Are my Damage Controlmen (DC) going to be up to this, if we are blasted by that cruiser? I need to go talk with them.

He headed below to encourage them.

Lieutenant Porter spun his combination hat around and around as he looked between Lieutenants Morgan and Marston.

Oh, shit!

"I will be in Combat."

The Captain looked around Combat. "Has anyone a reliable camera? If we pop into view of the Soviet task group, I want pictures."

Sorenson RD2, a bitter USNR, raised his hand.

"I do, sir. Great lenses and film."

The Captain smiled, pleased, and thumbed Sorenson to his locker. Sorenson took off for the compartment for his camera gear in his locker.

Captain Brown sat on the barstool, hunched down, and studied the vertical plot board. Lieutenant Porter eased in alongside him on the other barstool.

"Parks, draw in the northern blockade line on the vertical plot." Ordered the Captain.

"Aye aye, Captain." Parks got behind the SC radar operator and squinted at the display.

"Give me a range and bearing on the Manchurian North Korean international border, north of Sosura."

The SC radar operator nodded and began cranking his nobs to comply with Park's orders.

The SC operator shifted to manual drive and zeroed in on the coast, stopping on a particular headland, and cranked out the range marker.

"There it is, Parks." He reported.

"Okay, tell the Vertical Plot operator to use a Yellow wax and draw the line straight seaward from there."

The operator nodded and spoke into his headset. Across Combat, the vertical plot Radarman listened and nodded He pulled a long straight edge, laid it on the Vertical Plot, and began drawing a straight yellow wax line across the plot.

The Captain watched this with satisfaction.

They may not like what I am doing, but they are professionals.

"Distance to the Soviets, please." Politely, the Captain asked.

"Range is 9700 yards, Captain."

"Very well. Our distance to the Blockade line," as he looked at the Plot being developed.

"Range to Blockade line is 2200 yards, Captain."

"Very well." He reached above him to the 21mc.

"Wheelhouse Combat—all ahead one-third."

"Wheelhouse aye. All ahead one-third, Captain. Engine room answers all ahead one-third, Captain."

Click click

He turned to Lieutenant Porter.

"I want to ease up to the Blockade line and hold just on this side." In a louder voice, "range to both the Soviets and Blockade line, please."

"Captain, the Soviets have slowed. Range to the Soviets is 7100 yards and 900 yards to the line, Sir."

"Very well."

The Captain grabbed the message blank and scribbled on it. "Parks." He beckoned to him. "Here," as he thrust the message blank to Parks, "send this message to the Soviets very slowly on every voice channel we have. Then, take it to Radio and have them send it in Morse Code on 500 kilocycles very slowly as a Securite Message."

"Aye aye, Captain," Parks responded and reached for the radiophone handset.

SECURITE SECURITE SECURITE

SOVIET SHIPS EAST OF SOSURA NORTH KOREA THIS IS UNITED STATES SHIP HOQUIAM ON UNITED NATIONS COMMAND DUTY.

YOU ARE SAILING IN HARMS WAY. THE UNITED NATIONS COMMAND HAS BLOCKADED THE SEA OF JAPAN SOUTH OF THE MANCHURIAN BORDER WITH NORTH KOREA. TURN BACK NOW. DO NOT CROSS THE BLOCKADE LINE.

Parks continued to send this message on other voice circuits. Then he ran to the Radio shack, bursting through the door.

"James, send this immediately on 500 kilocycles. The Soviet Navy is bearing down on us and we need to stop them."

James read the message and cringed. "Holy shit! Is the Captain crazy?"

Mother Fuck!

"No, he's playing poker with the Soviets."

James turned to the RBA receiver and tuned it to 500, and listened. He could hear people sending CW. Turning to the transmitter, he flipped the switch to the low frequency band and turned it on. He didn't bother fiddling with the LM frequency meter. Instead, he keyed the transmitter and twisted the oscillator dial until he heard it on the RBA. Tuning carefully, he had the transmitter lined up on 500 and ready to go. A fast check on loading the Final—no change.

He slapped the back on Lloyd's chair. "Get the fuck out of there, Lloyd."

Puzzled, Lloyd moved out of the chair so James could sit down.

Jimmy, what the fuck are you doing?

James took over the Task Group Common position and sat down. Reaching in, he pressed the red power key and waited for the TDE filaments to glow. Tapping the key to make sure the transmitter was up, he began sending the Morse Code message slowly, beginning with the "Securite Code".

XXX XXX XXX DE NZCY NZCY NZCY

BT
SOVIET SHIPS EAST OF SOSURA NORTH KOREA THIS IS UNITED STATES SHIP HOQUIAM ON UNITED NATIONS COMMAND DUTY X YOU ARE SAILING INTO HARMS WAY X THE UNITED NATIONS COMMAND HAS BLOCKADED THE SEA OF JAPAN

SOUTH OF THE MANCHURIAN BORDER WITH NORTH KOREA X TURN BACK NOW X DO NOT CROSS THE BLOCKADE LINE
BT
AR VA

Jimmy Dean's brow was heavy with sweat. He did not like what he had just sent to the Soviet Navy.

"Combat Radio—this is Parks. James just sent that message on 500, Captain. Should he send it again?"

"Negative, Parks. I'm sure they got it. Return to Combat, please."

Click click

Meanwhile in CIC, "Captain, range to the line is approximately 200 yards."

"Very well."

"Wheelhouse Combat—come right to new course 090 true."

"Wheelhouse aye, come right to new course 090 true. Rudder is answering the helm, Captain."

"Steady on new course 090 true, Captain."

Click click

Lieutenant Porter leaned to the Captain. "We are still on a collision course, Captain. Range is now under 5000 yards and closing."

The Captain nodded. "Wheelhouse Combat—Mr. Hitchcock, slow to steerage way on course 090. Let me know the instant the fog lifts and the ships are in sight."

Click click

The Gunnery Officer, Lieutenant Morgan, spoke from his corner of Combat. "Shall I train out our guns, Captain?"

The Captain laughed and peered under the overhead radiophone units at Lieutenant Morgan. "Lord no. One shot and we'd be sunk, possibly starting World War Three. I intend to ram the cruiser if they cross the line."

He paused as Combat grew very quiet. "This is a game of draw poker, gentlemen, and he does not know what we will do. My bet is he will dash up to the line and turn west to Vladivostok. Range to the Soviets, please."

"2900 yards, still on collision course, Captain."

"Combat Wheelhouse—fog has cleared and a cruiser and two destroyers are in sight."

Click click

"Sorenson, get your camera and follow me."

The Captain grabbed his slicker on the way out, heading for the Bridge, Sorenson right behind him.

"Sorenson, you get as many photographs of those Soviet warships—as many as you can get. Understand?"

"Oh aye aye sir, Captain. I'm already shooting."

As they got on the Bridge, the Captain, looked around and found Chief Swenson.

"Chief, man all three lights and send this message to those ships. Tell them to turn away. Just keep repeating that. Turn away. Put the big light directly on the cruiser's bridge. Light 'em up! "Aye aye, sir."

Chief Swenson looked at his Signal crew. "Smitty on the 24 to the cruiser bridge, Curry and Barney on the 12s to the destroyers. Snap it up." The Chief called out.

One by one, the three signal light shutter levers began to clatter and squeak as the three signalmen slowly sent the Captain's message.

TURN AWAY TURN AWAY TURN AWAY

"Range 1400 yards to us, Captain. That's about 1200 yards to the line."

Click click

The Captain leaned over the voice tube.

"Wheelhouse—inform engineering to standby for flank speed momentarily."

"Wheelhouse, inform engineering to standby for flank speed momentarily, aye aye. Engineering acknowledges and is standing by, Captain."

Ensigns Hitchcock and Herbert appeared at his elbow.

"You play poker, Mr. Hitchcock, Mr. Herbert?"

"Yessir," came the puzzled reply from both.

"What do you suppose the Soviet commander will do when a hopelessly outgunned smaller ship suddenly closes at flank speed with every intention of ramming him?"

"Blow him out of the water."

"He can't do that, Mister. We're too close to him now." He reached up to the 21MC talk lever and pressed.

"Wheelhouse—all ahead flank."

"All ahead flank, aye. Engine room answers all ahead flank, Captain."

"Bridge Combat—range to cruiser 800 yards."

Click click

"As soon as we get beyond their little task unit, I will turn right, still building speed, and continue turning—circling—until we line up with the cruiser bow. We will either ram him or he will turn away. Right now, he's laughing up his sleeve because we are running away."

"Sorenson, you getting those photographs?"

"Yes, Captain."

"Combat Bridge—Mr. Morgan, evacuate Mount 31. Advise both 40's and 20's to engage the Soviets only if they fire upon us."

"Aye aye, Captain."

He leaned over the voice tube. "Right rudder fifteen degrees."

"Right rudder, fifteen degrees, aye. Rudder answers the helm, Captain."

"Very well."

"Bridge combat—the Soviets are 300 yards from the line."

Click click

The Hoquiam continued to build speed toward its maximum of 19.2 knots, as it turned in a wide circle.

"Mr. Hitchcock, return to Combat. Mr. Herbert, into the Wheelhouse. Aim the ship directly at the bow of the cruiser. Do not blink. Keep your crew and the helm on station."

"Aye aye, Captain." Mr. Herbert saluted and went below to the wheelhouse, as Mr. Hitchcock abruptly left.

The Captain watched as the bow swung around to the cruiser. "Meet your rudder, helmsman."

"Meeting the rudder, aye." The Helmsman's voice had a small tremor in it.

"Keep our bow on their bow, helmsman."

"Aye aye, Captain."

The Captain turned behind him and hit all the 1MC switches.

"All hands, brace for collision on the bow."

Mr. Porter's excited voice jumped over the 21MC. "He's folding his cards, Captain. The Soviets are turning and increasing speed away from here."

"Wheelhouse—left standard rudder, all ahead one-third."

"Bridge combat—you just crossed the line."

Click click

The Captain was alone on the Bridge. He stared at the Soviet ships beginning to show their sterns to him. For a moment, he shivered uncontrollably and had trouble swallowing. Then, it passed.

He opened the 1MC again. "This is the Captain. Resume normal routine; set modified condition one able. We won this round."

"Wheelhouse Combat—Bridge. I will be in my stateroom."

Click click

1215, 18 April 1951
USS Hoquiam PF-5
On Station, patrolling in vicinity of
Iwon, North Korea

Starboard Lookout Seaman Brewster, refocused his binoculars and steadied for a better look. "Oh, hoooo", he muttered and looked over his shoulder. "Mr. Dixon?"

Lieutenant Dixon stepped over to the starboard side and looked at Brewster.

"Sir, I just saw some troops go into a shack near the edge of that meadow there," pointing to the shack.

Lieutenant Dixon said, "Put your glasses on the alidade and line up on your target, then let me have a look."

Brewster, the tall Seaman from Second Division, removed the binoculars from his neck, leaned over and twisted around until he had the glasses dead on, and stood away.

Mr. Dixon hastily leaned over and checked the target. He looked up to the rangefinder where the man on duty was looking down at him. expectantly.

"Check the shack bearing about," he looked back to the alidade for the bearing, "about zero three seven relative."

"Got it, Mr. Dixon. Bearing zero three eight, range six two five yards and closing, sir."

Lieutenant Dixon waved in acknowledgment and buzzed the Wardroom. One of the Stewards picked up the phone.

"Wardroom, Ennis speaking, sir."

"Is the Captain in the Wardroom?"

"Oh, yes sir, Mr. Dixon." Ennis turned and passed the handset to the Captain.

"This is the Captain."

"Target of Opportunity, Captain. A house or shed where several Chinese troopers just ducked in. Permission to drop a few Commons with Mount 33? We could use Mount Forty-one or Forty-two."

"How do you know they are Chinese troops, Dix?"

"Intelligence told us their uniforms are yellow quilted jackets and that's what these guys are wearing. North Korean uniforms are dark."

There was a pause as he listened.

"Use the 40's. They don't have much opportunity to work on a target, Mr. Dixon."

"Thank you, Captain."

"Combat Bridge—we have a T.O.P., range about six two five yards, bearing zero three eight. Get an update from rangefinder."

Click click

He looked at the gun roster to see which gun crews had the duty.

"Boatswains Mate—Pass the word for Mount Forty-one gun crew man your gun on the double."

The 1MC opened and a reedy Bos'uns pipe wheezed 'Attention'.

"Forty-one gun crew man your gun on the double. Forty-one."

"Bridge Combat—we don't pick up the target. Must be made of straw or soft wood."

Click click

Dixon thought about it.

"Phone talker, go to the JC circuit for Mount Forty-one. Tell Rangefinder to switch also."

"Aye aye, sir."

"Rangefinder, I want a current range and bearing to the target and when Forty-one is ready for action."

"Aye aye, sir."

He whirled around and pressed the 1MC microphone.

"All hands stand clear of Mount Forty-one while engaging enemy forces." He paused for a moment. "Gun crew Twenty-five, stand by your machine gun."

He leaned over the 21MC: he snapped. "Combat Bridge—range to the beach," and leaned over the voice tube.

"Quartermaster—let me know the instant the Fathometer shows fifty feet."

He straightened up and turned when he felt the phone talker's hand on his shoulder.

"Range is five hundred yards and decreasing, bearing is zero four one, sir. Mount 41 and Machine gun 25 are manned and ready. Twenty-five wants to know if they should load a magazine now, sir."

"Very well. Insure Forty-one copies all ranges and bearings. Tell Twenty-five to load and cock, safe it, but do not fire unless specifically directed to fire."

"Bridge Combat—Range to the beach is now four hundred twenty-five yards and closing."

Click click

With bright, intense eyes, Mr. Dixon turned to the phone talker. This would be his first complete fire mission without the Captain around to take over. His elation and sense of responsibility for his next action showed on his face and in his voice.

He walked to the Bridge binoculars and leaned over them focusing sharply on the target. A drab small shed where a few troops had ducked, an equally small and skimpy fenced yard, a larger barn, and a single carabao.

"Phone talker, Forty-one fire one for position."

Blam

He waited for a few seconds. The proximity fuse went off about twenty feet in front of the shed.

"Up three degrees. Fire the remainder of the clip," (There are four rounds in a 40mm clip.)

Blam blam blam

The three projectiles fired, burst automatically, directly on target. The shed was demolished and burning.

"Sir, Forty-one wants to know if they can fire the next clip which is already seated."

"Standby"

He looked through the Bridge binoculars again for anything moving.

Just the carabao walking slowly away from the former shed.

"Bridge Combat—range to the beach is one hundred yards."

Click click

"Forty-one put one round way behind that carabao. Let's see if it will get excited."

Blam

Mr. Dixon chuckled. The carabao, tail straight up in the air had taken off at a trot.

"Forty-one put one round way in front of that carabao. Let's see if it turns around."

Blam

The carabao, tail still straight up on the air, wheeled about and went the other direction a little bit faster.

"Forty-one do not load another clip. Lay a shot way in front of the carabao again.

Blam

"Aye aye Fantail. Mr. Dixon, fantail reports we're churning up muddy water."

He whirled again to check the stern, and stepped quickly to the voice tube.

Holy Shit!

"All back one-third. Quartermaster, what's the Fathometer reading right now?"

"Engine room answers all back one-third."

"This is the Quartermaster of the Watch, sir. Repeat that?"

Oh Christ—the Sonar dome!

"Sonar Bridge—emergency—shallow water—raise the dome!"

"Quartermaster," he said furiously, "I sent word down to you to report when the Fathometer showed fifty feet under the keel. What is the current reading?"

"Very tight sir, about twenty three feet. I was never given that order sir."

"Very well. Log it. We're not out of the woods yet," he fumed.

"Bridge Sonar—Dome is housed. No damage."

The ship finally stopped and began backing down its track into deeper water.

"Combat Bridge—range to the beach."

"Range from rangefinder is forty-five yards, Mr. Dixon. Way inside our minimum."

"Thank you all."

He turned to his phone talker.

"Forty-one and Twenty-five. Cease-fire. Unload and report safe."

Jesus!

"All stop, rudder right fifteen degrees."

"All stop. Engine room answers all stop. Rudder is right fifteen degrees, sir."

"Very well. All ahead standard. Left standard rudder."

"All ahead standard, aye aye, sir. Engine room answers all ahead standard, Left standard rudder and rudder answers the helm, sir. Passing one eight seven degrees true, sir."

"Very well, steady up on one two zero degrees true."

"Steady up on one two zero true, aye aye, sir. Rudder is still at Left Standard, sir."

"Very well."

"Phone talker, advise JC circuit to revert to normal, and you return to JV."

The phone talker nodded and began calling the stations.

"Sir, Forty-one and Twenty-five are safe now."

"Very well, tell them they are still the active gun crews until relieved by the next watch."

"Aye aye, sir."

"Steady on one two zero, Mr. Dixon."

"Very well."

"Combat Bridge—let me know when we are out one thousand yards from the beach."

Click click

The rain hit him like a fire hose. One second it was cold and relatively dry: the next? Solid wet and very cold. The wind screamed across the Bridge.

Damn! What must have life been like on one of those big sailing ships when you were hit by winds like this?

He glanced at his lookouts. Both of them turned away and hunched over, protecting against the wind and rain. He yelled out against the wind.

"Lookouts—Mind your posts."

They looked at him guiltily and miserable. At the same time they brought up their glasses and tried to look through the soup.

R APRIL 18, 1951
FM USS W.L.LIND (DD703)
TO USS HOQUIAM
BT
THANK YOU X YOU CERTAINLY DO
A WONDERFUL JOB CONSIDERING
THE HANDICAPS YOU HAVE HAD
TO OVERCOME
BT

April 20, 1951
U.S. Naval Station, Anacostia, Md.
Bureau of Ships

BuShips Routing Slip and Office Memo
Hoquiam LtrSer 95: Allowance List. One N/R PF394, 99102
Vol II of III and III of III, mailed this date.

One gray day faded into the next: all miserable. The rain, wind, cold temperature, and high seas just never let up. Every day, they sailed in close to shore and fired at Targets of Opportunity. The real destroyers stayed out about 3,500 yards. The Hoquiam usually operated within 500 yards for targets of opportunity: a small troop concentration, a couple of trucks or bridges, cutting the rail line, closing tunnels every time they were repaired, and busting trains. The few friendly junks and sampans got escorted to the ROK Navy PC's—Patrol Craft—near Wonsan.

Sometimes, the Hoquiam worked independently; other times, she worked with destroyers to destroy large concentrations of troops or trucks. For sure, the Hoquiam expended between fifty and one hundred rounds of three-inch ammunition every day and night. Every so often, they operated in fifty foot of water—with the sound dome retracted—in order to use the 40mm mounts effectively. The 40's were useful in burning rail trestles. The 3-inch .50 caliber Main Batteries could not do it.

THIS IS A F R S TOKYO WITH THE EVENING NEWS APRIL TWENTY-SEVENTH NINETEEN FIFTY-ONE, STAFF SERGEANT ROSS HINES IS YOUR REPORTER. THIS STORY IS JUST NOW FILTERING OUT OF KOREA. THE CHINESE COMMUNIST FORCES APPARENTLY LAUNCHED THEIR SPRING OFFENSIVE ON APRIL TWENTY-SECOND. ACCORDING TO REPORTS RECEIVED HERE THIS MORNING, MORE THAN TWO HUNDRED FIFTY THOUSAND CHINESE TROOPS IN TWENTY-SEVEN DIVISIONS ARE ATTACKING ALL ALONG THE LINE, FORCING UNITED NATIONS TROOPS TO RETREAT TOWARD THE THIRTY-EIGHTH PARALLEL.

April 30, 1951
U.S.S. Hoquiam (PF-5)
Ammunition expenditure report
On North Korean and Chinese targets

During 22 days on the firing line in the month of April, Hoquiam operated in the northern section between Songjin and Chongjin on assigned targets, targets of opportunity, and interdicting fire, during daylight and night operations. Targets included sampams, junks, railroad beds and bridges, roadbeds and bridges, troop concentrations, trucks, and trains. Hoquiam operated independently, part of Task Element 95.22, or OTC Task Element 95.22, or in company with Thompson DMS-38, O'Brien DD-725, Lind DD-703, Massey DD-778, Hank DD-702, Walke DD-723, Bausell DD-845, and HMS Cockade.

3-inch 50cal	**1731 rounds of AA Common**
	2 rounds of VT
	26 rounds of Illumination
40mm	**438 rounds of HEIT**
	704 rounds of HEI
20mm	**240 rounds**

MAY

May 01, 1951
USS Hoquiam PF-5
On Station, patrolling in vicinity of Songjin, North Korea

It was May Day all over the world. Back at Songjin after two weeks off Chongjin, North Korea, it was grim, lousy weather in a grim, lousy war. Stewart came back in the Radio Shack from his 2000 Messenger Run, pulled all the messages that had been signed from the clip board, and dropped them into James's basket for checking. He was still shivering from the wet trip to the bridge with the nightly weather forecast from Naval Weather Center Guam.

The forecast suggested the Hoquiam might face high winds, heavy seas, and cold temperatures. The seas began piling up on the port bow as it was slamming the ship around pretty badly. Stewart had staggered a couple of times going up the ladder to the oh-three deck and the Wheelhouse.

The Officer of the Deck had moved his station from the Open Bridge after running into the harsh storm. The ship was at Darken Ship as it steamed on station just off Songjin. Stewart glanced around the Shack and discovered, gratefully, that someone had already swept down and put things away.

He had first seen tonight's movie, 'Tangier', on the Chilton after Operation Miki, and again while the Hoquiam was on Buoy 4 off Hungnam.

Stewart hung up the Messenger's foul weather jacket on the door hook and dragged the broken down chair into the unlighted dark corner to settled down under the RBO entertainment receiver. Stewart slipped the earphones over his ears and fiddled with the AM dial, making sure AFRS Honshu was coming in loud and clear.

Coyle was copying George Fox broadcast and Masters was listening to the Task Group CW circuit, hoping the Task Group Commander had some message traffic. It was boring to just sit there with nothing to do. Griffin was drinking coffee as he waited for the movie to start.

Stewart found the Jack Benny radio program. He settled down to listen to the adventures of Jack, Don, Rochester, Mary, Mel, and the gang. Rochester was driving Jack and Mary in the Maxwell to his bank. As usual, the guard and squeaking door were hilarious. It was a very funny show this evening.

Hands suddenly grabbed Stewart's arms and pulled him out from where he was sitting. Alarmed, he looked at James and Coyle who were holding on to him with concerned expressions. Griffin and Masters were watching with tight looks on their faces, too.

Stewart struggling to get free. "Hey, guys, what's wrong with you?" The earphones were still on his ears and the program was running strong.

Abruptly, James and Coyle let loose and backed off. Coyle was laughing while James shook his head. Stewart pulled the earphones down on his neck and looked around, puzzled.

"You dumb shit, Stew," James explained. "You were sitting there in the dark, way back in the corner hunched over, and bursting out in little laughs. We thought you'd flipped your lid."

"I was listening to Jack Benny down in his vault again," he said, pointing to the earphones.

"But we didn't know that. You were sitting in the dark and we couldn't see the black cans," Griffin said. By this time, everyone was laughing. James told him to go back to his program and keep the laughing quiet.

2130, 07 May 1951
USS Hoquiam PF-5
At anchor off Songjin, North Korea

Stewart stood up as the mess deck lights came on. He stretched and rubbed his butt, numb from watching the movie for nearly two hours. Hearing laughter at the passage way entrance, he moseyed back to see what was going on. Seeing nothing, he saw Barnes BM3 shaking his head.

"Hey Barnes," he called. "What's up?"

Barnes chuckled nastily. "Your buddy Percy Anhouse is down in Sick Bay, that's what's up."

Stewart raised his eyebrows. "First of all, that asshole is no buddy of mine. I repeat, what's up?" he asked.

"Asshole shot himself in the foot, that's what!" Barnes chuckled shaking his head. "He was Boatswain's Mate of the Watch on the Quarterdeck, getting relieved." He paused for a moment and looked at Stewart.

"Do you know how to properly hand over your Colt .45 when relieved?"

"Certainly—remove from holster, remove the clip, jack the receiver to clear the chamber, point in a safe direction and squeeze the trigger, then hand it over your shoulder to your relief —right?" he said.

"Exactly right. Percy baby didn't quite get it right. He jacked the receiver, removed the clip, pointed the weapon down and fired a .45 slug through his foot." Barnes grinned at Stewart. "Is that what they teach Radiomen to do?"

Stewart seethed and said, "Boats, he ain't a radioman, he's a fuckin' Boatswain's Mate striker. About the right intelligence level." Barnes glared at Stewart, growled something under his breath and stalked off.

Stewart choked down a laugh and ran up the ladder to tell the radio gang about the latest Percy Anhouse goof.

0730, 07 May 1951
USS Hoquiam PF-5
On Station, Patrolling in vicinity of
Songjin, North Korea

Crack
Crack Crack
Crack

Stewart steadied his coffee mug as Thirty-one fired again. He continued filing messages, reaching over to his mug every time one of the Main Batteries fired. Anymore, unless the firing was intense, he seldom went out. The only time they went to GQ was every dawn and dusk against a surprise attack.

It was interesting to go out when one of the 40's fired. That meant they were almost close enough to hit the beach with rocks. Griffin was growling as he continually retuned the RBS. As long as the Task Group Common was on a Low Frequency, they couldn't listen to a Guam Low Frequency. They never used the pre-War Two RAK or RAL receivers: useless as tits on a boar.

Finished with the filing, he got down on his hands and knees with a foxtail and swept under the two radio positions, tapping James and Griffin's feet as a hint to let him sweep under them. Completing that task, he stood up and tapped the dirt into the shit can. He was free. A little sack time maybe.

Blam
Blam blam

Aha! That's Forty-one.

He moved around into James's view and motioned out. James grinned and nodded.

Stew's curiosity is going to kill him one of these days.

Lee jammed his white hat on his head and stuffed his arms into his foul weather jacket and headed out through the port hatch onto the oh-one deck.

Blam
Blam blam blam blam

Hey, this sounds interesting.

He trotted aft beyond Secondary Conn and stopped, puzzled. He stared at some gray streaks on the deck.

Blam blam blam blam

What the hell had those deck apes been dragging across the deck?

He ducked as a bee buzzed by his ear. He looked around but couldn't see the bees, but a few more zipped by.

What the hell are bees doing this far away from land?

Then he looked where Forty-one was pointed at a hillside close to the beach.

That's funny: that flickering light looks like electric brush sparks!

"Holy shit! Machine gun fire!" he screamed and squatted.

Someone grunted, and then screamed in pain.

"I'm hit."

"Gun Control this is Forty-one. Harper, our pointer, says he's hit—I don't see any blood but he's doubled over."

A repeating metallic splat kept hitting the gun tub and ready ammo locker.

In the distance, a machine gun could be heard firing—faintly—and it was firing at the Hoquiam.

"Down everybody—machine gun fire," yelled the Gun Captain.

Stewart ducked inside Forty-two's gun tub and very carefully peered across the deck at Mount Forty-one where Harper was slumped over his Pointer crank handles.

A seaman from First Division was swearing steadily. He chose to duck behind the 40mm open ready ammo locker adjacent to rows of stacked empty brass 3-inch shells in canisters were located, but he didn't have any safer place to go.

"Get a Stokes for Harper." yelled someone.

From somewhere, the metal chicken-wire form fitting Stokes Litter came crashing and sliding across the exposed deck.

"Control Forty-one—I see people on the beach where the machine gun is. Request permission to open fire?

"But they hit Harper. Aye aye, sir. Cease fire—cease fire," the Gun Captain yelled in disgust.

Stewart crouched and scuttled across the deck scooting on his knuckles and knees to Harper just as the First Loader moved over to him.

Harper's face was scrunched up in pain; both hands were pressing his lower belly. The First Loader and Stewart stood up, hunched over to reduce exposure, and lifted Harper out of his Pointer seat. At the movement, he screamed sharply and whimpered.

The Gun Captain helped Stewart and the First Loader lift Harper into the Stokes Litter and strap him in tight. Harper's screaming had dropped to a whimper as they strapped him into the Stokes Litter. Harper's face was pale as the sheen of sweat suddenly appeared on his forehead.

"He's going into shock, we gotta move," whispered the Gun Captain.

Crouching and straining, the First Loader and Stewart lifted the Stokes with Harper, the First Loader on the front and Stewart on the rear. Both men stayed as low as they could and scurried swiftly across the deck to the midships hatch by Sickbay.

The First Loader stepped over the hatch combing, turned around, and began backing down the ladder. Harper was going down feet first, his head at Stewart's end. Harper was pale and gasping with his face screwed up as if he had severe stomach cramps. However, he did not cry out.

As the First Loader carefully backed down the ladder, he yelled over his shoulder at the top of his lungs., "Corpsman, Corpsman, he's hit, get the fuck out here!"

The Chief and Webb yanked open Sickbay's door and looked out. Seeing the Stokes litter coming down, the Chief motioned to Webb and they stepped back in to prepare the table for a patient.

Meanwhile, Stewart was forced to stand, beginning to lift his end of the litter up in the air, hindered by the chicken wire cutting into his fingers.

Oh shit! Am I due for a slug?

His back felt a very peculiar tingling sensation—a feeling of exposure as he stood full height to lift Harper over the hatch combing.

Lee already figured out what those gray streaks on the deck and the bees he had heard zipping by his head were. This strange feeling continued until his head was below the combing. Then he shivered once all over. The Loader looked back at him, and then grinned nervously as he guessed why Stewart had shivered.

They got the litter even with the steel table. The Chief and Webb hastily unstrapped Harper and lifted him onto the table. He moaned softly as if he had bumped a painful bruise.

"All right people, get out. Webb and I have work to do. Take the Stokes back where it belongs," ordered Chief Farmer intensely.

"Will you let us know how he is, Chief?" asked the Loader.

"Yeah yeah, go!" His voice was intense and harsh as he pushed them out the door and shut it.

Stewart and the First Loader looked at each other then realized there were other people crowding around them. They shrugged and waited.

The ship trembled as it picked up speed.

The 1MC clicked on

"Mounts Thirty-one and Thirty-three man your guns Mounts Thirty-one and Thirty-three man your guns."

The 1MC clicked off and right back on.

"Condition Two, set material condition able throughout the ship Condition Two, set material condition able throughout the ship."

Hatches began slamming shut and their dogs clanged as the ship sealed as best it could for watertight integrity. The sailors standing outside Sickbay looked at each other.

It sorta added up. We were going back in and fire at those babies.

Maybe this time they had something larger for counter battery against us. Collectively, they nodded and began leaving for their work areas. Stewart went back up the ladder and through the scuttle since they dropped the hatch and secured the dogs.

He walked over to the gray streaks on the deck and remembered the bees he heard. Stewart squatted and felt the graphite-like traces where the machine gun bullets had ricocheted or skipped along the deck.

I was walking through the raindrops on that one!

He stood, noticing that two destroyers were heading their way in a hurry.

Stewart quietly stepped into the Radio Shack and grabbed his mug.

"What's going on out there, Stew?" asked Griffin.

"We just got our first Purple Heart," he said shortly.

James slammed down his cup and yelled:, "Goddammit, Stew, don't stop there. What the hell you talking about?"

Stewart took a couple of minutes to explain the graphite trails, the bees, taking Harper down, the feeling in his back he had never felt before.

"Stewart, you should be proud of yourself. You helped rescue a man in a very dangerous situation. You could have been killed or wounded yourself," spoke Mr. Forsythe, who always showed up at the most unlikely moments.

Stewart stared at him mutely. He did not need reminding.

Sometimes, Mr. Forsythe, sometimes.

"Stewart, let me get this straight for the record. You went across the deck, helped get Harper into the basket, carried the back end back across the deck, and were last down the hatch. Is that correct?" Mr. Forsythe badgered with a certain amount of wonderment in his voice.

"Yes sir."

"What was that about the bees. I didn't catch that."

"He was trying to catch machine gun slugs with his teeth, Mr. Forsythe!" answered Masters.

Lieutenant (jg) Forsythe turned red, nodded, and left the Radio Shack, still not understanding.

Stewart sipped his coffee, staring out the porthole a few minutes swaying back and forth keeping his sealegs. The door opened. Stew glanced up: it was Billy Boy.

"James, can I borrow Stew for just a moment?"

James cocked his head at him, curiously. "Mind if I tag along, Chief?"

Chief Billons looked at James, thoughtfully.

"No, this is personal, a private matter, if you don't mind. Stewart is in no trouble a-tall, if that's what you're thinkin'."

James nodded his head at Stewart, who put his mug down, and followed Billy Boy out the door. Billy Boy didn't say a word; just led him out through the Port hatch to Secondary Conn where they were alone.

"Stew, I talked to the gun crew. Everett, the First Loader, told me you were the only other fella to help Harper. I want you to know that was a fine thing you did. You seem pretty cool in a tight. You can be part of my crew anytime, Stew. Put her there!" Reaching out with both hands, they shook hands tightly.

"You know Stew, I lost some of my gun crews in the Battle of Leyte Gulf in the Philippines in the last war. I thought I'd just lost another in this miserable war.

"Porky says he cannot find any wound entry or exit point, and there is no blood on him. His belly hurts though. Porky figures the pointer crank bucked backward and caught him in the gonads. Harper says that's not true. Anyway, he's going to stay in Sickbay for a while. That's all I wanted to say, Stew."

Stewart had been staring at the graphite trails as the Chief spoke, following his eyes. He recognized what they were, squeezed Stewart's shoulder, and headed forward to Thirty-one. Lee slowly walked back to the Radio Shack.

Lieutenant Porter opened the Radio Shack door and looked at James with a worried look on his face.

"Are we in contact with CTG 95.2?"

"Yes sir. I heard him less than," comparing the clock and his circuit log, "three minutes ago, Mr. Porter. Got something hot?" responded James.

"Yeah. Harper was wounded after all. He is in bad shape and Chief Farmer says we have to get him to a hospital facility. The Captain is making up a message now. Make sure we have 95.2."

James held up his finger meaning "wait one" and reached for the power switch by the CW key. He glanced over his shoulder at the TDE, to make sure it was switched to the Low Frequency side and pushed the power button. As the transmitter needles came up, he reached in and touched the key briefly. The needles flicked.

G4G4 DE NZCY K
NZCY DE G4G4 K
DE NZCY R AR

"He's got us loud and clear," turning to look up at Lieutenant Porter, "and you could hear him. Now, he's also alerted we are up to something. So, he will be prepared for our call. Tell the Captain it had better be Operational Immediate or better. Pretty heavy traffic on here."

Everyone slipped aside as the Captain, a very sober and worried Captain, moved in. He looked around, holding a message blank in his hand. James took it, read it once, looked at the Captain and pointed to the precedence line.

"Flash," said the Captain flatly, not leaving room for discussion.

Stewart, not about to mention it, wondered about that because the Flash precedence was only for initial Enemy Contact Reports. Then again, this was an enemy contact at that.

James looked at the clock, assigned a date time group, and called CTG 95.2.

G4G4 DE NZCY OC K
DE G4G4 ZBO1 AS (pause as that operator rolled paper into his typewriter) **K**
DE NZCY—T—P3U9
OC MAY 7, 1951
FM NZCY
TO G4G4
INFO P3U9
GR43
BT

COUNTERBATTERY WHILE FIRING 40MM INTERDICTION ON RAIL TRESTLE SOUTH OF SONGJIN RESULTED IN ONE WOUNDED MAN CRITICAL INJURY X HMC ADVISES MAN IN JEOPARDY UNLESS HOSPITALIZED X REQUIRES BLOOD X REQUIRES SURGERY X PATIENT HARPER GMM3 274 89 2338 USNR BLOOD TYPE ABLE POSITIVE X ADVISE
BT
DE G4G4 R AR

(CTG 95.2 relay to CTF 95, from Hoquiam to CTG 95.2, information copy to CTF 95.)

James drew the Time of Delivery message cross (TOD, Task Group Common, when CTG95.2 received the message, and who (James) sent it.) and scribbled out the delivery information. He nodded to the Captain, solicitously.

"We just have to wait for them to come back with an answer, Captain. I'm sure that message is flying around the Helena right now. Can you tell us what happened? We heard some from Stewart but nothing about the wound."

The Captain squatted behind James—and Mr. Forsythe hastily backed across to his room and grabbed his chair for the Captain. The Captain looked up at the Radio Gang, then to Stewart.

"I heard about your part in the action, Stewart." Stewart nodded slowly. "Forty-one had fired several rounds at a railroad bridge. The cordite smoke obscured the target. So, Harper stopped firing and stood up in the stirrups, looking over the iron sights, to see the bridge more clearly.

That is when he got hit in the groin, right up next to his privates. It left such a tiny entry hole and stayed inside so that Chief Farmer didn't find anything. Later on, Harper got an erection and started urinating blood." He paused. Then smiled whimsically. "Did you know his nickname is Lucky?"

"No sir, but he's still alive," commented James.

NZCY DE G4G4 K

James held up his finger, pulled his cans back on his ears and pressed the TDE power switch.

DE NZCY K

DE G4G4
OP MAY 7, 1951
FM G4G4
TO NZCY
INFO P3U9
GR31
BT
HELENA UNDERWAY AT 35 KNOTS FOR MEET AT POINT XRAY X PROCEED POINT XRAY BEST POSSIBLE SPEED TO TRANSFER HARPER WITH ALL SERVICE

RECORDS AND SEABAG X REPORT
ETA POINT XRAY
BT

G4G4 DE NZCY R AR

The Captain reached for the 21MC and flipped Bridge, Combat, and Wheelhouse.

"Bridge Combat Radio—All ahead flank. Make one six five turns. Lay in best course for Point Xray. Give me ETA Point Xray. Helena departed Wonsan a couple of minutes ago, SOA 35 knots, to meet us at Point Xray for hand off.

"Bridge aye aye Captain. Engine room answers all ahead flank one six five turns, sir."

Click click

"This is Combat—Recommend come to course two one eight true. ETA is 7.5 hours. Speed of closure will be 53.7 knots, Captain."

The Hoquiam was beginning to tremble and surge through the seas as she increased speed to her best output. For once, the weather chose to be clear and calm, albeit very cold.

"This is Radio—Very well. Mr. Dixon, come to two one eight true. I will be here for a few more minutes. Then I will be in Sickbay. I want to know when you pick up the Helena on radar, Combat."

"Aye aye, Captain."

Click click

He flipped all the 21MC switches up and asked for another message blank. Stewart had one prepared and handed him the clipboard. Commander Brown thought for a moment, printed the message rapidly, signed it, and handed the clipboard to James on Task Group Common. James looked at it, nodded and reached into the key.

G4G4 DE NZCY P K
DE G4G4 K
DE NZCY—T—P3U9
P MAY 7, 1951
FM NZCY
TO G4G4
INFO P3U9
GR9
BT
SOA 18PNT7 X COURSE 218T X ETA 7PNT5 HOURS
BT

NZCY DE G4G4 R AR

The Hoquiam drove Southwestward toward Point Xray, hour after hour, the ship trembling with exertion of an all out effort from her engines.

"Bridge, Combat—We have Helena on the 'scope. Recommend coming left to two one five true."

Click click

"Come left to two one five true, Helmsman."

"Left to two one five true, aye aye, sir. Rudder answers the helm. Steady on new course two one five, sir."

"Very well."

1530, May 7, 1951
USS Hoquiam PF-5
Point Xray
Rendezvous USS Helena (CA-75)

The weather had abated some but the sea swells were still relatively high. The Captain, several officers, and Chief Billons discussed whether they should use their own Motor whaleboat which now handled superbly, or ask the Helena to use one of their 50' Motor Launches.

The Captain and Chief agreed. They should use their own boat because it actually would give a much smoother ride through the rough water. The Chief left to make preparations and pick his crew.

"Bridge, Rangefinder—I have Helena masthead in sight."

Lieutenant Marston looked up and waved to the Fire Controlman. He and the Captain looked aft on the starboard side to see how Chief Billons was coming along. He had the boat snugged tightly against the hull at deck level.

His crew lashed a couple of planks to the thwarts where Harper would lay in his Stokes litter. The Chief's crew had even lashed an oar upright to hold a bottle of plasma for the trip across to the Helena. Chief Farmer had already stated he was going to give him another morphine shot about five minutes before they took him out of sickbay.

They did not slow down until the Helena was 2,000 yards distant.

"All Engines stop."

"All engines stop. Engine room answers all engines stop. Turns indicators moved to zero zero zero by the Engine Room, sir."

"Very well."

In the late afternoon, they coasted to a stop near the Helena. The Hoquiam was rolling a little bit, but not enough to cause any strain. Stewart turned to watch as Harper came up through the hatch from Sickbay. Involuntarily, he glanced down at the graphite trails.

With Harper's bearers holding the Stokes stretcher, Webb and Chief Farmer came across the deck where Chief Billons waited. The boat crew boarded the Motor Whaleboat as soon as they saw Harper's stretcher. Chief Billons looked up to the Bridge at the Captain who waved for him to continue. The two 'Hooks took one end of the Stokes and carefully positioned that end on the centerline forward. The Engineer and Coxswain grabbed the other end and brought Harper's feet aft along the centerline.

Four gray kapok lifejackets were fastened to the sides of the Stokes litter cage just in case. Two additional crewmen were coming along to jerk loose the basket tie downs and to handle Harper if the boat capsized. Everyone aboard and in place, Chief Farmer climbed aboard with a small red satchel.

Two men released the boat from the cleats on the roll in. As the roll reversed, the boat gently swung free. Chief Billons looked forward; raising a clenched fist, then extended a finger and slowly twirled it. The Hoquiam motor whaleboat began to slide gently down to the water's edge. Unfortunately, the water was rough. The Chief clenched his fist; the boat stopped.

Barnes, the Coxswain, checked everyone again for lifejackets tied and fastened properly and nodded to his Engineer to start the engine. The Engineer primed once, checked to make sure the transmission was in neutral, and pushed the starter. The engine caught on the second cylinder. Barnes looked up at the Chief.

"Any final instructions, Boats?"

"Yeah, easy over and come back safe."

"That's a roger, Chief."

The Chief looked up and twirled his finger again. As the boat splashed, the 'Hooks gave hard heaves on the pelican hook releases and the boat was almost free. The Bow Hook stumbled forward and when ready, looked back to Barnes. Barnes looked at his engineer, then up to Billy Boy and gave him thumbs up.

"Cast off, Barnes," called Chief Billons.

Barnes pointed to the Bow Hook who released the Painter, and reached for his bell lanyard.

Dingdingding—reverse—and pushed the 'tiller with his knees, left to force the bow out.

Dingding—neutral and straighten the 'tiller.

Ding—ahead slowly, moving away from the hull.

Dingdingdingding—full ahead and slight push to the left to place the waves on the bow.

Stewart went up where Mount 32 should be and watched with several others as their boat came under the Helena's crane. They could not see the actual hookup but damned if the stretcher wasn't gracefully lifted onto the Helena's deck where some medical staff waited for him.

They saw Harper being lifted onto a wheeled gurney and hustled through a hatch. Then nothing. The Stokes litter came back into the boat. Barnes headed back to the ship. If Harper survived, it was doubtful anyone would see him again since all his records and sea bag went with him in the basket.

The Chief swung in and stored the Motor whaleboat with its canvas cover attached. The Hoquiam came about and began a lazy 12-knot return to Songjin to help continue the blockade.

NZCY DE G4G4 R K

DE NZCY K

DE G4G4

R MAY 8, 1951
FM G4G4
TO NZCY
INFO P3U9
BT
HARPER OUT OF SURGERY X 150 VOLUNTEERS OFFERED BLOOD X NEEDED 19 PINTS X A PNT27 CALIBER UNJACKETED SLUG WAS REMOVED X MARINE DET G/SGT IDENTIFIED SLUG FROM KALISHNAKOV BURP GUN X HOW CLOSE DO YOU GET HOQUIAM X HARPER CRITICAL BUT EXPECT NORMAL RECOVERY X XFER TO NAVHOSP YOKO SOONEST
BT

G4G4 DE NZCY R TKS AR

di-dit

Roney and Stewart looked round-eyed at the last exchange. Thanks and di-dit were definitely number one on the no no list. Lloyd noticed their expression as he powered down the transmitter and made entries in the log.

"Fuck 'em. If the gumshoes caught it, let them kick me out of the Navy, but do not let me catch you doing either one or it's your ass," he said with a smile on his face.

"Roney, route the fucking board. Stewart, go eat chow before I starve to death."

0615, May 13, 1951
Fleet Weather Center,
Commander U.S. Naval Forces Marianas,
Agaña, Guam. Marianas Islands

Stewart trotted up to the Bridge with a weather message.

This must be the millionth weather message I've run around the ship.

It was different, though. A Tropical Depression had formed near the Equator. Fleet Weather Center (FWC) Guam was forecasting it would move northwesterly instead of westerly. The message precedence was Operational Immediate.

He saluted and handed the board to Lieutenant Marston.

"Got a tropical depression for you, Mr. Marston."

Mr. Marston automatically looked at the sky before he began reading the weather message.

Wonder how those aerographers handle those reports?

Messrs. Marston and Dixon were on the Bridge. They signed off and Mr. Marston hurried away with his Navigator's copy to plot the Depression.

Abert, (he pronounced it A'-bear) Aerographer's Mate First Class, or AG1, stood 5'6" in his bare feet, jet black curly hair, showing his French ancestry in his stance and coarse looks, stared eastward out the wooden-louvered window at the sunrise, absently noting the cumulus, or CU, and stratocumulus, or SC, cloud coverage this morning. They made a beautiful palette of yellows, oranges, and reds, turning silvery white as the sun came above the horizon. Just a typical, tropical day at Agaña, Guam, in the Commander, Naval Forces, Marianas building.

The headquarters was situated on the hill overlooking the Naval Base by Apra Harbor, and the town of Agaña, capital of Guam.

Abert was dressed in the Uniform of the Day: white trousers with white web belt and black buckle, white skivvy shirt, white hat, and black shoes and socks.

He carefully placed his coffee cup on the table and picked up a large stack of weather reports that had come in during the past hour. There were about a hundred of them. To save transmission time, all reporting ships, stations, and aircraft used the standard international weather reporting code. He tapped and shuffled the stack into a squared pile, licked his thumb and forefinger and began to sort the reports into four piles based on reported latitude and longitude.

Each International Hydrographic code group consisted of five numerals. The first group showed the time of the report in Greenwich Mean Time. The next two groups reported latitude north or south and longitude east or west. The next seven groups listed the barometric pressure, temperature, wind speed and direction, Sea State, kind and amount of precipitation during the last hour, type of cloud cover, and the amount of cloud cover, in ninths. Aircraft included their altitude at the time of the latest report.

The message 'originator' (FM) line stated which ship, station, or aircraft had sent the message. It was hard to make a mistake drafting, transmitting, or receiving this kind of message. Numbers were the easiest thing in the world to send or receive over the CW radio circuits.

Abert carried these to four sailors working on their section of the weather model, and dropped the weather reports at the table's four corners. The sailors were busy constructing barometric isobar gradients and wind information based on data received from each reporting party. Gradually, curved lines appeared from the mass of data.

He moved along to another table dropping off Winds Aloft data gathered from flying aircraft and radiosonde units hanging below weather balloons. This chart built a picture about cloud formations and upper air conditions, painting another part of the puzzle.

Lieutenant Melville, slim but not skinny, nearly 6'3", light brown close-cropped hair leaned over the last completed weather complex, waiting to overlay the new data. He believed he would upgrade this tropical depression to a Tropical Storm named Annabelle at the next reporting period in four hours. This storm could turn into a typhoon within twelve hours. Abert stopped alongside the lieutenant and folded his arms to stare at the chart, too.

"If this one follows the historical path, Mr. Melville, looks like it's going to cross the Ryukyus into the East China Sea," said Abert. Lieutenant Melville stepped closer to the chart hanging on the wall and traced the old route with his left hand, stopping as he crossed the Ryukyus. He leaned against the chart and looked over at his Leading Petty Officer.

He thought a moment, "Trouble is, which path then—Yellow Sea into China, or up the Korea Strait into the Sea of Japan? We should have a better picture once this new weather data is drawn. Let me see your preliminary reports as soon as you're ready."

"Aye aye, sir," Abert responded and went back to his desk.

Once the Fleet Weather Center declares a cyclonic Tropical Storm and gives it a girl's name, the message handling precedence bumps up to Emergency. At that time, all ships automatically increase the number of local weather condition reports they transmit from one every four hours, to one per hour.

R MAY 13, 1951
FM COMDESDIV 12

TO USS HOQUIAM
BT
BON VOYAGE X WELL DONE
BT

The Hoquiam was moving at standard speed in a southeasterly direction. C division was at Quarters for Muster at Fair Weather Parade and Lieutenant (jg) Forsythe was speaking.

"Men, as you may know, we will be out of the combat zone in about fourteen more hours on our way to Sasebo. After five days, we go home to Yokosuka for three weeks upkeep and repairs." He paused for a moment, looking for someone.

"Stewart," he continued with a grin on his face, "the Captain says to ask your girlfriend what we are going to do next. Got it?"

Stewart frowned. "Aye aye, sir," as he blushed deeply.

Comedian!

"Any questions?" No questions. "Relieve your quarters."

Stewart had just gotten off the mid-watch. He headed below to shower and shave before he hit the pad. After undressing and wrapping a towel around his waist, he headed back up the ladder with his shaving gear. But: first things first. He sat on the trough and relaxed sleepily. As he sat staring at the deck, he looked at some small scabs on his left knee.

How'd I do that?

Absently, he picked at a scab. It came off, stuck to the end of his fingernail. He glanced at the scab idly before flicking it into the trough below him.

Continuing to sit there, it came to him that something was wrong with that scab. He looked down and found another one. Carefully picking it off, he brought it up close to his eyes and inspected the scab.

Oh shit: it's got legs!

Stewart completed his assigned task, all the while looking for more little scab-like creatures. He grabbed his gear and went back down to dress. Hurriedly, he made is way aft to Sickbay and knocked. Webb opened the door.

"What's up, Stew?"

"I think I've got a problem, Doc. Can I come in and show you?"

Webb stood aside, allowing Stewart to pass through. Chief Farmer had already completed morning Sick Call, but Webb and the Chief knew the Radiomen worked weird hours.

Webb turned and waited for Stewart to say what was on his mind.

Stewart held up his little finger, right in front of Webb's eyes. Webb grabbed his hand and looked at Stewart's fingernail with interest.

"Well Stewart, you're not alone. You've got a dose of the crabs." Webb smiled and looked at Stewart, then leaned closer for a better look. "Even in your mustache and eyebrows. Christ, you are infested. Strip, I want to look you over."

Stewart slumped in humiliation.

How the hell could I have gotten the crabs? We've been to sea for almost forty-five days.

"Strip all your clothes, Stew, everything. I need to check your body, arm pits, and crotch a lot closer than I'd like to do."

Webb sat down on his little steel piano stool while Stewart stripped down. Webb had a wry smile on his face.

So far, twenty-seven people, including two officers, had showed up with crabs. Another present from the Soviet Navy.

The Chief had confided the information to Webb that other PF's were reporting alarming rates of crab infestation.

"Turn slowly around, Stew. Okay, spread your legs and hold your family jewels to one side. All right, raise your arms so I can see your armpits. Yep, you got a real good dose. Don't know why you weren't reporting this a couple of weeks ago. You must itch like all fury. Wait a minute."

"It's too damn cold to itch, Webb," Stewart answered in disgust.

While Stewart shivered, Webb opened a cabinet and took out a gray DDT bug bomb.

"Close your eyes and mouth pinch your nose shut. I'll start with your face and hair." The cool and gentle shush of the stinky bug bomb operating stopped.

"Okay, raise your right arm and look to the left."

The cool spraying concentrated on his armpit.

"Can you hear them screaming and choking as I gas the little bastards, Stew?"

This ship is full of comedians.

"Arm down. Give me the other arm and turn your face away."

Stewart moved in embarrassment, hoping no one else would notice.

Whew, it stinks.

"Spread your legs wide so I can get through all that hair, Stew."

"Okay, now turn around, keeping the legs wide and bend over."

The cold blast of DDT hit him in the crack, condensed, and trickled down to drip on the deck. Webb finished with the bug bomb and replaced the canister in the cabinet, and set a timer for fifteen minutes. Turning back to Stewart, he said

"Okay, go sit in that corner on these paper towels," Webb said handing him a bunch of paper towels and pointing to a place out of his way. "When the timer goes off, put your skivvies back on and go shower thoroughly with lots of soap and lots of hot water. If you don't shower when I tell you, you will blister all over your body. Got it?"

Stewart nodded miserably. He started to gather his clothes but Webb would not let him.

"As soon as you dry, put on some clean skivvies. Come back here with all the clothes in your locker, plus your mattress and fart sack, pillow and case, and both blankets—everything, got it?"

Stewart nodded again.

"While everything is being steamed and dried by the laundry, you're going to return and spray your locker."

Dingggg

Stewart stepped out into the passageway in his zoris and skivvy shorts only. He had to walk by several offices, through the Mess Deck and Galley, by the head, and down to his compartment. There was absolutely nothing he could do about the jibes he got along the way.

"Hey look, fellas, another dose of crabs walking by," said one voice.

"See, I told you. I swear I saw a thousand of them lil critters marching up and down his back."

"Jeez, Stew, use after shave lotion, not DDT."

"A better method is to shave one side of your balls, soak the other side with lighter fluid and light it. When the crabs rush out into the clearing, stab them with an ice pick. Works every time!"

He tried to ignore their hazing and ribald comments as he walked through the Mess Deck. It was hard to do. Stewart thought he must be blushing all over his body.

As fast as he could without losing his zoris, he got into the compartment, grabbed his shaving gear again and headed back up. A Master-At-Arms waited at the door to the head.

"Head is closed for an hour for cleaning, sailor. You'll have to wait."

"Hey, sheriff, I can't do that. Got to get this DDT stuff off me."

The MAA backed off a few inches and grinned. "In that case, have a nice long hot shower just like I did yesterday."

Stewart mumbled his thanks. He took his Gillette double-edged razor into the shower with a new blade. His mustache was coming off.

Dry, with clean skivvy shorts and shirt on, he carried all his clothes back to Sick Bay where Webb gave him the rest of his clothes and took him across the passageway to the laundry.

"Aranzas, here's another special job for you. He'll be sitting in Sick Bay waiting for you to get done."

Aranzas waved, took Stewart's clothing, and disappeared inside.

Stewart sat in Sick Bay while his neatly folded clothes were being tumbled in dry steam.

Not much sleeping off this midwatch.

Hoquiam was passing out of Area George toward the channel to Sasebo Harbor when Stewart showed up on the Bridge.

"Emergency, Captain," he stated, thrusting out the board and pen.

Commander Brown rapidly scanned the message and looked up at the sky. Then, he slowly went over the message very carefully.

The depression was now Tropical Storm Annabelle. At the moment, it appeared to curving toward Okinawa but you never knew how these storms would twist and turn.

"Make sure the Quartermaster gets a copy of this right away for the Navigator, Stewart."

"Aye aye, Captain," Stewart responded and passed the board to Lieutenant (jg) Trapp, Officer of the Deck.

"Shift Colors—shift Colors"

The Tacoma's line-handling crew caught the first line to the USS Tacoma PF3, moored to Buoy X-2, in Sasebo Harbor. Commander Brown watched Dix handle the ship as he leaned back into the Bridge forecorner. He pulled his hat down a little snugger in the increasingly strong wind, laid his arms along the top of the Bridge windshield, and gazed about his ship.

He had pride in his crew and ship. They had performed superbly. Tension was beginning to unwind out of the crew. Bellies began to relax. They had spent forty-three days on the line from Wonsan to Songjin to Chongjin and back to Songjin, firing the Main Battery and 40's night and day to keep the Chinks off balance, all the time aware the North Koreans were sowing Russian and Chink mines in those waters.

Wait a minute. What was it that staff message said?

UNC was upset to hear the uncomplimentary names—Gooks, Japs, and Chinks—applied to the Koreans, Japanese, and Nationalist or Communist Chinese. From now on, everyone is supposed to refer to their nationality with correct terminology. Japs or Nips must become Japanese. Gooks must become Koreans, ROK, NK or DRK. Chinks must be Chinese, ChiNats or ChiComs.

A smile grew as he remembered the goodbye speech by their ROK Navy advisor, Lieutenant Commander Arlin, last week. He kept referring to those goddammed gooks, meaning the North Korean troops.

He was going to have to sit down and count all the destruction they had accomplished. Six trains busted. It was awesome to believe they had fired over 3,500 rounds of 3-inch ammo from just two guns and about 450 rounds from both 40mm's.

Commander Brown stretched and relaxed. Tonight he would sleep in his stateroom, not the sea cabin.

R MAY 13, 1951
FM CTF95
TO USS HOQUIAM
INFO CTG95.5
BT
CTF95 SAYS WELL DONE TO CAPTAIN OFFICERS AND MEN OF HOQUIAM FOR EXCEPTIONALLY

OUTSTANDING PERFORMANCE DURING 43 DAYS IN OP AREA X REAR ADMIRAL ALLEN E. SMITH USN
BT

0520, 14 May 1951
Fleet Weather Center
Commander, U.S. Naval Forces Marianas, Agaña, Guam

Lieutenant Melville and Abert studied the finished chart for this period. Without a doubt, the typhoon season was starting with a roar. Annabelle now packed winds of 110 knots near the center. The eye of the storm was three miles across. Its speed of advance was an alarming twelve knots. Crossing the Ryukyus right now, Annabelle appeared to be intensifying and curving northward for the Korea Strait. This meant Annabelle would affect the Korean peninsula and Kyushu landmasses. Damage reports were coming in from Okinawa and Taiwan already.

Abert prepared a standard typhoon weather message for the fleet and brought it over to the board where Lieutenant Melville stood, checking more figures as they came in. Lieutenant Melville looked at the wall clock to see how much time they had.

"Task Force seventy-seven is going to have their hands full. I bet we get a direct message from CTF77 within an hour asking for a good place to hide."

He signed the message and handed it back to Abert.

"Get it out to NavCommSta Guam right away. They have to get it on George Fox broadcast to the fleet."

OI MAY 14, 1951
FM FWC GUAM
TO ALL AIRCRAFT SHIPS AND STATIONS WESTPAC
BT
TROPICAL STORM ANNABELLE UPGRADED TO TYPHOON X ANNABELLE ONE X 13/0800 GMT X WINDS NEAR CENTER 110 KNOTS X WELL DEFINED EYE CMA THREE MILE DIAMETER X SPEED OF ADVANCE TWELVE KNOTS X COURSE 325 X EYE FIXED BY RADAR CROSSING RYUKYUS AT PRESENT X EIGHT HOUR FORECAST X ANNABELLE INTENSIFYING AND RECURVING NORTHWARD TOWARD THE KOREA STRAIT X WINDS IN NORTHEAST QUADRANT TO 100 MILES EXPECTED TO BE 50 KNOTS INCREASING TOWARD CENTER X WINDS IN NORTHWEST QUADRANT TO 100 MILES OVERLAND EXPECTED TO REDUCE TO 35 TO 45 KNOTS X INCREASING TOWARD CENTER
BT

1730, 14 May 1951
USS Hoquiam PF-5

Moored Buoy X-2
Sasebo Harbor, Japan

The Chiefs' Mess Cook had closed the deck hatch to keep the Chiefs' Quarters dry when the rain began. He neglected to remove the deck-hatch canvas-hood because he was preparing the Chiefs' Mess for dinner. The canvas hood that covered the hatchway was tall enough that the Chiefs did not have to duck their heads. Normally, the deck hatch was up in port so the Chiefs could enter and depart their quarters without having to walk through the mess deck.

Chief Billons sat down to eat dinner just as the mooring chain over his head began jolting softly, sounding like a hollow drum. By the time he finished eating, it was near 1800 and the chain was banging pretty hard.

Frowning, the Chief stepped up the ladder and cracked the scuttle.

Christ, feel that fuckin' wind!

He was surprised when he felt the power of the wind.

Very unusual for Sasebo.

He pulled the scuttle shut without securing it and twisted a battle lantern from its bulkhead fixture.

Now for a looksee at the mooring buoy and chain.

The Chief cocked the scuttle open and climbed through. Dropping the scuttle and securing it, he peered around the canvas hood toward the bow into the wind and drenching downpour, pointing the battle lantern at the active mooring tackle. Snapping the light off, he ducked back into the slight protection of the canvas. Water streamed down his face and his khaki uniform was already soaking wet. Chief Billons considered his next move as he took care of some personal problems.

His glasses went into a shirt pocket. He snatched his combination hat as the wind tried to tear it from his head. He loosened the chinstrap all the way. Back on his head it went, chin strap under his chin. The Chief snugged the strap as tight as the strap would allow.

I'm not going to lose this fucker over the side!

He leaned into the wind and rain, inspecting the tackle, thinking it might not hold. Grimly, he headed aft to the Wardroom for Lieutenant Dixon, leaning back into the wind as he held onto the lifelines and walked carefully. The weather was building fast. The strong wind made it very difficult to open the thwartship hatch into Officers' Country, but he made it.

Chief Billons swept open the green curtain door to the Wardroom and stood outside. He saw no reason to drip water on to their deck. Conversation died as all officers looked at the Chief in surprise. Lieutenant Dixon, sensing the Chief had an important report for him, placed his fork on his plate and looked with raised eyebrows at the Chief.

"Mr. Dixon," he paused to blow water off the tip of his nose. "I think you'd better inspect the mooring lines, sir. This typhoon is beginning to raise a ruckus in the Harbor."

"Somehow, I don't think my raincoat or slicker would do any good in that weather out there. Let's go, Chief."

He and Mr. Dixon had their battle lanterns turned on, as they made their way forward to the bow. The battle lanterns spotlighted the mooring buoy, X-2. The Tacoma had gotten underway right after they pulled in. Chief Billon had suggested the port anchor chain for mooring when the Tacoma departed.

"Chief, what do you think?" asked Lieutenant Dixon, hanging onto Mount 31. "Is this going to hold or should we put the other anchor chain out? The harbor waters are high. and I am positive Small Craft Warnings are up now."

Chief Billons shrugged and shook his head.

"I don't know, Mr. Dixon." This storm could fizzle in a second or get worse."

There was a clatter and dragging sound. Both leaped to the bow and looked down to the Mooring Buoy. It was not below them where it should be. It was up ahead and seemed to be getting farther away as the wind pushed the Hoquiam backwards. The standard six inch preventer line was about to part under the pressure of 35 to 40 knot winds.

Chief Billons did not wait. He stepped back to the Windlass and released the handbrake. Lieutenant Dixon was retrieving the sledge hammer from its clips.

"Here, Chief, I've never done this," he panted holding out the sledge hammer.

The Chief pulled his knife—"Take the hand brake, Mr. Dixon,"—cut the mousing from the oyster clamp, and stepped back. He grabbed the sledge, roared, "Look out—stand back!" automatically, and swung the sledge at the oyster clamp holding the anchor chain.

Its clattering roar was heard throughout the ship as the starboard anchor dropped into the harbor. Mr. Dixon did not know how much clearance they had to Buoy X-1 behind them. He did know if the scope of chain were too short, the anchor would slip along the bottom, or drag through the bottom material. Nevertheless, he set the hand brake and held his breath.

"Now hear this—station the anchor detail on the double station the anchor detail on the double." That was Mr. Marston's voice.

Chief Billons placed his foot lightly on the chain and felt for dragging.

"Not dragging," the Chief addressed Mr. Dixon and the Captain," who had appeared out of the darkness. "We lost the mooring shackle on the port chain, sir. Lucky us, we happened to be here when it happened.

"Not luck, Chief, good seamanship," said the Captain shortly.

The Chief's grin almost glowed in the wet gloom.

"Captain, I'd like to put another preventer line back on the mooring buoy."

People began reporting to their anchor detail.

"Yes, permission granted. You'll need the Motor whaleboat, too. Is the JV phone talker here yet?"

"Yes, Captain. Lieutenant Unsenger is already on the Bridge. Bridge, Wheelhouse, Combat, and Engine room report manned and ready."

"Good. Tell the Boatswain's Mate of the Watch to call away the boat."

"Aye aye, Captain."

"Wheelhouse Foc'sl—the Captain says for the Boatswain's Mate of the Watch to call away the boat."

The 1MC opened and 'Away the Boat' warbled out on the pipe.

"Away the boat, away. Come to the Quarterdeck."

"Hays," called the Chief, "set up an eight inch manila preventer line. I'll go out with the boat and make sure it's done right. Give us lots of light, though.

"Right, Chief."

The Captain left for the Bridge, as the Chief made his way to the Quarterdeck.

The Chief walked aft rapidly but very carefully. The ship was moving about, pitched by the wind and choppy seas in the harbor. The ship's motor whaleboat was already drawn up to the quarterdeck Jacobs Ladder waiting for him.

"Barnes, you dumb shit, where's your life jacket?" yelled Chief Billons over the wind and rain.

"Right here, Chief," Barnes acknowledged, pointing down and stooped over for a soggy life jacket, soaked with rain water.

"Okay, let's get underway. The anchor detail is breaking out an eight-inch hawser to back up the anchor chain. Who's got the new anchor shackle?" One of the seamen held up a hand with the shackle in it.

"I don't see the pin. Where's that?" asked the Chief. The seaman grinned and held up his other hand with the shackle pin. Chief Billons nodded.

"Okay Barnes, go!"

Ding

Barnes cupped his hand to his mouth and yelled over the wind. "Let go the painter, Ralston."

The painter fell away as the boat moved slowly, bobbing and rocking in the chop, heading forward to their mooring buoy, itself swinging back and forth.

The winds and seas hampered Chief Billon's efforts. He turned and looked up to Hays. "Let's pick up the bitter end of the anchor chain first." Hays nodded and looked at the engineer. "Forget my bells. Watch my hand motions while we try to stay next to the buoy without getting crushed." The engineer nodded putting one hand on the gearshift and the other on the throttle.

"Ralston," yelled Barnes, "use the boat hook and grab the anchor chain." Ralston nodded, grabbed the pole and sat on the thwart bench with his legs locked under it. It took three passes before Ralston could grab the chain and pull it to him. Meanwhile, Barnes and the engineer jockeyed the motor between forward, neutral, and reverse to hold the boat steady.

"Great work, Ralston," the Chief said as he patted his shoulder. "Now, let's get on the mooring buoy."

Barnes brought the boat as close to the buoy as was safe. The Chief and Ralston leaped from the bouncing boat on to the rolling buoy. It was very difficult to stand on top of it. Ralston grinned at the chief as he countered the rocking buoy.

"Steady, Chief. You don't want to get wet—sea water wet that is," grinning in the heavy rain.

"No problem, Ralston. I'll just hang on to you if I start to slip and fall," he said, laughing.

Getting a new shackle through the mooring buoy ring was always the toughest job. By blindass luck, the shackle pin shoved through the buoy ring on the first try. Chief Billons used a marlinspike to make sure the pin was threaded properly and tightly.

The eight-inch preventer line, port mooring chain, and starboard anchor seemed to be holding, but the Captain did not like the ship's situation. The bow was lifting in the increasing winds. He was concerned the preventer or mooring chain or both could part.

"Talker, tell Mr. Hansen I want to talk with him."

"Aye aye, sir," he murmured and then spoke to Engineering.

"Captain, Mr. Hansen is on his way to the Bridge," reported the talker.

Nuts. I meant to talk to him on the JV or did he deliberately misunderstand so he could see this storm?

Lieutenant Hansen arrived in a moment, rapidly getting soaked. He appeared not to worry about the rain, though. He was eager to see. The Captain gave him a moment in the dark.

"Jim, what shape are the boilers in? How soon and how fast can you give me flank speed?"

Jim Hansen's eyes popped at the last.

Why would he want flank speed in here?

"Both boilers are on line now, Captain. A full head of steam on Number 2, and One should be ready in twenty more minutes. You can have over one hundred turns on both shafts now."

The Captain nodded and pointed to the bow. The Bridge Port and Starboard twelve-inch lights were steady on the mooring buoy. Jim now thought he understood.

"We're ready to answer bells, Captain. Permission to return to the Engine Room, sir?"

"Thanks Jim. Permission granted," the Captain agreed and turned to the Officer of the Deck.

"Mr. Unsenger, let's take some pressure off the mooring buoy. All ahead slow, make turns for five knots, rudder amidship."

"Aye aye, Captain." He opened the voice tube cover and blew it like a whistle. They closed the voice tube cover in the Wheelhouse to keep the water out.

"Wheelhouse, aye aye, sir."

"All ahead slow, make turns for five knots, rudder amidship."

"All ahead slow make turns for five knots, aye aye, sir—Engine Room answers all ahead slow and making turns for five knots. Rudder is amidship."

"Very well," he responded as he flipped the voice tube cover closed.

The ship pitched and rolled almost as much as it did in a storm at sea. After three hours, Combat reported they had Annabelle's eye on the 'scope and were tracking it.

The wind continued to intensify, applying more pressure on the ship and straining its connection to the mooring buoy. Gradually, the Captain increased the number of turns to meet the threat. For about thirty minutes in the early hours before dawn, the Hoquiam was making turns for eleven knots while moored at Buoy X-2.

May 15, 1951
Late afternoon
Green Swan Tea House
Sasebo, Japan

Rivas CS1 did not often leave the ship, and then usually for special fresh produce. His teeth grated as he remembered the first time he had tried to bring fresh produce back to the ship.

The Shore Patrolman at the entrance to the Fleet Landing looked at Rivas as he set two string bags down to pull out his ID and liberty card. The Shore Patrolman looked at the bags suspiciously. "Whatcha got in them bags, sailor?"

"These are fresh vegetables I am bringing back to the ship," he explained.

"Yeah? Untie them and let me inspect them." Rivas leaned over and pulled the bow knots free. "Have at it, fella."

The Shore Patrolman rummaged around looking for liquor bottles. "Where'ja get this stuff, sailor."

Rivas sighed. "I got them at a Japanese market. Listen, these are fresh and I need to get them aboard before they wilt. Fresh vegetables need to stay cool, you know."

What kind of ignoramus is poking his dirty hands in my bag?
He'll bruise those peaches.

He was beginning to feel tense because he had taken a long time to pick just the right greens and fruit.

"Sorry sailor, but we have to confiscate this produce. It's not legal to use Japanese grown fresh fruit and veggies, pal, because it's unfit for human consumption." Rivas's eyes bugged out as the shore patrolman threw his bags into the trash can.

"You can't do that, fella. That's mine for the ship's mess."

He gave Rivas a hard look. "Move along, sailor, before I take you into custody for interference."

Rivas thrust his jaw out at the shore patrolman, and in a rage, walked by him to the waiting area.

The second time, in Yokosuka, he attempted to bring Shiitaki mushrooms in the gate. During the ensuing heated argument, the Marine Military Policeman had been horrified to learn that all commercial mushrooms are grown in sterile manure. Still, the mushrooms stayed ashore.

He did not try it again. He decided to use diplomatic mail: the Hoquiam officers. No one searched their packages—even if they gurgled suspiciously. It was not diplomatic to search officers.

He wasn't on a buying mission today. The skies were clear and warm following Annabelle's passage two days ago. Rivas wanted to get away somewhere quiet where he could remember his Master Chef duties on the ocean liner. He found a pedicab driver with strong legs to drive him up the winding hill back of Sasebo.

When he saw the old teahouse overlooking Sasebo and the harbor, he nudged the cabbie to stop. Paying the pedicab driver one hundred yen, (about twenty-five cents) Rivas laid claim to a corner table where he looked out over the harbor at all the ships and tried to relax. A bottle of wine rested in front of him uncapped. A dainty sake cup filled with wine rested in his cupped hands. The aroma of plums teased his nose.

A rather large, rotund English Petty Officer of the Royal Navy walked in and sat down across the room. After glancing his way when he arrived, Rivas didn't pay any more attention to him. He would rather not have any companions today—just because he didn't want to think of anything.

The Petty Officer got up and strolled over, squinting at Rivas's arm.

"Excuse me, you are what your American Navy calls a Commissary Steward, is that correct?"

Annoyed that his peace was disturbed but a little curious what he was leading up to, Rivas answered, "Yes."

"Commissary Steward. Is that any relation to a cook or chef?"

Rivas looked at the English sailor carefully. "A Commissary Steward may be a cook, baker, butcher, or commissary stores specialist. On a very small ship, he might be all of them. In my situation, all of them."

The English sailor hesitated. "I see. I am one of the cooks on our aircraft carrier, HMS Triumph. That's her out there," pointing to the only carrier in the harbor. "We have 27 cooks and bakers. What ship do you have and how many cooks are you?"

"The Hoquiam PF5 at Buoy X-2, right there," pointing down on the very small ship near the inner harbor. "Three including me and four helpers."

"Oh. I was wondering, Cookee, if you could tell me how you American chaps always serve such great meals. Every time I have been offered a chance to eat in one of your messes, I have been impressed."

Is he pulling my leg? I've sure eaten many lousy meals aboard our ships—even some I have cooked!

His disinterested face moved into a friendly smile. "Care for some wine?" he asked and pointed to a chair. The Englishman looked at the plum wine and shook his head. "Rather have this ale but thanks," he said and sat down.

They began talking about different canned foods and military stores: how to sauce something up, as the Englishman said, to make it palatable. Rivas told of his attempts to bring fresh produce aboard and how he finally accomplished it.

"You know, Ransome, there's one thing that's always made me curious," Rivas offered.

"What's that, Cookee?"

"I've eaten on some of your large and small ships back in World War Two quite a few times. If it was lamb chops, roasted potatoes, honeyed carrots, and apple crumb cake for dinner, it was delicious. Every other meal I ate was between bad and worse."

Ransome laughed uproariously, slapping the table several times. "That's easy, chappie. Our cook school teaches us how to prepare lamb chops, roasted potatoes, honeyed carrots and apple crumb cake, over and over, until we get it right. They didn't teach us anything else."

Ransome and Rivas continued to talk, drink, and eat into the late hours of the evening. By the time Rivas and Ransome returned to the Fleet Landing, Rivas knew that the next day was going to be a very tough day, as he would suffer from a nasty hangover.

Barney and Lee had not taken liberty together in a long time. Barney had some shopping to do for his Mother. Lee was feeling guilty about his Mother's birthday and Mother's Day. But, he had been able to find a set of Noritake china dishes and shipped them to her from the Navy Exchange.

Lee wanted to get a special present for Ruth, back in Seattle. He had in mind a silk print pajama suit. He had seen some in Yokosuka but didn't like the pattern assortment or sizes, either. They were strolling on the street behind the main drag where most of the good shops were to be found. He spotted an interesting shop and tugged Barney's sleeve. Glancing at the sky, he could see the next rain shower was almost upon them.

"Let's look in here, Barney."

Inside were mannequins with all sorts of women's romantic clothing. Barney knew what he was looking for and they split up as they checked the wares.

"Barney, think I've found 'em," he called.

He looked at the style, and then looked for the right size. That was going to be tough because the Japanese women were so much smaller—all over—and designed their dress patterns accordingly. Slowly, the Japanese were catching on that they needed to make things on a larger scale for the American market.

"Ah sa ror, yo see sumsinga yo lika?" The sales girl had come up behind Lee while he was looking at patterns, colors, and sizes.

"Hai!" He spread one arm wide and grinned.

She's cute.

"My American girl is this big." He put his hand above her head and pulled it straight back toward himself so she could see the height. "Her shoulders are this wide." Then he pantomimed, on himself, the width of her shoulders. "Her boobs are this big." He started to put his cupped hands in front of her and thought better of it. Instead, he cupped his hands on his chest to show the size of her breasts as she giggled. Then without touching her, he put his hands where Ruth's waist and hips would be.

"That's what I want."

"Ohhh, I unnastand. Yo stay hyah sa ror. I look. Okay Joe?"

"Hai!" Lee said with a grin.

She scurried off in the little store, calling for help from other people. He watched her go through the sizing he had given her. There was more conversation and a very old bent woman picked up three pieces of material and shuffled them over to him.

She laid out three basic patterns: bamboo, girl in kimono standing on bridge, and trees.

"Yo say," waving her hands over the patterns.

Lee liked all three but thought the bamboo pattern was the best. He picked up the bamboo material and gave it to her. She smiled, bobbed her head a few times, and backed away. Another girl brought several bamboo patterns for him to look at. He liked the one with little birds flitting through the bamboo. She giggled and went away.

"Lee, what the hell is going on?" laughed Barney.

"I'm not quite sure, Barney. I think they are trying to zero in on everything I want on this pajama suit for

Ruth. If I am right, someone is going to come back with a whole series of color swatches for me to look at and select a color. Yep. Here she comes."

"Joe. What a co rah yo wan'?" the first sales girl asked. Lee picked up the swatches and picked through them.

After a few minutes of struggle and muttering from Barney, he picked the white piece and held it up.

"This is it, okay." She nodded and turned away.

"My name is Stew. What's your name?"

"Muh namu Michko. Yo wait, Stoo," she giggled and ran to the back of the store. Barney was getting impatient, and Stewart did not understand what the deal was.

In a few minutes, the first salesgirl came in with a young man who had a broad smile pasted on his face. "Hello sa ror. I study Eng rish in schoo. So, for five hundred yen, I make sure they understand, okay."

Hmmm, this might get a little tight but worth it if it all comes out right.

"Okay." Lee pulled out his wallet and handed him five one hundred-yen notes. "Now, how does this work?"

"Yo waita, prease." He turned to talk to Michko, and came back to the group. After talking and laughing for a couple of minutes, he and Michko returned.

"She says no suit that big but they can make one in two hours. It cost you five t'ousand yen. Okay?"

Less than fifteen dollars? I can handle that.

"Will that include packing so I can mail it?"

"Yes. Now, you come to back of shop, prease. They show you clotha and check measurements. Okay?" Lee nodded and turned to Barney.

"We can eat, grab some snatch and be back here in a couple of hours, right?" Barney was getting tired of Lee's shopping spree, but it was almost over. He nodded, too.

The shopkeepers led him back to the bolts of cloth with two for him to choose, both white with birds. He squinted at both and took the left one because it had smaller birds.

"This is special deal, so you have to pay now. Okay, Joe?"

"Yeah, no problem." After so long at sea, Lee had a fair amount of money. He pulled five new thousand yen notes from his wallet and handed them to Michko.

"Thank yo, Stoo," she giggled.

The interpreter said, "They want to check those measurements, and the girl will help. Okay?"

"Sure."

Now what?

Michko spoke sharply to the interpreter who stood straighter and almost bowed. "Michko say to you this is her shop. It belonged to her parent's who died in an air raid. She says they going to take better measurements now.

Giggling, Michko came next to him and snuggled up close, facing him.

That's nice. She can do this some more.

Then, she put her hand over her head and raised it up and down.

"She wants to know how tall. The old one will measure." Lee put one hand behind her back to steady her, and pulled the other one up to where the top of Ruth's head would be. Still holding her close, the old woman measured the height, just as Junior began to grow in curiosity.

Oh shit.

Michko's bright eyes flashed to his eyes but she didn't pull away. Then she turned around, brushing against Junior as she did.

She did that on purpose!

The old woman spoke sharply at her. Michko moved back against him knowing very well what she was doing.

Lee was having the time of his life. Barney noticed and grinned but kept quiet about it.

"Put your hands up to show the size of your girl friend's breasts. It's okay to touch. This is business." Barney laughed outright. "Can you handle all that, Lee?"

Lee brought his hands gently into her breasts, whose nipples were hard as rocks, moved his hands ever so little to tease—himself as much as her, and pulled them away to where Ruth would be. Barney whistled as he saw the nice size.

Meanwhile, the girl leaned forward to let the old woman pass the measuring tape behind Michko, which caused her bottom to press into Lee.

Oh yeah? Take this, Michko!

He flicked Junior a couple of times. It was just too good to resist.

Michko turned around inside his arms with a big smile and pulled his arms easily to her waist. Lee realized the fun was over and visualized Ruth's waist, putting his hands away from her waist. Once again, the tape had to come between them. As she leaned back a little and thus let her hips move in, she looked up at him and smiled a tiny smile. She brushed Junior with her belly and straightened.

Barney was enjoying the show and had sense enough to keep quiet. They didn't know the interpreter's relationship to Michko. The hips were next and final. She didn't touch him this time, except to talk.

"Michko needs to know all your name for the order. She says to ask for her when you come back. But you must get back before eight PM because that is when she closes the store and her workers go home."

Did I hear what I thought I heard?

He glanced at Barney who picked up the same thing.

I won't bring up a girl friend until I test the waters later.

But he nodded slightly to Barney.

"When we come back to the store just before eight o'clock, will Michko be waiting with the pajama suit for my inspection before it is wrapped?"

The interpreter asked her the question and heard her response.

He turned back with a smile on his face.

He's not so fuckin' dumb!

"Yes, that is correct. She wants to know if her girl friend who helps close the store should leave or continue to help tonight."

"We think she should stay to at least keep her company in case Barney and I are delayed a few minutes."

"Hai, Stoo San." She responded directly with a very nice smile.

Everyone bowed and smiled at Lee and Barney, as they returned the courtesy.

"Barney, I think it is time we do your shopping now, don't you?" Barney nodded and walked toward the front. Lee was close behind but looked back to see if Michko was watching. She was. He waved. She giggled and ran to the back of the store.

They stepped out into the rain showers that were passing through. Each time the rain appeared, they would step into some store, like this one a couple of doors farther along Sasebo's Black Market Alley. Not exactly like this one but Lee thought it would do. The shelves were absolutely filled to the brim with Japanese figurines; some were in porcelain; others looked like baked clay with very finely painted features.

Here a fisherman sat on a rock repairing his net, and there a man stood, mallet in hand, caulking his sampan. On another shelf, a samurai had his sword drawn and stood ready to swing it.

Man, this detail work is something else.

He found a tattoo artist sitting working on a woman's bare back.

That kind of work must be difficult because she was very close to him where he sat. I wonder if the artist's name is on the bottom.

He looked at the shopkeeper and motioned with his hands, asking if he could pick up the figure. The woman smiled broadly and nodded, bobbing her head several times. He picked up the figurine and turned it over, casually looking along the edge for some scratches.

Holy shit!

Lee almost dropped it and looked at the shopkeeper to see if she noticed. She was laughing silently!

He inspected the artistic efforts at great length.

"Hey Barney, could you come here a minute?" Lee asked, turning the tattoo artist upright again.

"Whatcha got, Stew?"

Lee handed him the figurine with a straight face. "What do you think of this one, Barney?" Barney admired it silently for a while, and then automatically turned it over to check. Lee caught it as it dropped from Barney's numbed hands.

They both admired the artist's handy work. His penis was deep in her vagina, in fine, painted detail. Lee looked up to see the proprietor looking at them.

"Kore wa ikura des'ka?—How much is this, please?" asked Lee.

Barney looked at him in amazement.

"When did you start speaking Jap, Stew?"

"Since I last looked in my little red Japanese-American phrase book, Barney!" he said with a big smile.

The lady had a big smile on her face as she held up three fingers and said,

"san zen yen."

"Three thousand Yen, Barney. You know what? If Customs opened the box back in the States, they'd trash it and charge me with trying to bring in pornographic dolls—if you could get it by the MP's on the gate."

Lee was moving along the shelf, lifting each piece of art to check the bottom. There were quite a few delightful statues. Barney was right behind him studying the artwork.

Barney got an idea. He motioned to the lady and using his hands, showed her he wanted the bottom filled with dry rice and covered with green felt. He figured the MP's and Customs would never figure that one out. Barney paid her an extra five hundred-Yen to make that change, and pre-pack it. The two young men went off to dinner.

"You know Stew, I'm sending this to my old man at his office. He will put it on his desk where Mom will never see it. I'll write a letter to him there warning him. He'll have a ball with that."

"If it gets that far, Barney, only if it gets that far."

"Lee, do you suppose Michko has a friend for me?"

"I think that's the second girl who will be there when we get back. Anyway, I think Michko lives in the back of the shop. Unless we take them out to eat, we'll never leave until time to return to the ship. I think we ought to get a couple of bottles of wine to take back with us to Michko's, don't you?" suggested Lee.

A couple of minutes before eight, Lee and Barney approached Michko's clothing store. Her shop was easy to identify because kimonos were still outside and other stores were dark. They decided Barney would carry the wine and clink the bottles if he felt the time was ripe.

A young woman was taking in the kimonos as they walked up. She glanced at them, smiled shyly, and called out.

"Michko, Michko" Lots of Japanese words followed, but her name was all either sailor understood.

Michko appeared in back and waved Lee and Barney toward her. As they walked back, they heard the sliding door closing the store. The other girl called out something and Michko responded. Some lights went out but three light bulbs in the tailoring area stayed on.

Lee spotted the pajama suit right away. It was beautiful and would fit Ruth very nicely.

"Oh, this is nice, Michko. He ran his hands lightly over the material."

"Stoo San, you rik-a?" She looked up at him with an anxious face.

"Hai! Very nice." He bobbed his head up and down. "I like you, too." Michko giggled and said something to the other girl.

Michko stood back by her girl friend and said, "Dis-a Ariko, okay? Ariko, my frand. You unnastand? She talk yo. I put dis-a gone." Michko promptly began wrapping and preparing Ruth's suit for shipment, watching and listening to Ariko and then Barney.

"Hi Ariko," Barney said as he stuck his thumb on his chest, "I am Barney."

"Bah nee San?"

"Stoo San, yo rik-a records? I hav-a Merican records. Yo rik-a?" asked Michko timidly.

"Oh yes, I do, Michko."

"Yo come, prease." Michko led the way to the back wall, removed her sandals, pointed to his feet, and stepped sideways into another room.

Oh, this is her home, I'll bet.

Lee removed his shoes and stepped inside, looking around. Looked to be only one room nicely set up. She was standing at a shelf with quite a few 78rpm records. All of them were in dust cases, some homemade. She pulled one out and set it on a small windup record player. Tinny, but he recognized Star Dust.

"Stoo San, yo dance, yes? Yo teach Michko Merican dance, yes?" Lee nodded and opened his arms. She stepped into his arms at a proper distance and placed her hands properly. She looked up at Lee.

"Lik-a dis, Stoo San?" and before he could answer her, she moved very close and asked, "Maybe lik-a dis, yo." They danced without a word while he hummed Star Dust to himself. When the record scratched at the end, she reached over and restarted at the beginning, this time winding the crank till it stopped.

Barney and Ariko came in, holding glasses of plum wine out to Michko and Lee. Barney and Ariko began dancing as Lee and Michko stood swaying and sipping the wine.

She looked up at him out of the top of her eyes, smiling at him. "Yo rik-a?" His hardon was square in the middle of her belly, rubbing slowly back and forth. Junior was beginning to leak a little. Lee nodded and offered her some plum wine from his glass. She stopped and pressed closer, leaning back to watch him as she sipped.

She nodded and laughed. "Yo lik-a!" She spoke softly to Ariko and put on another record as Star Dust ended.

How appropriate, Lee thought as "I've got my love to keep me warm," began.

By this time, Lee's ears were pounding. Michko came back in his arms to dance some more, then looked up for a kiss. With both of her arms around his neck, he dropped his hands to softly play with her bottom. When they came up for air, Michko asked, "You lik-a Michko ver' mooch?"

"Oh yeah, Michko, very much." He looked around to tell Barney to take Ariko somewhere. They were not there. There was just one little light left. Lee turned it off as they danced by it.

Michko stopped and Lee was afraid she was going to turn the light back on. He heard some rustling and Michko called to him from the floor, "Oh, Stoo Sannnn."

He leaned over and touched a bare leg in the dark. Off came his uniform and he got down beside her. Those hard little nipples tasted just like he thought they would.

Afterward, Michko lay snuggled up next to Lee. Both of them were sweaty and hot as if from some sort of strenuous exercise. Lee thought he was completely relaxed from his toes to his crew cut. Michko was practically purring as he gently stroked her body.

"Stoo, yo see Michko some mo'?" she asked drowsily.

"Oh yeah, Michko. I'll see you all the time. You have another boy friend?"

She rose up and looked at him in the nearly dark room. "Boy fran go way. No see him t'ree monts. Yo nice man, Stoo. I like yo stay hyar fo me. Yo hava gir fran?"

I don't think this is the time to mention Kiki up in Yokosuka.

"No girl friend here. Only back in States."

"Okay Stoo. Yo stay me. I take care yo," as she snuggled up and rubbed against him.

A tapping on the wall brought them back to here and now. "Hey Lee, we gotta go back to the ship now."

"Barney, you got lousy timing, ya know." Lee stopped Michko's hand from stroking Junior and pushed it away. Barney laughed. "Come on, we gotta hurry."

Lee was up and dressing in a moment. "Michko, Barney and my ship sails tomorrow for Yokosuka. I'm not sure when we will be back. But as soon as I can, I will come to you."

Michko looked shocked. "You doan lik a me?" she whimpered as she stood close to him.

"Oh yes, I do, Michko. But I have to go with my ship. Okay?" Lee held her in his arm, his hands busy on her body. He kissed Michko goodbye, promising to see her as soon as he could. Grabbing their packages, Lee and Barney hurried out to find a cab.

0700, May 16, 1951
USS Hoquiam PF-5
Underway for Yokosuka, Japan

The Bos'uns pipe shrilled its early morning greeting. "All hands not actually on watch, Quarters for getting underway. Undress whites for enlisted men; informal khaki uniforms of Chiefs and Officers without ties. Quarters for getting underway."

After the hassle the Yokosuka girlfriends received from their surprise visit down in Sasebo, none of them had been waiting when the Hoquiam arrived in Sasebo. This was good because Lee got to meet Michko, which otherwise would not have happened. Without fanfare and a great deal of gladness, the Hoquiam sailed for Yokosuka for three weeks of welcome yard work at SRF.

May 18, 1951
USS Hoquiam PF-5
Moored Pier A-7
Outboard of U.S.S. Sausalito PF-4
SRF Yokosuka, Japan

The Hoquiam arrived late last night and temporarily moored alongside the Sausalito before she went into Dry Dock 2 for work on the Sonar Sound Dome.

As before, they offloaded all ammunition from the ship. Stewart's fortunes took a turn for the better. He had the day watch while this all hands evolution was in process. Not only that, he had the duty first day in Yokosuka.

"Stewart!" Dean called out.

Lee looked up from his filing task with raised eyebrows.

Dean held out the duty belt and bag. "Make a run for unclassified Guard Mail now." He ordered.

"Okay, Dean. Do you suppose I could stop by the Hospital and see how Harper is doing?"

Dean looked at him for a second. "Sure, Stew. Say hello for the rest of us, will you?"

"You got it, boss."

He grabbed the duty belt and leather mailbag and headed for the gangway.

"Good morning, sir," Lee said saluting the Officer-of-the-Deck, one of the new ensigns. "I am making the morning Guard Mail run. Request permission to leave the ship?"

"Permission granted, sailor," the officer replied, returning Stewart's salute.

Lee turned, saluting the colors on the fantail, and left the ship.

He rode the bus around to the Naval Hospital and got off. He stretched and looked at the peaceful surroundings.

Lots of trees, lawn, and walkways with benches and quiet.

Men in wheel chairs, blue or maroon bathrobes, some with crutches, moved slowly around in the warm sun and cool shade. Most were wounded Marines brought here to recover before being shipped back to their units or stateside. Stewart was relaxed in the setting but intimidated by all the wounded men. He strolled inside, taking off his hat, and looked around. He walked to the information desk.

"Excuse me, ma'am," he asked the Gray Lady, softly.

She looked up at him and smiled back. "Can I help you, young man?" she asked warmly.

"Yes Ma'am. I am looking for a wounded shipmate, name of Harper, Gunner's Mate Third. He was wounded May 7th off Korea and is supposed to be here."

She nodded and looked through her cards. Holding a card with her fingernails, she wrote something on a slip of paper and handed it to Stewart.

"Your friend is in Ward East Six." She pointed down the wide corridor on her left. "Take the aisle to your right and walk to the third cross aisle. East 6 is on your right. Check in at the desk to find out his bed number."

"Thank you, Ma'am." Stewart smiled and followed her directions.

The aisles, or passageways, had very high ceilings. About every ten feet, a hanging fan rotated slowly to move the air a little bit. The only noise he heard was his heels on the deck and the whispered moan from the fans. The hospital was very quiet. He turned to his right into Ward East 6 and stopped at the desk. A Corpsman looked from his filing.

"Harper GM3?" Stewart asked.

"Tenth bed on the right," he said jerking his thumb in that direction. "You from his ship, too?"

"Yeah. What do you mean, too?"

"He's the only guy in here that has had visitors the last couple of days, other than Chaplain, Red Cross and Gray Ladies."

Stewart nodded and tiptoed along the ward. The odor of alcohol and something else was pervasive. Most of the wounded were sleeping. A couple of guys tracked him silently with their eyes. He nodded at them, respectfully. They just stared.

There he is. He looks a little pale.

Stewart stood at the foot of the bed, rolling his white hat through his hands until Harper looked up.

"Hey Stew, come to look at my Purple Heart?"

"Aw, just wanted to see how you are and whether you need anything."

"Nah," he said with a thin smile, "the Captain, Exec, Mr. Morgan, Mr. Dixon, Chief Billons, a couple of other guys and now you. It's great to see you all."

"Are you coming back to the Hoquiam?" Stewart asked.

"No sir. The Navy promoted me to Second Class, gave me this Medal, and will ship me home for release from active duty. They said I served my piece."

"That's great. We'll miss you but it's great for you."

"I'd just as lief still be aboard and not go through this pain."

"Still there?"

"Oh yeah. They did a lot of cutting and searching before they found the slug." He reached over and handed him a small glass vial. "That's the little bastard they dug out of me.—Understand you helped get me below to Sick Bay. That right?"

"Uh—yeah." He studied the little slug and gave it back.

"Thanks." Harper said with a thin smile.

"Yeah."

Stewart stood up and looked down at Harper. He leaned over and shook Harper's hand.

"Well—see you around, Harper."

"Yeah, take it easy," he said with the same thin smile.

Stewart turned and walked away.

THIS IS A F R S TOKYO WITH THE EVENING NEWS MAY TWENTIETH NINETEEN FIFTY-ONE, SPECIALIST FOURTH CLASS SUSAN ROSS IS YOUR REPORTER. THE NAVY IS IN THE NEWS TODAY. FROM WONSAN, WE LEARN THE DESTROYER BRINKLEY BASS DD-887 SUSTAINED A NEAR MISS FROM SHORE BATTERIES WHILE FIRING HER FORTY-MILLIMETER GUNS AT UMI DO. ONE MAN WAS KILLED AND NINE MORE WERE WOUNDED. AT KANGSONG, THE BATTLESHIP NEW JERSEY BOMBARDEDED THAT WHOLE AREA.

May 21, 1951
Ltrser 273/20
FM COMDESDIV162 in ZELLARS (DD777)
TO COMCORTRON FIVE
COPY to C.O. HOQUIAM

> 1. During the period 7-13 April 1951 HOQUIAM (PF5) operated under my command as a unit of Task Element 95.22, Songjin Element, Patrol and Escort Force.
> 2. It is a pleasure to report that HOQUIAM performed all missions assigned her in an outstanding manner. She impressed me as being an alert and effective unit.
>
> /s/ J.D. Whitfield, Capt, USN

May 23, 1951
Early Morning
Kiki Hashimoto's apartment
Yokosuka, Japan

Lee woke slowly as morning sounds penetrated his mind.

My first overnight liberty and oh boy, has it been worth it. Don't have to be back until tonight.

He stirred, stretched, and rolled over on his side to snuggle closer to Kiki under the quilt. She was on her side, backed up to him. Kiki wriggled a little bit, then giggled.

"Not yet, Lee. I have to go to the benjo, first," she whispered as she twisted around to face him. Depending on which face you saw, that was or was not the best move to make.

Kiki rolled out, stood and stretched, then stepped back from Lee's groping hands. She laughed while covering herself, then raced for the benjo. She was still laughing later when she called out quietly to Kimiko in the room across the hall. Charles' voice joined in.

"That's a great idea. Lee, we are going to see the Great Buddha today. Go take a bath while I take care of something else." Kimiko giggled and was suddenly quiet.

Charles and Lee were in their Dress Blues. The girls surprised them by wearing traditional kimonos and parasols. They walked down the hill to the Yokosuka Train Station and boarded an old but serviceable local diesel rattletrap that departed Yokosuka for the Yokosuka rail junction.

Lee had enough time to admire the Yokosuka Junction operation and read the signs (they were written in Japanese and English) before they changed to a newer fast express train for Zushi. At Zushi, they boarded another local train for Kamakura.

The four of them sat on the front side seats in the electric interurban train. They would get off at the Kamakura train station and use Pedi-cabs to ride to Kita Kamakura and the Great Buddha Shrine. Lee was fascinated with the Japanese interurban electric trains. He compared these to trains in America.

He liked the way you stepped straight on or off an elevated platform without having to climb steps in and out of the cars. The Jap trains ran on time. The clear voice announcement when you came to a stop was almost as good as the signboards at each station. Each board had three names. The one in the center, big and bold, named 'this' stop. Two smaller names to the left and right listed the previous and next stops on the line.

The girls took complete charge of the trip when they got out of the station at Kamakura. Kimiko and Kiki selected two Pedi-cabs after considerable haggling. Lee handed Kiki into their Pedi-cab and climbed in beside her. It was a tight fit, hips pressed against each other. They were in the lead leaving the station.

"Lee, we are going to take the old way to the Shrine. Just before we get there, we're going to get out and walk the rest of the way. We want you two to appreciate our Great Buddha."

Lee settled back and enjoyed the ride in the warm, clear sun. It was not hot or muggy. It was just a great morning after the golden light was gone. He absorbed the pleasant moving scene as they passed through the countryside.

The ubiquitous, effervescent odor from the farm fields wrapped itself around your nose and would not let loose. That was the only sour note in an otherwise great ride. U.S. military personnel were under strict orders not to eat Japanese field-grown vegetables because they fertilized their fields with human feces. Of course, it was okay to eat hydroponically grown vegetables fertilized with chemicals.

The foursome got out of their Pedi-cabs onto a hard-packed grit pathway. It was wide enough for driving. People in all forms of dress walked in both directions. Many children dashed around, shouting happily among themselves. The adults were subdued and did not talk—at least not loudly. Lee started to ask why so quiet, but Charles motioned with his hand to stay quiet for now.

About all Lee could hear above the children's chatter was the scrunch of grit under people's getas, zoris, and shoes. Lee walked next to a wooden rail fence in a row of trees. When they walked around a sweeping turn, Lee gasped and stood stock-still.

My God! That thing is enormous.

He was looking at the Great Buddha Amitabha of Kitakamakura.

The seated, cross-legged, squat, bronze statue towered over its garden and shrine. Kiki explained that the Shogun ordered construction of Daibatsu Buddha in the late 13 century; it was cast, assembled, and completed in the middle of the 14th century.

A long line of people inched their way around back of Buddha where the line seemed to disappear. Lee compared the height of people to the Buddha and figured it must be thirty-five to forty feet high. People stood quietly in the line as it moved forward ever so slowly. Kiki and Kimiko refused to tell Charles and Lee why the line was so slow or what happened to the people.

Lee and Charles began to snicker, then shut up as the girls kicked them. Kimiko and Kiki each paid 20 yen to a man in a gray kimono for the privilege of walking on the muddy ground behind the Buddha and through a tiny doorway where even the Japanese had to stoop or duck, going inside Buddha.

A large scaffold made of the ubiquitous bamboo rose inside the back of the Great Buddha. People walked on two-by-twelve wooden planks in a zigzag pattern. Lee did not like the plank walkway; it flexed up and down and trembled too much. The plank walkway climbed its way up to Buddha's head.

All the people moved along in a side shuffle, stopping long enough to gaze out each eye for a few seconds, some to take pictures. A lady attendant kept them moving, speaking softly and touching shoulders. Suddenly, they were exiting out of another lower doorway into the gardens. People spread out all over the grounds. Some sat, others prayed, even more just looked around in curiosity.

Kimiko told them of great floods in the Fourteenth and Fifteenth centuries, which tore down Buddha's protective building.

By this time, they had been there nearly two hours. Kimiko led the way to a small food stand on wheels for some hot noodle soup.

"It's Chinese noodles called Ramen, Lee. The dry noodles are dipped in a hot broth of your choice—chicken, pork, or beef. Do you know which you would like?" asked Kiki.

Charles spoke up: "It's pretty good, Lee. You ought to try some."

Lee decided to try the chicken broth. Kiki followed suit. Lee watched with interest as the old man selected a square of noodles and dipped it into the chicken broth for a moment. Lifting it out of the broth, he dropped the noodles and some broth into a cone shaped paper container and smilingly handed it to Lee. He sipped from his paper container and decided that hot Ramen was a tasty soup.

He watched the old man prepare Kiki's hot ramen. Lee thought the old man was a former soldier or sailor from World War Two; he had that look.

Kimiko nudged Charles and Lee. "Now is the time to leave. The early people have already left, so we can find Pedi cabs and go back to the train station," commented Kimiko.

They strolled slowly back to the dirt walkway. Two Pedi cabs later; they were on the way back to Yokosuka.

Red and Stewart reflected about the whole two-day liberty they had just completed. It was the first overnight liberty that either had been granted since they arrived in Japan. They would not see the girls for a couple of days. Kimiko had to return to Tokyo on family affairs; Kiki had to work hard to make up for one day lost being with Stewart.

May 31, 1951
U.S.S. Hoquiam PF-5
Ammunition expenditure report
On North Korean and Chinese targets

During 8 days on the firing line in the month of May, Hoquiam operated in the northern section between Songjin and Chongjin on assigned targets, targets of opportunity, and interdicting fire, during daylight and night operations. Targets included a 6-truck convoy, railroad beds and bridges, roadbeds and bridges, troop concentrations, trucks and trains. Hoquiam operated independently, part of Task Element 95.22, or as OTC Task Element 95.22, or in company with Thompson DMS-38, Bausell DD-845, and HMS Cockade D-34. One Russian mine type M-KB destroyed.

3-inch 50cal	**1084 rounds of AA Common**
	32 rounds of Illumination
40mm	**946 rounds of HEIT**

JUNE

1130, June 1, 1951
USS Hoquiam PF-5
Mess Deck
Moored Berth 16
SRF Yokosuka, Japan

Red, Barney, and Stewart were relaxed, eating slowly, not saying a word. They paid no attention to the clattering on the ladder and the hurried footsteps. Smitty stopped behind Red and tapped him on the shoulder.

"Excuse me, Red, the Chief told me to tell you your girls are trying to get hold of you." Red nodded and looked at Stewart in surprise.

"She's never contacted me this way before. Wonder what's up?"

"I'll come up with you and see if Kiki is involved, Red." They both got up, chugalugged their milk and carried their trays to the scullery. Stewart grabbed his cookie from the tray and they headed to the Signal Bridge.

Chief Swenson had the Bridge binoculars aimed at the hillside. "There is one girl there, Red, and I think it is Stewart's girlfriend." Red bent over the big bridge binoculars and refocused.

"Yeah, that's Kiki, Stew. She's looking at us with her glasses." Red stood away from the binoculars and raised his hands in the letter K, and bent over the glasses again.

Stewart could make out she was semaphoring to Red. Chief Swenson, using regular binoculars, breathed "Oh shit" under his breath.

Hey, what's going on over there?

"What's going on, Chief?" Stewart whispered.

"Kimiko's in the hospital—went in late last night—she tried to abort a pregnancy—by herself—bleeding pretty bad—Kiki wants Red—to go see Kimiko—ASAP—needs blood transfusion—and money."

The Chief looked over at Red, who was shaking and sobbing quietly as he read the semaphore. The Chief leaned back to Stewart and whispered to him. "This is bad shit, Stew. Go get a special request chit from the Cubby. Fill it out for Red and I will walk it through to Mr. Marston."

"That's a rog, Chief." He hurried into the Cubby and began filling out the spaces on the Special Request chit.

He still could hear Red crying quietly over the big glasses and the Chief's soothing voice as he stood next to Red.

"Red. Roger for it. You get ready for special liberty now. I'm going to see Mr. Marston to get you early liberty." Red looked over his shoulder, tears wet on his cheeks. He nodded and straightened, semaphoring to get her attention. Chief Swenson pulled the chit from Stewart's hand and headed down the ladder to CIC to find Lt. Porter, who would have to sign off first.

Red semaphored that he would be leaving the ship in about a half-hour. Could Kiki meet him at the Main Gate in a taxi, so they could motor to the Japanese hospital, wherever that was? She would.

"Hey Red, uh I'm sorry as can be. Here is thirty dollars you can have if that will help." He thrust the money to Red.

"Thanks buddy, but I don't know what it is going to cost yet. I'll tell you all about it when I get back."

"Okay, if she needs blood, I have O positive."

"Thanks, I'll remember." He dashed off.

1745, June 2, 1951
USS Hoquiam PF-5
Mess Deck
Moored Berth 16
SRF Yokosuka, Japan

Stewart looked up from dinner as Red sat down beside him.

"You been gone long enough. How is she, Red?" Red had a thin smile.

"She's going to be okay. God, I didn't know her being hurt would affect me that way, Stew." He sat with his arms alongside his tray and head bowed. "I guess I love Kimiko, Stew. Ain't that a bitch?"

"Uh huh. You making some sort of plans I ought to know about, Red?" Red turned his head slowly to look at Stewart, face tight and eyes glaring.

"Now, tell me you ain't going to be a shit about this, Stew."

Stewart stopped chewing and met him eyeball to eyeball. "We're buddies, I think, Red. Just be damned well sure of what you haven't said yet."

"This morning in the hospital, I asked her to marry me. She said yes."

Here is as good a chance I know to really screw things up between us.

"Then, I went to the Navy Exchange and got her a ring."

"Congratulations, Charles. Are you going to stay out here, or haul her back to the States?"

"We haven't gotten that far yet. I do know she wants to be married in accordance with Taoist practices, though."

"Is that legal in the States."

"I think so. Anyway, I laid a Special Request chit on Lt. Porter a little while ago, requesting permission to get married to a Japanese National."

"Well, good luck. However, you know this will fuck up things for me with Kiki. She is going to expect me to follow suit, and that, buddy, ain't gonna happen." Lee looked at Red expectantly. Life could get very complicated.

Red, finished with dinner now, swung around and lit up. He grinned at Stewart.

"Yeah, I guess so. When are you going to see her again?"

"Duty today. That leaves tomorrow, the next day and the last day. Then we sail on the seventh."

Stewart laid his hand on Red's arm and looked intensely into Red's eyes. "You gotta be awful sure about this, Red. Think of her family and your family back home. How are they going to take to this? You know, it's kinda like a Jew and Catholic getting married. That's real tough because the Jew's family disowns him or her, and the Catholic—well, he or she gets discombobulated from the church, if not the family." Lee was really worried about how Red was going to react to his thoughtful comments.

"Never thought of that, but my family doesn't go to church anyway. I get what you mean. So, we'll cross those roads when we come to them.

The 1MC opened. "Now Crosley Quartermaster Third Class, lay to the Executive Officer's Stateroom. Crosley." Red looked at Stewart. "Boy, that was fast." He got up with his tray and headed for the scullery. Lee watched him leave.

This yard period was great as far as the Radio Gang was concerned. The only thing off the ship for maintenance and repair was one of their two communications typewriters. This was a seasoned crew now. Everyone took turns listening on the UTE (Underway Training Element) CW training circuit for the fun of it. One does not transmit when one's ship is in dry dock without any water around it.

1800, June 7, 1951
USS Hoquiam PF-5
Underway to Sasebo, Japan

The wheezy pipe shrilled its introduction. "Make all preparation for getting underway. Department heads report readiness to the Officer of the Deck on the Quarterdeck."

Coyle, Romey, and Stewart, already in whites, were eating dinner as the initial call sounded. Just getting off watch, they were doubling back to the midwatch, but would have to stand to Quarters for leaving port. Romey was a non-smoking, non-coffee drinker, but sure guzzled the beer when he had liberty. Coyle leaned over and lit Stewart's cigarette in exchange for the two cups of coffee in front of them.

"Are things tight with you and Kiki, Stew?' Coyle asked with amusement. He knew the uproar the impending marriage of Red and Kimiko was causing on the ship and up on the hill at Kimiko's and Kiki's apartments. Red, a Third Class with over four years in the service was going to have a Navy Dependent Allotment for Kimiko. Kiki was wild with anger. Stewart was not biting at various subtle hints.

"I'd say things were not too swift at the moment. She's beginning to ration it," he said with a twisted smile.

The 1MC came on without fanfare. "Station the Special Sea and Anchor Detail. The Officer of the Deck is shifting his watch to the Bridge. All hands not actually on watch, Quarters at Fair Weather Parade for getting underway. Uniform is undress white trousers, skivvy shirt and white hat for enlisted men. Chiefs and officers uniform is khakis without jacket, with tie and combination hat."

The three Radiomen got up and headed to the scullery with their trays.

1430, June 11, 1951
USS Hoquiam PF-5
Steaming in company
Seaward of Songjin, North Korea

"Secure from General Quarters. On deck, Section One, relieve the watch. The Smoking Lamp is lit throughout the ship." The 1MC snapped off. The Radiomen removed their helmets and lifejackets, and stored them. Romey helped Griffin with his gear because he was copying George Fox.

Most of the day, the Rupertus DD-851, Titania AKA-13, Manatee AO-58, Tacoma PF-3, and Hoquiam PF-5, had been firing, in column formation, at assigned targets in the Songjin area. Hoquiam's Mounts 31 and 33 had fired 114 rounds of AA Common during that period. Most of the month was going to be like this. Escort the Replenishment Group from port to port, act as Anti-Submarine Warfare, or ASW-Barrier patrol, and fire upon targets.

THIS IS A F R S TOKYO WITH THE EVENING NEWS JUNE TWELVTH NINETEEN FIFTY-ONE, SPECIALIST FOURTH CLASS DAVID HAMLIN IS YOUR REPORTER. THE NAVY IS IN THE NEWS TODAY. A MINE OFF HUNGNAM, NORTH KOREA, HIT THE DESTROYER USS WALKE DD723.

TWENTY-SIX OFFICERS AND MEN WERE KILLED AND AN ADDITIONAL THIRTY-FIVE WERE WOUNDED IN THE EXPLOSION. THIS IS THE LARGEST SINGLE NAVY COMBAT LOSS OF THE WAR.

1230, June 13, 1951
USS Hoquiam PF-5
On Station, patrolling in vicinity of
Songjin, North Korea

Lt. Marston's eyes were red, stinging from the salt spray. He, and the entire crew, was tired of bobbing around in the Sea of Japan off the coast of North Korea.

By damn, this is Wednesday and we ought to be able to have a Rope Yarn Sunday to rest in the afternoon, instead of Condition Two steaming watches.

He looked around the wardroom table. All the officers were staring back at him with the same worn out expression.

"All right Gents, if you can stay awake long enough, I have some intelligence information to share. It will explain a lot of things." He cleared his sore throat and sipped the grapefruit juice.

"The Stickell landed some ROK soldiers from those sampans they towed to the area of this bridge we keep knocking out. They captured a man who was boss of the repair gangs all the way from Songjin to Sosura, near Manchuria. He says many trains are in tunnels waiting to make dash following repairs on this bridge. After the repair gang finished fixing our favorite target, the ROK's (he pronounced it rocks) used a whole shitpot of plastique explosives to make kindling of it.

"Now, pay close attention. The Thompson closed to within 3000 yards of beach looking at possible targets. Four 3-inch camouflaged, mobile guns commenced firing on her. Thompson beat a hasty retreat after she took 13 hits. Thompson suffered three killed and three wounded.

He glanced at Ensign Hitchcock. "I don't know about your friend Peter, whether he was one of them. Now that's about all I have.

"Oh, wait a minute. We're off to Sasebo on Friday for a five-day rest. Then, back up here on the line."

1430, June 16. 1951
USS Hoquiam PF-5
Moored Buoy X-6
Sasebo Harbor, Japan

The 1MC came on and the Bos'uns Pipe shrilled Attention vigorously. "Secure from Special Sea and Anchor Detail. On deck, Section Three, relieve the watch. The smoking lamp is lit in all authorized spaces."

The speaker paused for a moment. "Liberty will commence immediately following Captain's inspection of the upper decks. Liberty expires on board for non-rated personnel at 2230, for petty officers at 2330, and Chiefs at 0200. Liberty uniform for enlisted personnel is undress white baker with neckerchief, white hat, and ribbons."

Barney and Lee stood drinking coffee next to the flag bags. They watched the Captain as he made his rounds.

As soon as they heard steps on the Starboard ladder, they tiptoed down the Port ladder to the 02-deck and around to the Starboard side to get out of his way. They wanted no part of the Captain while he was inspecting the Bridge. When they heard steps going down on the Port ladder, they climbed back up to the Signal Bridge area of the Open Bridge, and refilled their coffee cups.

Already, the Chiefs and petty officers were gathering between the fantail depth charge racks. They would ride the second boat unless a LCM took pity on them and came alongside to remove the entire Hoquiam liberty party. Lee and Barney had already gone to Sick Bay for milk down and received their liberty card from Webb.

"You going to see Michko, Lee?"

"Yeah, I thought we'd trot around there to see how the land lies. You liked Ariko, didn't you?"

"Oh yes, she wiggled all over the place. Kept me hopping, I'll tell you. Ya know, a friendly nipple puts me into a feeding frenzy!"

Lee laughed, spilling a few drops of coffee. "Uh huh, although I wasn't thinking of hopping so much as being buried deep inside." He got a rag and wiped up the coffee from the Signal Bridge clean deck.

Barney stretched and adjusted his pants as though things had gotten tight, all of a sudden. "I just hope they remember us. There's no telling how many guys have shared that little love nest."

"Too true, but do you remember how much it cost us? I think I'm going to invite her out for dinner, and see how that goes over."

"Why waste the money, Lee. If she is offering it for free, take it without losing money."

"For one reason, I think Kiki is going to drop me right after Red and Kimiko's wedding. Michko is a much better piece than Kiki. Michko cannot speak a lick of English, which is the same amount of Japanese I know. But our hand signals work miracles," laughing at his own joke. Then he pointed at the LCM heading their way.

"Liberty call for Sections One and Two. Muster the liberty party between the depth charge racks." Barney and Lee dumped their coffee in the urinal, dunked their cups in the bucket to rinse them off, and hung them on the cup hooks. They casually dropped down the ladder and headed for the fantail because seniority has its privilege. The whole liberty party was able to drop into the LCM for a ride to the Sasebo Fleet Landing.

As Lee and Barney came out of the Fleet Landing, Lee looked nervously for Kiki. He breathed a sign of relief since she was not there. The two of them hailed one of the Jap bicycle "taxi" cabs, and jumped in. They had him deliver them to the alleyway across from Michko's Dress Shop.

Barney and Lee stood across the alleyway from the Japanese dress shop. They had already spotted Ariko, but had not seen Michko yet. Barney was standing in the shade and wasn't squinting like Lee out in the sunlight. Barney straightened up and jabbed his arm into Lee's ribs and pointed toward a girl that just came into view. "There, isn't that Michko?"

"I think so. Been a while since we were here but that looks like her. Let's walk over there and see what happens."

Lee and Barney were taller than most people, especially the Japanese of shorter stature. Michko saw the two sailors walking toward her but didn't recognize Lee until he was at the doorway. Her hand darted to her mouth as she gasped. Lee wiggled his fingers at her and she smiled and laughed at the same time.

"Ariko, Ariko" and that is all they understood. Ariko peered around the corner from the sewing table and came running out, calling "Bar nee Bar nee."

Michko came up close to Lee and brushed non-existent lint from his chest. "You wait hyah, Stoo. Okay?" Lee nodded, smiled, and feinted to brush lint from her chest. Michko giggled and ran down the alleyway. Lee turned to say something to Barney but he and Ariko had disappeared into the sewing room. He grinned as they disappeared.

This is not the time to go back there.

Michko came back with the same interpreter she had used before. He was full of big smiles and giggles and sucking in his breath.

The man bobbed and bowed to Lee and Barney. "Hello, Mr. Stewart. We so grada see you again. Michko says why you stay away so long, and Ariko says why you here now."

Lee laughed. "Our ship PF-5—you know PF-5." The interpreter shook his head.

Michko and Ariko not know PF-5 or they know we sail away next day. PF-5 come here from Korea and Yokosuka this afternoon." Lee waited while that information has passed to Michko and Ariko whose eyes are darting back and forth between all three men.

"We came back because we like Michko and Ariko and would like to take them out for a nice dinner to show how much we like them." While the interpreter was telling the girls what he had said, Barney leaned over and whispered, "Let's not get too carried away, Lee."

Lee and Barney saw immediately results from this last exchange. The girls fairly glowed with excitement and warmth.

"Ariko say where you take us.

Michko ask if Japanese or American Japanese restaurant?"

Lee and Barney looked at each other.

"Lee, have you been to a Japanese restaurant. I don't know what kind of food they serve."

"Yeah. Red, Kimiko, Kiki, and I went to one in Kamakura when we saw the Buddha last month."

Oh hell. That wasn't a good idea to mention the girls' names.

"It is fish and other sea food served raw with various sauces. I was really surprised. Very colorful and in tiny bite sizes. Wanna try it?" Barney nodded doubtfully.

The interpreter was ready for them. "Michko say who Red, Kimiko and Kiki?"

I knew it.

Lee nodded as Barney snickered.

"Red is shipmate who loves Kimiko. They get married when we go Yokosuka again."

With arms folded across her chest, she looked a little grim as she spat out a question.

"Michko she say . . . ."

"I know. She wants to know about Kiki. You say she was girlfriend, no more. When her girlfriend Kimiko and Red say get married, she want me marry her. I say no. She go. Not girlfriend maybe two months."

Barney decided to cough and Lee pounded his back just a little stronger than needed. "Does that help, Barney?"

"Yeah yeah, I got it."

Lee turned back to the interpreter again. "You say we go Japanese restaurant."

He did and Michko clapped her hands happily, jumping up and down in her excitment. Michko and Ariko discussed restaurants, made up their minds, and told interpreter.

"She say that good. Barney and Stoo go beer hall one hour, then come back. But no drunk. Okay?" Lee and Barney both nodded agreement.

"Okay, she say close shop early. They clean and dress for you. Take you nice place you like."

Michko handed the interpreter some money. They exchanged bows and he left. Michko came to stand very close to Lee and squeezed his hand, then shooed them out. He and Barney looked both directions for a place to sit and have beer.

Ariko ran out and pointed down the alleyway. With sign language, she said, "go six doors on that side of alley." They nodded and counted off doors and went in and looked around. This was a quiet, non-military kind of bar.

Lee looked at the shopkeeper and politely asked: "Asahi, kudu sai." The shopkeeper bobbed his head and pointed to a table. Lee and Barney sat down at the tiny table and slouched to relax in those hard chairs.

They lit their cigarettes and slouched back further in the chairs.

The shopkeeper shuffled back with two liter bottles and two glasses.

"Two hunnad yen, prease."

Barney beat Lee with two hundred yen. He turned to Lee, looking very seriously at Lee.

"Is that true, Lee? You and Kiki are quits."

Lee nodded.

"Thought you really had something going there. You left me in the lurch and always went up the hill with Red."

"True, Barney. Very true, but when Kimiko fucked up her abortion and almost died, so did Red. He realized he loved her and decided he was going to marry her. But, hey, I don't love Kiki. She is a great girl, and very nice in bed. A real biggee is her ability to speak English. But ho ho ho, Kiki is expecting me to do the same thing. No way. Shit, oh dear. She is just a girlfriend."

Barney nodded here and there soberly, as he listened.

"And, I expect when we get back to Yokosuka, it will be officially over. She was pissed last time I saw her."

"Gotcha. You figure Michko is going to take her place? I sure like Ariko."

Lee looked sideways at Barney with a nasty grin. "Barney, aren't you the guy who's got to try them all, always on the lookout for the perfect ass?" He sipped his beer and grinned at Barney.

Barney lit up a Lucky Strike before he answered, sheepishly. "You gotta admit that Michko and Ariko are free ass. That makes a big difference."

Lee chuckled. "Oh Barney, Barney, you got to learn that it will cost more this way than going to a house and knocking off a piece for a few hundred yen. What do you think tonight's adventure is going to cost? Don't forget, we gotta be back by ten-thirty."

Barney hastily looked at his watch. "You mean we might not even get some pussy tonight?"

Lee grinned and nodded his head. "But think of it as money in the bank. You'll get a lot of interest later. How's our time coming along, by the way?"

"Pretty soon now." They lapsed into silence, watching other customers and people walking by in the alleyway. Lee was first to realize there were no business girls in here.

That's why the girls sent us here, I'll bet.

"You notice Barney. No girls."

Barney looked around, nodding. "We got a couple of smart girls, we do." He looked at his watch and looked at Lee. "Time to head back to the store." Lee looked at the bartender and shuffled his fingers for the bar bill.

Learning the bill was only about 300 Yen, Lee left a 500 Yen note on the table. Lee and Barney heaved out of their uncomfortable chairs and walked back into the alley. Leading the way in the dark, Lee headed out. Actually, the alleyway was lit by many colorful oil lamps hanging on the walls.

The taxi stopped in front of a large building set back from the road. Candle-lit lanterns shaped like balloons swung back and forth in the light breeze. Square lanterns casting yellow-orange light were spaced along the grit walkway to the front entrance. The girls chattered as Lee and Barney looked around in hushed silence.

"Lee, are we going to have to wash dishes, do you think?" Barney asked quietly.

Lee shook his head. "But I don't think we'll come here very often. And look at the girls. They are a knockout, aren't they?" Both were dressed in traditional garbs. Michko was dressed in an emerald green kimono with a bird in a juniper tree. Ariko was in striking gold with flowers and butterflies. By comparison, the boys were drab in their whites.

The door opened before they got there by a pair of doorkeepers. The Maitre d' stood behind them, smiling and bobbing to Michko and Ariko. They talked and laughed for a couple of minutes; then Michko turned to Lee. "Stoo, disa mah brudda, Tanaka. Disa house his." She made a circling motion indicating the restaurant. Lee and Barney reached out with their hands to greet him. He looked shocked but touched, not shook, their hands briefly.

Then she spoke to Tanaka introducing him to Barney, indicating Ariko, and Lee, indicating herself. He appeared a little stiff in accepting the fact she had an American sailor as a boyfriend.

After a moment, a waiter took them down a sunken walkway by private dining areas. Barney and Lee sucked in their breath as they recognized Navy officers' brown shoes as they walked as they walked by.

Holy shit! This is that officer rest house we've heard about.

They continued to walk very quietly and stopped in front of a shoji. The waiter slid the shoji open and pointed to the boys' shoes. They took off their shoes and stepped up inside, the girls following so they could sit closest to the shoji. Ariko closed the shoji.

This was not a public place. Not only that, it was an officer's place. Not only that, this was Michko's brother's restaurant. There will be no grab ass in here. All proper decorum and such shit.

The shoji opened, a serving woman slid a small rectangular tray on the table with warm saki and four saki cups. The serving woman backed away and closed the shoji. Michko said something to Ariko, and Ariko poured the saki while Michko served first to Lee, then to Barney. Then she served Ariko and herself. Lee watched Michko and Ariko to see how they drank the saki. They sipped delicately. Lee sipped not quite so delicately. Barney slugged it down.

"This is better saki than I have had. I didn't even know it came in different grades," commented Lee.

Michko and Ariko tittered behind their hands at Barney. Barney, looking at the other saki cups realized he goofed. Smiling, he held out his cup "Dozo!"

Ariko poured more. This time, Barney barely sipped any and the girls giggled and clapped.

"Must be the way to do it, Lee."

"Think so, and don't forget, that stuff can really knock you for a loop."

Michko slid her hand under the table and lightly rubbed Lee's thigh. Up popped the devil. Lee slid his hand under the table and tried to do the same thing, just as the shoji opened and the serving woman delivered a tray of colorful food. The shoji closed and the girls snapped apart the chopsticks. Now, Lee tried again reaching for her inner thigh. She glanced at him, smiled sweetly, and let his hand start sliding up her leg. Michko clamped her legs shut tight, holding his hand where it was.

She picked something yellow from the tray, watching it carefully as she dipped it in one of the sauces, and brought it to his mouth.

Smells spicy.

Then she smiled and relaxed her legs just enough that he could have pulled his hand out if he wanted to, but not enough to slide up further as he wanted to.

Michko sipped her saki delicately and took a bite of the same yellow stuff, savoring it. Lee wasn't sure what it was. It was not any meat he knew.

Across the table, Ariko and Barney were doing the same thing above the table.

I wonder if I can feed Michko without messing up her pretty kimono?

Lee reached out for the chopsticks that Michko held. She looked at him in surprise and amusement. "You do?" Lee nodded, tapped the chopsticks to even them up, and selected the white stuff.

Lee selected the white seafood and was able to pick up the stuff on the third try. Looking at her with eyebrows raised, he slowly moved the seafood over the sauces until she nodded. He carefully dipped the chopsticks with the white stuff surprisingly still attached into the sauce as he had seen her do, and brought it up to her mouth with his hand under the chopsticks and sauce. She took it. A little drop of sauce fell onto her breast. Without thinking, he reached over, wiped it up with his finger, and licked it off.

She looked at him with a big smile, "no no Stoo, you no do dat." Even so, she let her thighs open a little more. He moved his hand back and forth very softly and very slowly. Her thighs were warm and moist. Junior was trying to rip a hole in his pants.

For another hour, they fed each other saki and food. It was finally time to settle up. Barney looked at his watch. "Lee, we may have time for one if we leave now."

Lee studied his watch, taking his hand from between her thighs for the first time.

"Michko, we go ship this time," Lee said pointing to ten o'clock. "Take boat to PF-5."

"Okay Stoo. We go now." She called out and the serving woman opened the shoji and stood up where she had been on her knees, waiting to serve more. Michko and Ariko exchanged words with the serving woman and stepped out. Barney and Lee slid over grabbing their shoes to put on.

"You know Barney, this has been one very interesting meal. Won't find the likes of this on the Hocky Maru." Barney laughed and suddenly shut up, listening to something.

"We need to get the fuck out of here now, Lee." he whispered. "I just recognized the Captain's voice."

Holy Toledo, that's all we need. Captain's Mast in a Japanese restaurant.

Lee listened carefully. He whispered, "I think Mr. Forsythe is right in the next room. Let's move it."

Tugging his shoes on, he tied his laces and stood up, just as the next shoji opened a crack so someone could look out. Lee saw a dark red mustache, then one blue eye, and then the other. The shoji opened further. Lee and Barney turned pale.

"Mr. Porter, Mr. Forsythe." Stammered Lee. "How are you this evening?"

Roger Forsythe stared and shook his head slowly. "Mind telling me how you got in this Officer's Club?"

Holy shit, worse than I thought.

Lee tried to clear his constricted throat. "Sirs, may I present Michko and Ariko. Michko owns a dress shop in town. Her brother Tanaka, the Maitre d', owns this restaurant, and the girls brought us here. We had no idea, and I'm sure the girls did not understand, this is off limits to us."

"Stewart, this is a special place for us. We can only afford it once in a great while. How the hell can you afford it?"

"Noooo. You wouldn't like the answer, Mr. Porter."

Michko and Ariko were watching the exchange between the four men. They knew something was amiss. Michko turned to the serving girl and said something. She ran down the hall and came back with Tanaka. Michko spoke to him and Tanaka answered rather sharply.

Tanaka turned to Stewart and asked in passable English. "They you officers?"

"Hai, Tanaka San." He pointed to Lt.,(jg) Forsythe. This is my officer; he pointed to Lt. Porter, he is Barney's officer. We are not supposed be here."

Tanaka looked back and forth between the officers and sailors. He turned to the officers and reached for a slip on their table. He made a show of tearing it up into little pieces and putting the scraps into his pocket. "No pay dis night. So sorry." Mr. Porter recovered first. "Arigato, Tanaka San, arigato."

Tanaka San bowed, said something to Michko and left.

Michko and Ariko stared after him. "We go now, Stoo. We go now," tugging hurriedly at his sleeve.

Barney looked at their officers and shrugged helplessly as Ariko pulled him away. "We had no idea. Sorry, sirs."

Lt. Porter frowned, then smiled in amusement. "Roger, that's twenty-five bucks each we didn't have to pay tonight. We can thank them tomorrow when it is convenient. I sure want to hear more about Stewart's girlfriend. Isn't he the one with the English speaking girl in Yokosuka?"

"That's past tense, Bob." He will not marry her as Crosley is marrying his girl. Think she took a powder."

The four got into a taxi outside the restaurant. Michko gave directions. "You go ship now. You come tomorrow, nei?"

Lee looked in disgust at Barney. "I think Tanaka San had a hand in this." Michko looked downcast and burst into tears.

Now what?

“Tanaka San plenty mad. He say we no pay dis night, but other no pay. Him mad.” She reached down and squeezed Junior. “We do dis nudda night, okay? You no mad me.”

“No Michko, no mad. And no do this,” as he reached down to touch her short hairs.

They all rode in silence back to the Fleet Landing where Michko and Ariko dropped them off. Barney and Lee submitted to search and dropped into the LCM for a ride back to their ship.

Not the best liberty in the world, but not bad, either.

19 June 1951
Letter
From Commander United Nations Blockading and Escort Force,
To C.O. HOQUIAM

> Upon being relieved as Commander United Nations Blockading and Escort Force and Commander Task Force NINETY-FIVE, I express to you, your officers and men, my personal appreciation for your outstanding cooperating and “can do” spirit during the time you were under my operational control and especially during those extremely cold wintry days and rough seas. I sincerely hope that the future will again bring us together. It is a source of satisfaction that this Force, though composed of ships of several Navies and varied languages and usages,

has been welded into a single fighting unit. With due consideration of the need for maintenance, morale and rotation, Task Force NINETY-FIVE's outstanding characteristic has been its "will to fight"; the one basic essential of any fighting force. To you your officers and men of the U.S.S. HOQUIAM, "Well done".
/s/ Allan E. Smith, Rear Admiral USN

June 23, 1951
New York City, New York
United Nations General Assembly

Soviet delegate to the United Nations, Jacob Malik, proposed cease-fire discussions between protagonists.

1030, June 25, 1951
USS Hoquiam PF-5
Escorting Replenishment Group
On station, near Songjin, North Korea

The Hoquiam and Brinkley Bass were working over the combined rail and truck bridge, and the road bypass at Pukch'ong, 45 miles south of Songjin. Ensign Herbert had the deck with the Captain maintaining his corner of the port windscreen.

The Brinkley Bass was cruising slowly back and forth, maintaining 2,900 yards from the nearest point of land, in lazy eight patterns. She was operating in slow fire mode, dropping two or three five-inch AA Common on a suspected target before moving on to the next.

She fired each of the twin Mounts—51, 52, and 53—exercised all six of the five-inch, thirty-eight caliber rifles. Maximum effective range was about seven and a half miles.

Inshore, about 750 yards off the nearest point of land, the Hoquiam paralleled the Brinkley Bass. Of course, her two single three-inch fifty caliber rifles had a maximum effective range of about five miles. The five-inch rifles packed a powerful punch that three-inch rifles could not match. Indeed, experience taught the shooters that the three-inch was fine for personnel, trucks, rails, and trains.

It was not effective for deep bunkers or caves. To their surprise, they discovered that their two single 40mm's were more effective than the two three-inchers on rail and vehicular bridges, starting fires in the bridge framework and sticking around until the fire was fully developed.

WhaWhoom

Two columns of water spouted about one hundred yards away between the Hoquiam and the beach suddenly appeared.

The Captain leaped to the voice tube.

"All ahead flank, maximum turns." The orders came rapidly and clearly as the Captain wanted to maneuver out of the ChiCom battery range. "Come left fifteen degrees. General Quarters." The gong started before the Wheelhouse answered.

"All ahead flank, maximum turns. Captain, they rang up 170 turns."

"Very well."

"Rudder is left fifteen degrees, Captain. No new course."

"Very well."

The Captain picked up the Task Group Command radiophone.

WHITE TIGER WHITE TIGER THIS IS LASHING PETER LASHING PETER WE HAVE COUNTER BATTERY FIRE FROM UNKNOWN SOURCE OVER

A whiff of dark smoke appeared on the Brinkley Bass stacks as she began turning toward the Hoquiam.

Whoom Whoom

Two more spouts appeared fifty yards astern and one hundred yards farther out.

LASHING PETER THIS IS WHITE TIGER WE HAVE IDENTIFIED SOURCE OF COUNTER BATTERY FIRE. RECOMMEND YOU CLEAR THE AREA OVER

THIS IS LASHING PETER WILCO OUT

"All ahead two thirds. Make big smoke. Shift your rudder, Helmsman."

"All ahead two thirds, Captain. Engine Room answers all ahead two thirds. Mr. Hansen wants to know if that's enough smoke for you."

"Rudder is shifted to right fifteen degrees, Captain."

"Very well." He moved to the 21MC. "Combat Bridge—can you identify the ChiCom battery yet?"

The Brinkley Bass now had a full head of steam on, charging in at ever increasing speed. Mounts 51 and 52 were in rapid-fire mode. Mount 53 was out of it until the turn.

"Bridge Combat—we can see the outgoing rounds from White Tiger and where they are impacting, out of our range, Captain. Bearing to the ChiCom battery is 283 degrees True, range based on impact area is 9,200 yards."

Click click

He leaned over the voice tube. "Rudder amidships. All ahead standard."

"Rudder amidships. Rudder answering the helm, Captain."

"Very well."

"All ahead standard. Engine room answers all ahead standard, ringing up one three five turns, Captain."

"Very well. Engine room stop making smoke now."

"Stop making smoke, aye aye, Captain. Engine Room answers stop making smoke, sir."

Whoom

A column of water appeared fifty yards inshore off the bow.

The Captain had a tight smile on his face as he looked at the Bridge crew. "It's working." He leaned over the voice tube again.

"Left standard rudder. Come left to one one five degrees true. All ahead flank, one six five turns and do not make smoke."

"Left standard rudder, aye aye, Captain. Rudder answers the helm, Captain. Coming left to one one five degrees true, Captain."

"Very well."

"All ahead flank, one six five turns, Captain. Engine room answers all ahead flank and rang up one six five turns, Captain. No smoke, aye aye, sir."

"Very well."

Captain Brown turned to look at the Brinkley Bass less than five hundred yards outboard of the Hoquiam. All three mounts were now firing, as Mount 53 had came to bear.

She is beautiful!

"Steady on new course one one five True, Captain."

"Very well, all ahead one third."

"All ahead one third, Captain. Engine Room answers all ahead one third, ringing up 85 turns, Captain."

"Very well. Secure from General Quarters. Set modified condition able."

"Aye aye Captain." The 1MC came alive. "Secure from General Quarters. Set modified condition able."

1700, June 28, 1951
USS Hoquiam PF-5
Nested with USS Burlington PF-51
Moored Buoy X-6,
Sasebo Harbor, Japan

"Liberty call for Sections One and Three. Uniform for enlisted men is undress whites with neckerchief, white hat, and ribbons. Liberty expires on board at 2230 for non-rated men, 2330 for petty officers, and 0200 for Chiefs. Liberty call."

Lee stood in inspection ranks between the depth charge racks. He was ready for liberty. They just finished their second tour of escorting the groups up and back. Last time in, they were here overnight and gone. The Hocky Maru would be here for a few days.

Wonder if Michko knows we are in port or not?

He was a little gunshy when he came out of the Fleet Landing. Almost on tiptoe, he looked around to make sure Kiki was not here to surprise him again. When he arrived at Michko's dress shop, she had been watching for him.

"Where Bah nee, Stoo?"

Wonder if she will understand?

"Today Barney on ship. Tomorrow Barney here. Tomorrow I stay on ship. Must work—duty."

"Dooty? Oh sooo. Unnastand dooty. You hava dooty next day, yes? Lee nodded. "Bah nee hava dooty this day?" Lee nodded. He held up his watch again. "Go Fleet Landing this time."

"Unnastand, Stoo. Me tell Ariko, okay." Lee nodded. Michko disappeared into the sewing room and came back with Ariko.

"Bah nee hava dooty, Stoo?"

"Hai, Ariko."

They giggled at him. Ariko pushed at them. "You go now, okay." Michko had his hand and led him outside, then dropped his hand. He saw she held binoculars on her other hand.

"Where we go, Michko?" She pointed to the top of the hill nearby.

We look you ship."

Lee thought about that for a moment. That will take up some time.

When we get back, time to close store.

They stood sweating in a little park or religious center at the top of the hill. Michko had walked him up this hill.

Wow! What an amazing view of the Sasebo Harbor.

He had no idea that many ships could anchor in there at one time. Not only that, there were many merchantmen off at one side out of the way of the warships.

"Stoo, where you shipa PF-5?" Lee squatted down and drew the number five. Standing, he pulled her in front of him and looked with the binoculars over her head. The '5' stood out like a sore thumb. Then he lowered the glasses to her eyes.

She studied the ship for a while. "You shipa littul."

Lee laughed. "Yeah, it is."

Michko turned around inside his arms and looked into his eyes. "When you come hyah, Stoo?" Lee carefully considered the question. Either it was simple or tight with complex issues. He took the simple way out.

"PF-5 here," pointing to ship. "I come two days, stay ship one day. You understand."

She nodded and he continued. "PF-5 no here—go Korea or Yokosuka, I no here. You understand? She nodded again and asked, "Bah ney da same?" He held up his hand, meaning wait while I think about this.

"You understand Barney duty this day?"

"Hai!"

"Barney is duty two," he continued while holding up two fingers.

Made no sense to her.

He squatted down to the grit again and scratched three numbers—1, 2, 3,—into the grit. "Barney this duty," pointing to the two. "Me this duty," pointing to the three. "Barney and I come here on this duty," pointing to the one. "You understand now." She nodded.

Lee looked around. "Good. Now, what will we do?" He asked. Lights were coming on as dusk advanced.

"You come dis way, now." She tugged at his sleeve and they walked down the hill a different way. Halfway down, she turned on a side alley, and ducked through an open entryway. She sat down and took off her street shoes, pointing to Lee's shoes also.

A couple of soft lights showed further in. Michko took him by the hand and led him into the courtyard. One stone lantern was burning a pure white candle, which glowed, in the near dark. She walked around the carefully raked Japanese formal garden to a small house and opened the door.

"Stoo, you go hyar. I be back." Lee stepped inside where pale yellow candles burned in three tiny alcoves. The important thing was the sunken bath filled with steaming water and perfumed oils. Lee thought he should get partially undressed and removed his uniform, folding it carefully, dumping wallet, watch, Camels and lighter into his white hat on top of his uniform. All he had on was his skivvy shorts and dog tags.

Michko walked in wearing a gray kimono and carrying one for him. She put his kimono on his folded uniform and motioned for him to take off his skivvies. He did so, self-consciously, and tossed his skivvies onto his uniform. Junior was sort of at parade rest. Nothing was going on but he was ready if everything else was ready.

Without touching him, she leaned forward and removed his dog tags. Then she stood back with a nice smile and slowly walked around him, looking at every square inch of his body. She stopped in front of him and placed his hands on both sides of her kimono.

"Stoo, you take now." Lee's eyes lit up as he slowly removed the kimono. He saw what he had only felt and tasted last month. Nice little breasts with big nipples. Typical chunky calves, a tiny waist, and a cute bottom. He broke the spell by leaning over and kissing her cheeks. Startled, she jumped and whirled around, laughing. "No no, Stoo. We go in now."

The bath was much deeper than he expected. The hard part of it was, she wanted him to sit at one end while she sat at the other. The second hard part of it was, the water was damned hot, and it took him a long time to drop all the way in, while she laughed at him.

Finally, she stood and stepped carefully around his legs until she was next to him. He ran his hands softly around her body and legs, surprised at how slippery she was. Then he remembered the oils.

Michko settled down facing him. Wriggling this way and that until everything was just in the right place. Leaning forward, she kissed him. Up to now, everything had been in silence.

She broke that. "You lika me, Stoo?"

"Yes Michko, I lika you." She sort of cooed and snuggled down a little more relaxed and closer to him, moving just a bit now and then to tantalize him.

When it was time to go, Lee was tempted—just tempted, to stay over. The new stripes had been hard to come by and he didn't want to fuck it up.

He stood alongside Barney on the Signal Bridge. There was not a drop of rust left in him. Michko had seen to that. Red came up alongside the two and sniffed. "Lee, what the hell have you been into? You smell like perfume." Barney snickered, then laughed uproariously.

"He took a bath with Michko, Red. He has stinkum foo everywhere." Stewart grinned in the dark, fully relaxed.

Nothing could rattle him now.

"She certainly took care of the cobwebs for me."

Red looked at him sadly for a moment. "Does that mean you and Kiki are done, Lee?"

"Charles, she wants me to marry her, like you and Kimiko. I do not love her and that is not my cup of tea at all. I am very happy for you and Kimiko but doubt very much Kiki wants to see me anymore."

"Well, I can tell you she has done a lot of crying over you."

"I don't think she is crying over Lee Stewart, Charles. I think she is crying because she lost another chance at an American husband. Don't get me wrong. She is very nice. End of story."

"That is interesting to hear. Mind if I cut in?" They all whirled and saw Lt (jg) Forsythe standing there. Stewart looked at him in disgust.

"You know, sir, I'm going to find a goat bell to hang around your neck. You are the sneakiest guy I know." Mr. Forsythe laughed.

"What I'd really like to know all about is that episode at the officers' rest house the other night. What's her name?" Stewart sighed and Barney slipped away to make his circle looking for yardarm signals.

"I met Michko when Barney and I went shopping. I wanted to find something very cozy for that special girl in Seattle—Ruth. Ruth is pretty big and Michko is damned small. So using hand signals we got Ruth's sizes just right for the pajama suit I ordered." Mr. Forsythe and Red nodded understanding.

"She invited Barney and me back later when the pajama suit would be ready. The other girl, Ariko for Barney, was waiting when we got back. One thing led to another, and so on.

Turns out Michko's parents owned the dress shop and were killed in World War Two bombing raids here. She was a young teenager at the time. The shop passed to her because her brother wanted nothing to do with it. Tanaka got a chunk of money and decided to open a very good Japanese restaurant. Your officer type shit came later." Mr. Forsythe's eyebrows went up at the comment, but he was grinning.

"That's the background. That all happened when we were here last time around in May. She was so delicious, shall we say, that I wanted to strike up something.

"Looked like things were dying out with Kiki, anyway. Barney went along with my plan to take her, he with Ariko, out to dinner at a Japanese restaurant. She could pick the place to go.

"We drove up to this elegant place. Barney and I immediately recognized it as something out of our price range, but what the hell, we could always wash dishes, right?" A couple of snorts of derision answered that.

"Two things we didn't know. This was her brother Tanaka's establishment, and it was going to be a surprise free dinner as Tanaka's present to his little sister.

"Second thing. We hadn't the foggiest idea that place was an officer's place. Nothing to show that it was. I'm still not sure whose face was being saved by giving you two a free evening, do you?"

Mr. Forsythe slowly shook his head. "You could have knocked me over with a feather when I heard your voices mentioning PF-5 and the Hocky Maru. Then seeing you two there was a real shocker. So, you going to be seeing this girl Michko for a while?"

"Oh yes indeedy, Mr. Forsythe. Tonight we had a lesson in duty sections. She knows I won't be there tomorrow and Barney will be. Then, I had a sweet lesson in a hot bathtub with her as my instructor. She was using Tanaka's house for the evening."

Red was chuckling over the whole incident. Mr. Forsythe just shook his head.

"Mr. Forsythe, how deep a shit am I in?"

"None at all, Stewart. Although, there are a couple of new ensigns that want to sneak along behind you and pick up the leavings."

"You mean the whole wardroom knows about this?"

"Oh yes. We operations types have bragging rights, too, you know."

Oh, crap! Looks like it is going to be fun routing the board for a while.

June 30, 1951
United Nations Command
Tokyo, Japan

General Matthew B. Ridgeway, Commander in Chief, United Nations Command, suggests meeting in Wonsan harbor aboard the neutral Danish Hospital Ship Jutlandia.

June 30, 1951
U.S.S. Hoquiam (PF-5)
Ammunition expenditure report
On North Korean and Chinese targets

Hoquiam had only one opportunity to fire on Assigned target in the northern section near Songjin before being relegated to escorting replenishment ships between Yokosuka and Sasebo to the bombline Hoquiam operated as OTC Task Element 95.22, in company with Thompson DMS-38.

3-inch 50 caliber 114 rounds of AA Common

JULY

July 1, 1951
Pyongyang, North Korea

Premier Kim Il Sung rejects the Danish Hospital ship Jutlandia, and counter proposes Kaesong on 38th parallel.

1300, July 2, 1951
USS Hoquiam PF-5
Nested with U.S.S. Sausalito PF-4,
Buoy X-4
Sasebo Harbor, Japan

Michko and Ariko had arranged to meet Lee and Barney at the Fleet Landing. The girls wanted to take their boyfriends to a special place for a picnic. Michko had told her salesgirls she would be gone for the day, not steal her blind, and lock up at the usual time if she were not back yet. The girls tittered because they knew about the American sailors.

Barney and Lee came out of the Fleet Landing looking for their girlfriends. Sharp-eyed Ariko spotted them amongst all the sailors and called to them. Veering out of the crowd heading for taxis, they trotted up to Michko and Ariko, already sitting in Pedi-cabs. Surprising Lee and Barney, the Pedi-cabs went the opposite direction into a steep valley, stopping at a little park.

"Stoo, you take," pointing at a little package on the Pedi-cab floor. Lee leaned over and casually picked it up.

Hey, this sucker is heavy. What'd she put in this thing?

He started to untie the string. Ariko giggled. "Stoo San, you no open, nei?"

"Hey, Lee, whatcha got there?"

"Beats the hell out of me. Looks like you're carrying some kind of mat."

Barney nodded. "Yeah, feels like very thin tatami, rolled up very tightly and tied with string." By this time, they were following the girls into a private enclosure.

"Bah nee, you close, nei." She was pointing at the high wooden gate.

A tall hedge about four feet inside the wooden fence seemed to add more privacy. Michko turned and led them to the right and stopped. Looking back at Lee and Barney, she pointed through an opening in the hedge. "Come Stoo, you see." He walked up next to her and was surprised to see water. It was either a very large bathtub or very small swimming pool. Hard packed grit surrounded three sides. Close-cropped grass covered the fourth side.

"What's this, Michko?"

"Disa Merican pik neek fo you and Bah nee. Yo lika" Ariko took the roll from Barney's hands, trotted over to the grass, and bent over to lay out two wide and long mats about ten feet apart.

Hope Barney appreciates those buns.

"Bah nee, disa you an me," Ariko indicated by pointing to one mat.

Michko grabbed Lee's free hand and led him to the other mat. He stood there a little confused as to what was going to happen next. Michko and Ariko showed them. They took off their clothes and lay down. Michko giggled at Lee. "Stoo, taka u ni foam off. Come hyar," she said patting the mat next to her. "We sun now."

I'm supposed to lie quietly and suntan with that sweet little body next to me? Hoo boy!

He looked over at Ariko, admiring her body, too. Michko slapped his shoe. "You no do dat. Not nice to see Ariko."

He grinned at her and began removing his uniform. Everything folded; he stashed his clothes on top of hers and moved them out of the way. He couldn't help his erection, not helped at all by Michko giggling and chattering at Ariko. Lee saw her eyeballing his erection. "No, no Ariko, not nice to see Stoo."

Michko handed him a bottle of dark oil. "You like rub me, Stoo?"

Uh, hoo boy!

She laid down, sunny side up. Michko already had a sheen of perspiration combined from the high humidity and direct sunlight. Lee dropped to his knees, poured some oil between her shoulders and watched it pool in the arch of her back. He began gently rubbing, working from her neck down, savoring—that is to say, not quite drooling—when he would reach her bottom.

"Stoo, you go all way my feet, nei," she giggled and wriggled around. He worked down to her feet and finished.

Now, I can lie down and work on my suntan.

Michko turned over and presented all her glory in the sunlight.

"You rub me more, Stoo. You like?"

"Hai!"

I gotta start with her feet; otherwise, I'll never get down that far.

Lee worked on her glistening skin, watching her nipples grow dark and hard, then soften and lighten, depending upon where he ran his hands. Her small, dark bush also glistened from the oil. Quivering from delight without full pleasure, Lee laid down on his back alongside Michko, erect and aching.

It would be a long time until they got back to her shop and get very physical.

"Stoo, I rub you, okay?"

"Yeah, sure," he answered, just a little grouchily. She smiled gleefully, dropped to her knees, and splashed oil liberally all over her front.

What the hell is she doing?

Michko pivoted on her knees and lifted one leg to straddle him. With all that oil, he slid right into her.

Oh yeah!

Now Michko laid down on top of him and slowly moved all over his front without losing him.

Oh, I like this.

Lee couldn't hold on to her slippery back. His hands slid all over her.

After a while, as they laid there in exhaustion, Lee stole a glance at his buddy, did a double take on where his head was, and quickly averted his eyes.

Don't think I will say a word now or later. He is liable to pound me into the ground.

Michko eased back and off Lee.

"Stoo, you turn ovah." He did and she laid tummy down on his back squirming around to spread oil on his back. This was a new way to arouse his senses to a keen desire.

"Stoo, we go water now." She got up and ran, jumping into the pool. Lee followed slowly, drained of energy.

In the late evening, just after dark, the two couples arrived at Michko's dress shop and apartment. She read a couple of notes her salesgirls had written, then grabbed Lee's hand stopping him from playing with her bottom, and took him into her small room. Lee heard cloth rustling as though someone was removing his or her clothes.

A match flared. Michko lit a small candle. Her skin glowed in its light. Lee took off his uniform while she selected a record to play. She held her arms opened, swaying to the sound of Star Dust. Lee did what any man would do under the circumstances. Junior leading the way, he took her in his arms. Lee and Barney had two hours before they had to be back at the Fleet Landing.

THIS IS A F R S TOKYO WITH THE EVENING NEWS JULY TENTH NINETEEN FIFTY-ONE, STAFF SERGEANT BILL WORKMAN, YOUR REPORTER.RECAPPINGANEARLIER STORY DATELINED KAESONG, NORTH KOREA, THE TRUCE TALKS HAVE FINALLY BEGUN. VICE ADMIRAL JOY LEADS THE UNITED NATIONS DELEGATION TO THE PEACE TALKS. WE UNDERSTAND THE INITIAL TALKS ARE TO SET THE STAGE FOR DELIBERATIONS. FIGHTING STILL GOES ON AS THE PEACE TALKS BEGIN.

THIS IS A F R S TOKYO WITH THE EVENINGNEWSJULYSEVENTEENTH NINETEEN FIFTY-ONE, SPECIALIST FOURTH CLASS DAVID HAMLIN, YOUR REPORTER. DATELINE

WONSAN. THE NAVY WAS INVOLVED IN AN ARTILLERY SLUGGING MATCH YESTERDAY. NORTH KOREAN ARTILLERYMEN APPARENTLY HAVING ENOUGH OF THE UNITED NATIONS INTERDICTION BOMBARDMENT RETALIATED WITH AN ESPECIALLY SEVERE GUN BOMBARDMENT ON THE USS O'BRIEN DD-725, THE USS BLUE DD-744, AND THE USS CUNNINGHAM DD-752. THE COMMUNIST FORCES FIRED AT THE SHIPS IN WONSAN HARBOR WITH MORE THAN FIVE HUNDRED ROUNDS SPLASHING AROUND THOSE SHIPS. THE DESTROYERS COUNTERED WITH MORE THAN TWENTY-THREE HUNDRED ROUNDS OF FIVE-INCH SHELLS ON UMI DO, KALMA GAK, AND HODO PANDO. COUNTER BATTERY FIRE WAS SO HEAVY THAT SHRAPNEL FELL ON TWO LST'S ANCHORED NEAR YO DO. REAR ADMIRAL DYER, COMMANDER TASK FORCE NINETY-FIVE NICKNAMED THIS ENGAGEMENT AS THE BATTLE OF THE BUZZ SAW. HE ALSO ORDERED ALL SHIPS ENTERING WONSAN HARBOR TO REMAIN UNDERWAY AND NOT ANCHOR AS PREVIOUSLY HAD BEEN THE CASE.

Stewart rolled a sheet of paper into their standard typewriter. He hadn't written to Ruth in quite a while. He needed to catch up on the news with her. One of these days, he was going to return to Seattle and see her.

July 24, 1951
Yokosuka, Japan.
Hey Luscious One,

We left Sasebo on July 7, escorting the replenishment group as usual. It was different this time. Constant steaming until we arrived here this afternoon. I'd be over guzzling down a few Asahi's with a steak dinner but got the duty tonight.
Another thing different, we worked with a Royal Thai Navy PF, a Columbian Navy PF, and three of our own PF's, in the process of escorting the cargo ships, tankers, and ammo carriers from place to place. Our skipper is senior, so he is usually the screen commander in charge of all the escort ships.
These ships really eat up the supplies. We keep hearing rumors of a big stevedore strike in San Francisco. The only ones those birds are hurting are us. Even though we didn't fire on any targets this trip, when we do fire,

we use up ammo at the rate of over 100 shells per day.
Hey Baby, did you get a package from me yet? If you haven't, not going to tell you what is in it. Enjoy it alone or when I get back. Not for your other boyfriends to enjoy.
We don't know what is happening with the Hocky Maru. Had a mass transfer of a bunch of guys to the Helena right after we got in. A message came in about the Reservists getting out on points. If we have any guys with enough points, those guys will leave for home in a couple of days. This keeps up we're not going to have enough crew to sail back to Korea.
The ship is supposed to have some major work accomplished, which means we ought to be here about three weeks. Time to cool down and relax the belly muscles again.

I really miss you, Luscious. Need to get you in my arms again. It is imagination time again. Think thoughts, Sweet One.
Lee

1630, July 27, 1951
USS Hoquiam PF-5
Radio Gang Party

Karazu Restaurant
Yokosuka, Japan

This is a special liberty, a really special liberty. The gang has arranged with the Tacoma PF-3, to take their communications guard over night. This is Jimmy Bob James's last night aboard the Hoquiam. In fact, it is his last night in Japan. For tomorrow, he and twenty-four other sailors and chiefs are heading home for separation. Their Reserve time is over. Chief Quartermaster (Signalman) Swenson is a special guest. He is being transferring to the Fleet Reserve. President Truman had frozen his retirement. Another special guest is Lieutenant (Junior Grade) Roger Forsythe, Communications Officer, and our division officer. Everyone kicked in 3,600 yen to pay for the room, food, dancers, and liquor. [*3600¥ was equivalent to $10.00*]

It is fitting that the Officer of the Deck is Lt. Porter, Operations Officer. Although he was politely invited to attend, he just as politely declined to attend. However, these were his people and he hoped the party would be a success.

Mr. Forsythe approached the Officer of the Deck. Saluting, he asked "Request permission to leave the ship, sir?"

"Permission granted, Mr. Forsythe. Have a good party."

"Request permission to leave the ship, Mr. Porter?" asked Chief Swenson with a smile.

"Permission granted, Chief. Don't forget, hangovers and planes don't mix well."

"Then, guess I'll have to go by ship, sir." He saluted and turned to the Colors, saluting.

One by one, the Radiomen approached and received permission to leave the ship.

Mr. Porter watched in amusement as each sailor saluted the Colors, and then tugged the bottom of his white jumper down after it had crept up during the saluting procedure. They bunched at the bottom of the ladder and walked off to the bus stop to ride around to the Main Gate.

Their party room was long and narrow with a door at each end. They entered at a door at one end. Everything else came and went through the other door.

Lee was happy that Kiki had finally arrived. They were excited because this was only his second overnight liberty. Having Kiki there gave the crew another advantage. She spoke English, a fact that most of Lee's shipmates didn't know until tonight.

She had helped make the party go smoothly. Lee told her all about the party when he invited her. Kiki, with Lee in tow, had immediately visited the restaurant and made sure there were no unanswered questions in the owner's mind. In addition, she explained why the party was so special. Kiki arranged to have young Geishas attend the members who did not bring a girlfriend. Lee made sure that each guy understood you don't tamper with these Geishas.

By 8:30PM, the party was roaring along in overdrive. One of the Geishas pointed at Lloyd and giggled, explaining to Kiki that he was passed out and slowly sliding down the tatami under the table.

"Kiki, it looks like he is sinking into the sea," laughed Lee.

Coyle, who was the new Leading Petty Officer, looked over at Lloyd. "I just knew he couldn't last. He's been bragging for a couple of days about how many sakis he could drink. Ha!"

Mr. Forsythe frowned, then smiled in anticipation of seeing Lloyd tomorrow. Occasionally, his mischievous side came out.

I'll just have to stand next to him tomorrow morning at quarters while I loudly give instructions.

Chief Swenson showed up with the WAVE Yeoman First from the Legal Office, surprising Lee. She was the one who had taken his deposition on Betty Echols.

"Hey, Stewart, front and center. My friend has a couple of questions for you," ordered, so to speak, that Lee approach the Chief and his girl friend.

Oh yeah, do I remember that sweet looking First Class.

Lee struggled off the slippery tatami, as Kiki sprang to her feet, and they both approached the Chief and his girlfriend. The WAVE looked at Kiki with curiosity.

"Stewart, Kiki, this is my fiancée, Peggy Ware. Peggy, you remember Lee Stewart from the deposition, and this is his lady friend, Kiki, whom you have heard of from Charles."

"Hi Lee, Kiki. Lee, what was the final disposition of those charges of fathering that baby, or would you rather not talk about it?"

Kiki snapped a look of surprise at Peggy, then Lee.

Oh shit!

Lee glanced at Kiki who had never heard about this.

"Well, ONI proved she wrote the letter after she claimed I had forged it. She finally confessed that she did not want to marry that Air Force guy because he was a bum. She had wanted me all along." Peggy nodded with knowing eyes. Lee continued. "Her folks were so pissed, they disowned her and shipped her and the baby off to some small Mormon village on the southeastern Utah desert. I got a no-return-address letter from her telling me to kiss off."

"So, everything has been dropped and all is well?" she smiled.

"Seems that way. But," he continued nodding at Roger Forsythe, "he and the Exec sealed everything up and placed it in my service jacket for safekeeping—just in case."

"Lee, what's this all about?" Peggy's eyebrows shot up at Kiki's English language skill.

"I'll tell you all about it later, Kiki. Was a long time ago." Kiki looked at Lee out of the side of her eyes, very doubtfully. Peggy chuckled and the Chief grinned.

Peggy laid her hand on Kiki's arm. "Let me explain. I work in the Legal Office and transcribe various hearings and court-martials. Lee was falsely accused by this girl of fathering her child.

"In a letter before the baby was born, she wrote that another guy got her drunk and made love to her. She found out she was pregnant and told the guy. He skipped out, joining the Air Force the next day. The girl tried to contact Lee at his base. They had been going together before this happened. However, Lee was already out here. When her mother discovered the pregnancy, the girl said Lee did it. Her parents fell for it because they wanted Lee as a son-in-law. If the girl hadn't screwed up and wrote the letter to Lee telling him what happened, he might be married now."

"I see. Lee," Kiki in a demanding voice said," did you make love to her before that?"

"No, Kiki. Never got that close to her. Besides, that's none of your concern. Why are you asking these questions about something that happened before I met you?" Her eyes flashed as she whirled around and went back to the table.

"Hey, Stewart, I think you just got cut off." The Chief laughed quietly. Peggy looked at Lee, then snapped at the Chief, "Sweetie, you better look to your own interests!" While Chief Swenson was pleading with Peggy, Lee walked over to Kiki and sat down beside her. He was sure he knew what was troubling her and he refused to touch the concept.

She wants me to marry her and take her back to the States. That is not going to be, and I sure as hell have given her no hope in that direction.

"Wanna tell me about it, Kiki?"

She looked at him with angry eyes. For the first time, Lee heard a slight accent to her English.

"You have been serious about a girl before me, Lee, and that hurts."

"Not true," said Lee. "The girl, Betty Echols, and her folks too, were serious about me. We kissed and felt each other up but that's all. I never saw her after the day her folks announced in church that "we" were keeping company. Now that you bring it up, I do have several girls with whom I write and visit." Kiki scrambled to her feet.

"I go home now. You stay and go back to ship." She spoke in Japanese to one of the Geishas and ran out of the room.

Roger Forsythe watched and shook his head.

"Hey, Lee. Is that the end of the grand love life?" Lee looked at him in exasperation.

"Well, let me put it this way, Rog." Lt (jg) Forsythe blinked at Lee's familiar address.

"Can I turn in this over night pass for one in Sasebo with Michko? I can't understand a word she says, but the body English is fantastic." He stared moodily at Peggy and the Chief who caused the eruption. "I do think Kiki is past tense."

"Hey, Lee," yelled Jimmy Bob from the end of the table. "What happened to Kiki?"

"I think she just figured out I'm not the marrying kind, Jimmy Bob." Jimmy Bob laughed his ass off.

Peggy and the Chief walked up behind Lee and nudged him. Seeing who it was, he stood to face them. They both had sorrowful, if not embarrassed looks on their faces.

"Lee, if it will do any good, I'll try to catch her and apologize for bringing up the deposition."

"Nah, Peggy. I think things have run their course. She didn't like that, but when I figured she was putting on the squeeze, I mentioned other girls I see and so forth. That is when she took a powder."

"What are you going to do now, Lee?" asked the Chief.

"Have one more saki with Rog there and go back to the ship. Looks like our old gang is beginning to break up."

Someone began knocking loudly on the table.

"Quiet down, I got something to say to you all," called out Jimmy Bob, breathing heavily from all the saki. Except for the noise from the other parts of the restaurant, all talk stopped and people looked at Jimmy Bob, except Lloyd who was snoring quietly.

"I hated it when I got recalled. I hated it when I saw this rusty bucket of bolts in the dry dock last year. I was scared to death when I found out I was L.P.O. and all my P.O.'s were in just as bad shape. I hated this last April worst of all. All that night shooting messed up my sleeping for a long time. However, I am going to remember everyone here for a long time to come. If you come to Birmingham, in good ole 'Bama-land, I'm in the telephone book. I'll treat you to some real southern belles. Roger, you ain't such a bad feller. Just keep a cool tool."

He held up his saki in toast to everyone and downed it. Everyone else did the same.

0830, July 28, 1951
Quarterdeck,
U.S.S. Hoquiam
SRF, Yokosuka, Japan

The radio gang stood by Secondary Conn as the twenty-five people lined up to leave the ship. Jimmy Bob James was the third man to leave the ship. Just before he got to the Officer of the Deck, Lt (jg) Unsenger, he looked at the radio gang, grinned a wide shit-eatin' grin, and gave thumbs up. He carried his sea bag and gym bag down to the bus and got on, never looking back at the Hoquiam. When everyone had boarded the bus and settled in their seats, a long beep came blaring up from the bus horn and it was gone.

"Okay gang, back to business. We got work to do before the next trip out." They stared at Coyle RM2 for a moment, and then remembered he was now their Leading Petty Officer.

July 28, 1951
02-Deck, forward of CIC
U.S.S. Hoquiam (PF-5)
SRF Yokosuka, Japan

LeBerge came back into the radio shack and dropped the message board into its wire basket. Freckle-faced with straight brown hair and dark brown eyes, he stood five feet, eleven inches, and weighed 148 pounds. A great smile was overcast with crooked, stained teeth. LeBerge tended to bray when he laughed.

"Hey guys, those Japanese yardworkers are getting ready to install a gun in front of the Bridge." Masters, Griffin, and Stewart looked at him. Coyle and Roney were on Fox and the Underway Training Element CW circuit, respectively.

As one, Masters, Griffin, and Stewart ambled out, heading for the 02-deck. They arrived in time to see the gun mount swing in over their head and drop to within inches of the deck.

"Son of a bitch, we're getting Mount 32 back," chucked Griffin.

"Bet the Captain is happy about that—more guns to fire all at once." Griffin looked at Masters. "Maybe so, but never for night interdiction. That's right over the Captain and Executive Officer staterooms.

"Holy shit, this one has electric drives." Stewart continued to look at it. Then, thoughtfully added, "Wonder what kind of sights this one uses?"

"Dunno, but that damned RBS receiver is going to jump right out of its shock mounts," Masters grumbled.

The three radiomen continued to watch a few more minutes, then returned to the shack for daily business.

AUGUST

0630, August 6, 1951
USS Hoquiam PF-5
Moored Pier A-8
SRF Yokosuka, Japan

The Bos'uns Pipe shrilled Attention. "Make all preparations for getting underway."

Stewart and Barney sat eating breakfast, completely ignoring the announcement. Red slid in and joined them. "Pass the sugar, asshole!" Red's voice was stressed.

"Barney, that must be you," said Stewart as a wide-eyed innocent. "We both know that Charles would never refer to me in quite that manner—sonofabitch, yes, but asshole, never."

With that, Red stood up and reached over for the sugar. "Fuck you, Stewart."

"Dammit Red, Kiki had hopes I was going to marry her and that never was and is not on my list of things to do. Besides, Chief Swenson's girlfriend Peggy spilled the beans about Betty and that's what started it. Come on, it's been over a week since then. You haven't given me any notes answering my note to Kiki, so what gives that's got you so upset?"

"Kimiko was up early this morning. She said Kiki disappeared yesterday without a word. She is worried and blames you, and therefore blames me."

"And you are blaming me for this? Hey Red, I am in the middle of her desires, and about something that did not happen back in the States. I don't buy it."

He thought about Kiki for a minute.

"Why don't you ask Kimiko if Kiki's stuff is gone? If it is, she may have gone back to Sendei with her ill mother. Who knows, maybe she got the word her mother took a turn for the worse." Stewart got up with his half-eaten breakfast, no longer hungry. "Gotta relieve the watch, guys. See you later."

The Quartermaster's whistle blew loud and clear.

"Shift colors—Shift colors." Stewart cocked his eye up to the clock. 0808.

I've got first duty in Sasebo. Wonder if Barney and I can go see Michko and Ariko? I'll ask him next time I go to the Bridge.

He continued copying George Fox as he reached for another 8 x 14" sheet of paper and laid it alongside the typewriter, ready to insert the sheet after this current sheet rolled to the bottom of the page. The current message and paper ended at the same time. He rapidly inserted the new sheet, lined it up, and caught up as the code continued without ceasing. Masters was sitting next to him checking routed messages.

The ship won't check into Task Group Common until tomorrow.

Masters made a sound of disgust and looked over his shoulder.

"Roney, take Leberge out again and show him where these offices are located." He pointed to three messages. "Coyle will chew him a new one if he keeps seeing addressees that don't get their traffic."

"He's routing the board right now, Hank. Want me to chase after him?" Asked Roney.

"Nah. Wait until he gets back, then herd his ass around. After three weeks, he should have learned this shit. He has to start standing messenger watches on this trip to Wonsan. We're only stopping in Sasebo long enough to refuel at the Jasco Fuel dock and pick up the next replenishment group and other escort—Burlington, I think."

Crap! I thought we were in port for a couple of days. Bye Michko.

1700, August 9, 1951
USS Hoquiam PF-5
Underway to Wonsan, North Korea
Escorting Replenishment Group

"Secure from Special Sea and Anchor Detail. On deck, Section One, relieve the watch. The smoking lamp is lit in all authorized spaces. Enlisted underway uniform is dungarees with skivvy shirt and white hat."

Stewart was glad they were underway. The humidity and temperature were high this August and Sasebo Harbor was a bowl that collected heat. He leaned against the chain lifelines just outside the radio shack, absorbing the hot breeze. They were escorting the Replenishment Group to Wonsan again, this time with the Glendale PF-36, as fellow escort.

Stewart was thinking about Charles and Kimiko, and Kiki. When the ship went back to Yokosuka, Charles was getting married to Kimiko.

When the four of them had been close, Stewart was supposed to witness the Taoist wedding for Charles, as Kiki did for Kimiko. What with Kiki's disappearance and Charles's unrelenting anger at him, he didn't know whether he should talk Charles about the marriage plans or just try to let Charles cool off for a while.

Barney told Stewart that Charles had made nasty comments about Stewart and Michko. That, he could ignore. She was a Sasebo flame that would eventually burn out.

She is a fiery one, though. I wonder how long I'll be able to keep up with her demands.

The ship trembled, increasing speed after passing through the submarine nets.

2000, August 11, 1951
USS Hoquiam PF-5
Underway for Songjin, North Korea
Escorting Replenishment Group

All three main battery gun crews were just finishing up, cleaning their guns. When they arrived at Wonsan this morning, the Task Group Commander (CTG95.2) assigned the Hoquiam to respond to Fire Missions. All day long, the three gun mounts, 31, 32, and 33, shot at assigned targets. By the time they weighed anchor to leave, the ship had fired 133 rounds of AA Common and 5 rounds of VT at Wonsan Harbor island targets.

1619, August 12, 1951
USS Hoquiam PF-5
Underway for Sasebo, Japan
Escorting Replenishment Group

"Bridge Sonar—Possible submarine contact bearing 115 degrees true, range fifteen hundred yards." The Captain rapidly ensured all the correct levers were down on the 21MC.

"Bridge aye Sonar. Combat—Label contact Sugar One and track."

"Combat aye aye Captain. Sugar One tracking."

The Captain leaned over the Wheelhouse voice tube.

"Boatswains Mate—General Quarters Condition One Charlie set condition zebra throughout the ship."

The Officer of the Deck, Lt (jg) Forsythe, pulled the Task Group Common handset from its holder and confirmed the Navasota's voice call sign.

"Boatswains Mate aye aye Captain." He wheeled around and moved the GQ lever to ON.

BONG BONG BONG BONG

"All hands man your battle stations. Condition One Charlie. Set condition Zebra throughout the ship." BONG BONG BONG BONG . . . .

That quickly, hatches began slamming shut. You could hear the dogs being wrenched tight to seal the hatches. Running feet attested to the urgency of a submarine attack.

Lt (jg) Forsythe pressed the handset mike switch.

CLANCEY THIS IS LASHING PETER FLASH BLUE I SAY AGAIN FLASH BLUE OVER

THIS IS CLANCEY ROGER AM PROCEEDING INDEPENDENTLY OUT

The U.S.S. Navasota AO-106, an empty fuel tanker heading in for a refill, damn well knew there were no friendly submarines in the Sea of Japan. She increased from standard speed to flank speed, passing close aboard the Hoquiam, in her haste to move out of range of the possible submarine. Tankers, even empty ones, are prime, fat targets for submarines.

"Bridge Sonar—We have lost contact in the Navasota wash."

"Bridge aye—I am going to cross the Navasota track. See if the contact is on the other side, Sonar."

"Sonar aye aye, Captain."

"Wheelhouse Left standard rudder, come to new course one one zero True."

Helmsman aye aye Captain left standard rudder. Coming to new course one one zero True."

"Rudder is answering the helm, Captain."

"Very well."

Bridge Helmsman Steady on new course one one zero true, Captain."

"Very well."

Captain Brown tried to regain contact by searching a square pattern surrounding the last known position. A little more than two hours later, Sonar was not sure whether the contact had been a submarine or a whale.

At that point, the Captain returned to the base course and headed for Sasebo. Suspicious by nature, the Captain continued searching at various courses and speeds in accordance with ASW doctrine without further contact.

August 21, 1951
Mount 33 Gun Tub
USS Hoquiam PF-5
Moored Buoy X-5
Sasebo, Japan

Stewart was downcast. Out of the original radio gang, only he, Masters, and Griffin were left. Griffin was the new L.P.O. and did not like it one bit. Oh sure, they had picked up two new strikers and a Radioman Third Class, but it wasn't the same. There was no party this time.

The word came day before yesterday in the morning Guard Mail run that Coyle RM2 and Lloyd RM2 were going home for separation that day. With yells of joy, they ran around the ship checking out and packing their sea bags.

The new Third Class, Frontella, as well as Roney and LeBerge took the watch as what was left of the old gang sat down to noon chow together for the last time. Coyle and Lloyd were cutting up and trying to outdo each other.

"Man, it's been so long I'm going to have to take out a training course before I tack my wife to the mattress," Lloyd chattered.

Coyle looked down at his crotch. "Son of one big gun! It's up! I thought it was never going to come up again." He looked at Lloyd. "Tack her? Shit, I'm going to rivet mine!"

Lloyd laughed and laughed, then got a serious look on his face. "Do you suppose our jobs are still waiting for us?"

Coyle choked on his coffee. "No sweat for me. I'm a mailman." He looked around at everyone staring at him. He smirked and preened. "You don't think I'd let anyone know that I worked for the U.S. Post Office, do you? You have any idea of what it would be like back there in the mail room."

Lloyd's face got a little longer. "Yeah, well I was a fairly successful new car salesman for Nash. I hear they aren't doing so well. Maybe I could get a job on a Studebaker lot."

Masters looked around. "You know what? I'm a house painter and that's a shitty job. Maybe I'll stick around like Stewart here and see the world."

Stewart looked around. "I've got nothing to go back to, just forward. I expect to make Chief Radioman in a few years and retire after twenty or thirty years. It ain't a bad life, to my way of thinking."

The others threw pieces of bread at him.

The 1MC cracked open and a Bos'uns Pipe shrilled Attention. "Those seventeen sailors departing for the U.S. for separation muster on the fantail with sea bags and orders. The uniform of the day is Dress Blue Baker."

"Dammit, they told us in Personnel that traveling uniform out here is dungarees," Coyle muttered as his coffee sloshed on the mess table.

"Shit," said Lloyd, "I've got to go down and change and repack my fuckin' bag."

The 1MC shrilled Attention. "Belay that last word. Those seventeen sailors departing for the U.S. for separation muster on the fantail with sea bags and orders. The uniform of the day is dungarees with shirt and white hat."

Lloyd grinned at Coyle. They got up and looked at the last three. Silently, both of them shook hands with Griffin, Masters, and Stewart.

"Bon voyage, guys."

"Yeah, you too, Stewart. Hope you're really happy after twenty or thirty years in this rat trap." Coyle shut up, took the sneer from his lips, and headed for their compartment for his gear.

Lloyd looked at the three. “Good luck,” and he too, went down in the compartment for his sea bag and gym bag.

Griffin, Masters, and Stewart joined some of the other Operations Department men and officers, aft in the Mount 33 gun tub. Mount 33 overlooked the fantail where seventeen men presented their orders to the Officer of the Deck who proceeded to inspect them.

Ensign Herbert waved to the coxswain in the Motor whaleboat, which was arriving from the Officer’s Landing. Lt (jg) Forsythe rode in the cockpit with an orange cloth bag. He had been on R and R the past four days and picked up Registered Publications before returning to the ship.

“Oh shit,” whispered Griffin, “Mr. Forsythe is about to get the shock of his life. He doesn’t know Coyle and Lloyd are in that draft of men.”

Some of the others chuckled and snickered. Mr. Forsythe was a nervous soul.

The Motor whaleboat pulled alongside, held closely by the ‘Hooks. Lt (jg) Forsythe requested permission to come aboard, was granted, and climbed the ladder up to the Quarterdeck, saluting the colors hanging limply at the fantail. As he did, he saw two familiar faces holding sea bags next to them.

Lieutenant (jg) Forsythe turned to Ensign Herbert. “Where are those men going, Carl?”

"They have been relieved of duty and are about to board the Motor whaleboat. They are going home for separation."

Lieutenant (jg) Forsythe stared at the two grinning men. He looked at Ensign Herbert, heard the shuffling above and looked up at Mount 33 gun tub with all its sightseers who were grinning at him, too. Lieutenant (jg) Forsythe gave a long sigh, squared his shoulders, and fairly marched up to Coyle and Lloyd.

"You two assholes could have given me some warning, dammit."

Coyle laughed. "Hey Rog, you'd already left on R and R when our immediate orders came in. We are gone as soon as you let us pass, sir."

Lieutenant (jg) Forsythe studied their faces for a moment and stuck out his hand. "We'll miss you. Been good serving with you both."

Lloyd said it. "Yeah, you too, Mr. Forsythe. Hope you get orders for separation soon, too." He came to attention and saluted—"By your leave, sir?" Lloyd, followed by Coyle, raised their hands in salute. Lieutenant (jg) Roger Forsythe looked at them a fleeting instant and returned their salute. "Permission granted," he said and stepped aside.

The seventeen began to debark the Hoquiam and board the motor whaleboat, handing down their sea bags and gym bags before requesting permission of Ensign Herbert to leave the ship. Once they were all in, voices from the Main Deck and 01-deck called down wishes for good luck.

"Coxswain, carry out your orders."

The coxswain saluted, “Aye aye, sir,” and pulled his bell lanyard once.

DING

He gave the tiller a little shove between his legs, and the Motor whaleboat eased away from the side of the Hoquiam.

DING DING DING DING

The bow lifted a little as the Motor whaleboat came up to full speed, getting smaller as it aimed at the Fleet Landing.

“Okay guys, back to traffic. We got work to do,” said Griffin RM2, the new L.P.O. Masters and Stewart looked at Griffin and nodded their heads.

0530, August 23, 1951
Underway for Wonsan, North Korea
Escorting large Replenishment Group

The 1MC crackled. “Set the Special Sea and Anchor Detail. Muster on stations. All Prisoners-at-large and Restricted Men muster with the duty Master-at-Arms on the Mess Deck.”

Wow! That's a new call. Wonder what brought that on?

Stewart was downcast as he poured coffee in the radio shack. He looked at Masters's coffee cup and refilled that. Masters nodded as he continued to copy Fox. Parks RD1 in CIC was now the L.P.O. of the Operations Department. No more Chiefs. Chief Hathaway, the Chief ET, had gone to the Naval Hospital Yokosuka with some kind of galloping crud on his right foot last month. He was not expected back.

The ship trembled as it got underway. Most ships were just sounding reveille as the Hoquiam and Bisbee PF-46 headed down the channel toward the submarine nets.

They were escorting this large group. Four ships, the Chara AK-58, Leo AKA-60, Graffias AF-29, and Chemung AO-30, were going up this time. Usually, they escorted one or two ships. Later, the Columbian PF, the Almirante Padilla, with her charges, the Platte AO-24, and Paricutin AE-18 joined the two escorts.

By 1300 the next day, the convoy slowed to less than ten knots because of typhoon-related heavy seas and gusty winds. Many hours late, the convoy arrived at the port of Pohang, South Korea. Released, the Hoquiam sailed back to Sasebo, Japan.

THIS IS A F R S TOKYO WITH THE EVENING NEWS AUGUST TWENTY-FIFTH NINETEEN FIFTY-ONE, SPECIALIST FOURTH CLASS DAVID HAMLIN REPORTING. FROM GENERAL RIDGEWAY'S UNITED NATIONS COMMAND HEADQUARTERS, WE LEARN THAT JCS FINALLY APPROVED

AN AIRSTRIKE ON THE RAIL MARSHALLING YARDS AT RASHIN, NORTH KOREA. FAR EAST U S AIR FORCE B TWENTY-NINES, ESCORTED BY NAVY PANTHER AND BANSHEE FIGHTERS, DESTROYED THE MARSHALLING YARDS, A TURNTABLE, A ROUNDHOUSE, A BRIDGE, AND SEVENTY-FIVE FREIGHT CARS BEING READIED FOR A RUN DOWN THE COAST.

SEPTEMBER

R SEPTEMBER 2, 1951
FM CTE 92.11
TO USS HOQUIAM

BT
A SPLENDID JOB OF HANDLING THE SCREEN X WELL DONE
BT

0955, September 9, 1951
USS Hoquiam PF-5
Inbound to Yokosuka, Japan

"Set the Special Sea and Anchor Detail. All hands shift into the uniform of the day for entering port. Undress blue baker for enlisted men, khakis with tie and jacket for Chiefs and officers. All hands not actually on duty, Quarters at fair weather parade for entering port."

There was a chill in the breeze that flowed over the Hoquiam. They had been underway on Replenishment Group escort duty since August 22. Now, the ship was being given a well-deserved yard period to correct some problems.

The 1MC came on with a long blast on the police whistle.

"Shift colors, Shift colors."

A few minutes later, the 1MC came on again.

"Liberty will commence at 1300 for Sections One and Two. Liberty expires on board for non-rated men at 2400, petty officers at 0200, and Chiefs at 0700."

Stewart thought about Red, or Charles as he preferred, and decided to go to the Bridge. Red still hadn't told him if he was to be his Witness at his marriage.

"Hey Griff, you mind if I run up to the Signal Bridge for a moment?" Griffin looked up and frowned. Then he nodded. "Not too long, please. You're making the unclassified guard mail run shortly."

"Who's making the Registered Pub and classified message run, you or Mr. Forsythe?

"I am," Mr. Forsythe replied from his stateroom. "Be back in fifteen minutes, Stewart."

"Aye aye, sir." Stewart wheeled out of the shack, through the hatch and up to the flag bags.

The new Signalman striker was making sure all the flags were properly stowed and one flag bag was covered, a pot of coffee made for the Signal watch, deck gratings up for full sweep down, and a fresh water clamp down.

After that, until time for liberty call, he could work on brass and chrome, or wipe down the bulkheads with fresh water and toweling to get rid of salt crystals. Stewart peered around the Cubby to the Bridge.

No officers—where the hell is the Officer of the Deck?

The 1MC opened. "The Officer of the Deck has shifted his watch to the Port Quarterdeck."

Barney was starting to lift the deck grating away so the new guy could get to work. Stewart helped him for a couple of minutes. "Barney, what's the new kid's name?"

"Umm, shit, I can't remember." Barney looked around and spotted the kid drifting around, not working.

"Hey, get over here, kid." Poor guy right of out Boot Camp almost peeled shoe leather. He was on a dirty detail and had dungarees on. His name, Watson, appeared on his shirt pocket.

"Listen, Watson, this is Stewart from the Radio Shack. He's my buddy and we help each other occasionally. He also routes the message board to the officers around here. You will carry semaphore and flashing light messages down to his shack for typing."

Watson watched wide-eyed as Stewart poured a cup of their coffee. Barney followed his eyes. "Yeah, the whole operations department has coffee privilege in each other's spaces. So, if you run down to the Radio Shack, you can get a cup down there. Got it?"

"Yes sir."

"Gawdammit, you already got told twice, only people you sir to, are officers. I'm Barney."

"Okay Barney"

"Good. Get hot and get this work done. Hubba hubba, nei?"

Stewart laughed. "He ain't gonna understand that shit yet."

Barney grinned. "You and Red speaking to each other yet?"

"That's why I am here, to find out the plans. Where is he?"

"I'm right above you, shit for brains." Red was standing on top of Sonar with his binoculars looking where Kimiko and Kiki always stood.

"Lee, can you see Kimiko's window from there?" Stewart squinted across the Inner Harbor at their hillside, picked up their semaphore position, and looked up to the left.

"Yeah, but it is pretty small, Red."

"Why don't you try to nail that window with the Starboard light? Maybe that will attract her attention."

Sounds like Red may have forgiven me, or at least decided I didn't have any choice.

He sauntered to the light, turned it on, and spun it around, looking through the ring and point sight until he had her window lined up. Then, he opened the shutters.

"I can't tell if you're painting her window with light or not. It's not strong enough. Oh wait, either Kiki is back or someone else has her old room. Hit her window and send her name. See if that gets a rise." Stewart began to send KIKI very slowly, over and over.

"She disappeared.—Got 'em. Both are in Kimiko's window, and now they are gone."

Stewart turned off the light and trained it forward.

"I gotta go Red. Guard mail run. You still pissed at me?"

"Nah, but Kiki probably is. I'll find out things and tell you before liberty. When was the last time you saw her, Stew?"

"At Jimmy Bob's farewell party. Gotta go now."

Masters was giving the new RMSA a lesson on how to correct a publication. Meanwhile, Stewart had already finished correcting one pub and was starting on another one. Masters was pointing to how Stewart was doing it. Therefore, Stewart, looking at Richards, the new striker, did it very slowly.

Red appeared in the doorway. "You busy, Stew?" Masters glanced up at him, nodded and told the new kid, "This is Red Crosley from the Signal Bridge, Richards. He and some of the other guys bring semaphore and flashing light messages down to us to type. They can drink our coffee because we can drink their coffee." Richards nodded understanding.

"Stewart, let Richards continue correcting what you've started there. Take care of your business with Red, then get back and monitor how Richards does this."

"Thanks, Hank." Stewart motioned to Red and they backed out to the shady area out side of the Radio Shack.

"What's the word, Red?" Red looked at him crookedly.

"I'm not sure how you're going to take this, Lee."

Oh well, was nice while it lasted.

He raised his cup for a sip of coffee.

"Kiki got married in Sendei and her husband is here with her." Stewart choked on his coffee and sprayed it all over the place.

Red slapped Lee's back as Lee swallowed his coffee the wrong way.

"This a joke?"

"No sirreebob. Kiki had a real close Japanese friend in Sendei and after a couple of days there, he told her how much he had missed her and loved her and would she marry him. She let him sweat for a couple of days and shyly, maiden-like, said yes."

"Maiden-like?" Lee grinned.

"That's the term she used. Also, when you see her, you barely know her cause the only time you have ever seen her is when you came up to see Kimiko and me. Otherwise, you are dis-invited to the marriage ceremony," Red continued seriously.

"I'm just floored, that's all. After all the fuss, she threw me over. Does not hurt me at all. Was a lot of fun while it lasted. However, I got a secret for you. Michko is one hell of a lover and I'll be glad to get back down to Sasebo to her, later in October. Sure, I barely know her— what's her name again?" Lee joked.

Red grinned and he-he-he'd at him. "Gotta pass the word to them. They are waiting to hear. You promise not to fuck with Kiki's new husband."

"Hey Red, that's not in my bag of tricks. Better yet, why don't I hit the beach with Barney today? That way, there is no question of dirty tricks." Red waved and pounded up the ladder to the Signal Bridge. Stewart went back in to work with Richards on pubs.

1730, September 10, 1951
Kimiko's apartment
Yokosuka, Japan

The Taoist ceremony was over and they were back in her apartment. In a surprise move, the Captain showed up for the marriage ceremony and visited Kimiko's apartment long enough to toast the couple and munch a couple of crackers.

Lt. Porter also put in an appearance but seemed somewhat uneasy the whole time. He left right after the Captain. That left the two couples, and Barney and Lee.

Lee completely ignored Kiki except a polite greeting at the ceremony. Her husband's name was Hiro who understood absolutely no English. Kiki offered to translate anything for Lee.

"Yes Kiki. Why don't you offer my sincerest congratulations? I knew you would make some man a great wife." Her eyes flashed fire momentarily and then she turned to Hiro and told him what Lee had said. Hiro's smile could not have gone wider. He talked at length.

"He said he always thought Americans didn't know a good thing when they had it in their hands. Now he understands that is different. They are just too stupid to know."

"Hey Kiki," Charles said with a big smile. "Lee is playing by your rules. Don't insult him for being proper to you." She turned away from Hiro so he wouldn't see her glare at Charles and Kimiko.

Lee stood abruptly. "Come on Barney, those girls are waiting for us." Barney got up, looking back and forth. Lee bowed to Hiro and hoped he had a long successful marriage with such a beautiful woman. Kimiko hurriedly translated before Kiki could do anything. Hiro bowed back with a big smile and stuck out his hand. Lee shook it warmly. When Hiro turned to Barney and shook his hand, Lee gave Kiki the finger and opened the shoji to leave.

Kimiko and Charles laughed because it was so out of character. Kiki was speechless. Hiro and Barney had no idea what the laughter was all about.

"Barney, it's a long walk from here to a Pedi-cab, but at least I know the way."

"Where we going, Lee?" Lee stopped dumbfounded and looked at Barney.

"Your favorite place, Barney." Barney looked down in the mouth.

"That place went belly-up while we were gone. I did not like the place where I went last night. You got any ideas."

"Well, we could go window shopping for girls. Mamasans don't like that, though."

"Fuck it, let's go back to the ship. We can start out fresh tomorrow."

Lee thought a moment.

Anything we do now could really be wrong. He's right, back to the ship.

"You're right."

Lee's eyes picked up the tall galoot in a pink kimono that came down to his knees, the gatas, and a farmer's conical sun hat. He was arguing with the MP's at the Main Gate. The closer they got, the more familiar he looked.

Then the guy's voice clicked in Lee's mind. "Holy shit! That's Parks. What the fuck happened to him?"

Barney started laughing.

They walked around in front of him and looked at a very angry man.

"Jeez, Parks, what the fuck happened to you?"

"Some bastard stole everything I had, right down to the skivvies. This is all Mamasan had for me to wear."

Barney grinned at Lee. "Ahh, Parks? Exactly where is this house."

Parks looked at him suspiciously. "Why the fuck you want to know, dipshit?"

"Well, we're looking for a new house, and yours is definitely on the no-no list." Lee and the Marine MP's began laughing. The Marine Sergeant looked at Barney and Lee.

"Your ID and Liberty Cards, please." They handed them over for inspection. After looking at the cards, the Sergeant asked, "Do you recognize this man?"

Both of them grinned, "Yes, Sergeant."

"I take it he is on your ship."

"That's right, Sergeant." Lee began walking around him. "Christ, I wish I had a camera for this."

"Damn you, Stewart, don't you even think it or I'll rip your tongue out of your head and stuff it up your ass."

"Oooo!"

"Stewart," cracked the Sergeant, "Identify this man so I can write him up for being out of uniform." This, of course, began another round of laughter. More people were coming in and stopping to watch. The Marines waved them on, but laughter and comments continued to torment Parks.

"He is Parks Radarman First Class, Leading Petty Officer of the Operations Department on the U.S.S. Hoquiam PF-5. Can you release him to our custody, please? We'll be very happy to escort him back to our ship," oozed Stewart with an insincere promise. Barney and Stewart had large grins on their faces.

An unintelligible growl escaped Parks lips.

"Well, we normally escort out of uniform personnel ourselves, but in this case, if you will sign for him, we'll let you escort him."

"Sure—where do I sign?" asked Lee.

Parks, seething with anger and humiliation, had nothing to say all the way back to the ship. A few sailors walking faster recognized Parks and raced ahead. By the time, Parks, Barney, and Lee arrived at the gangway, many officers, chiefs, and enlisted men lined the rails near the gangway. It was indeed a hilarious sight.

"Permission to come aboard, Mr. Hitchcock?" asked Parks. In further humiliation, Lieutenant (jg) Hitchcock, newly promoted from ensign, was Parks's division officer.

"Where the hell is your uniform, Parks?"

"Mr. Hitchcock, everything from the skin out, including my wallet, was stolen. Mamasan gave me this while she tries to find out what happened to my uniform."

"I see." Lt.(jg) Hitchcock, vastly amused, critically looked him slowly, up and down. "As I see it, your kimono is too short. She should have issued a longer one. Your getas are not polished, and that hat is definitely not uniform. I suggest you get below before the Captain sees you.—Oops, good evening, Captain. Didn't see you there." Parks slumped, humiliation complete.

"Parks, didn't I hear you discussing this ship's uniform policy with one of your men for being out of uniform this morning?" It was all the Captain could do to keep a stern face on. "How discouraging," he sighed, "to see one of my senior petty officers so attired." Parks's face in the Quarterdeck light was as red as could be.

In agony, he begged, "Sir, Captain, may I go below?"

The Captain turned away, a huge smile on his face. He waved his arms. "Be gone."

Griff had the duty and was checking traffic when Stewart walked in for a cup of coffee. He looked up at the clock on the bulkhead.

"Hey Stew, you're back early. No pussy available?"

"Nah, we gonna save it for tomorrow. Kiki's still pissed at me even though her husband was right there. Don't think he caught on though. At least Red and Kimiko aren't mad at me."

"How was the wedding ceremony?"

"You know, I don't know the Taoist religion, so I have nothing to base it on. They stood in front of what looked like an old stone relic, clapped their hands several different times, and bowed at other times. The Taoist priest spoke only in Japanese, I think.

After a while, the priest handed them a piece of paper, which they immediately brought to me to sign, then across to Kiki with her husband alongside, to sign. The Japanese guests began speaking gently and laughing quietly. I guess it was okay." Lee sipped his coffee.

Not to be put off, Griffin asked, "And Kiki, what did she say to you."

Stewart snorted. "Since her husband can't speak a word of English, plenty. The point of it was, I never had it so good, so why did I leave her?" She got a little huffy and Kimiko cut her off before her husband thought I had said something bad. So Barney and I came back to the ship, escorting Parks from the Main Gate."

Griffin looked up at him from the message he was checking. "Why?"

"Well, you see, the House of Park's choice fucked up. Everything he had, from the skin out, was stolen. Mamasan, beside her self with shame, issued him a kimono, gatas, and hat. Barney and I met him at the Gate where he was pleading with the Marine Sentry to let him through."

Lee chuckled, then roared with laughter. "We got him assigned to us to escort back to the ship." He was having trouble keeping the laughter down. Some guys saw him as we walked to the ship. When we got here, the lifelines and Quarterdeck were lined with half the ship's complement. Then, the Captain, appeared." Lee roared with laughter again. Then stopped. "Ya know, Griff, I think Barney and I are going to pay for it in the next few days."

Griffin thought it funny, too.

R 14 SEPTEMBER 1951
FM USS HOQUIAM
TO BUSHIPS
INFO SRF YOKO
BT
HOQUIAM NOW UNDERGOING ANNUAL OVERHAUL AT SHIPS REPAIR FACILITIES YOKOSUKA X REQUEST INFORMATION CONCERNING APPROVAL OF HOQUIAM ALTERATION REQUEST L92 SERIAL 304 DATE 9 JULY 1951
BT

R 14 SEPTEMBER 1951
FM USS HOQUIAM
TO BUSHIPS
INFO SRF YOKO
BT
DECK OF ONLY CREWS HEAD ABOARD HOQUIAM BADLY PITTED AND UNSANITARY X REQUEST AUTHORITY FOR SRF YOKOSUKA TO INSTALL NEOPRENE TERRAZZO SURFACING DURING PRESENT ANNUAL OVERHAUL X DECK AREA 285 SQUARE FEET
BT

17 September 1951
Bureau of Ships
Washington, D.C.

BuShips Route Slip and Office Memo.

Re Hoquiam 140542Z. PF's have an indefinite status determined by their employment in the Far East; they are also weight and moment critical; extensive and expensive alteration program not considered desirable unless and until it is determined that future length of employment in active service would be of sufficient duration to warrant such program.

/s/ Mooney

R 18 SEPTEMBER 1951
FM BUSHIPS
TO USS HOQUIAM

INFO COMCRUDESPAC
COMCORTRON 5
BT
HOQUIAM ALTERATION REQUEST L92 SER 304 DTD 9 JULY 1951 NOT RECEIVED BY BUREAU
BT

R 20 SEPTEMBER 1951
FM BUSHIPS
TO USS HOQUIAM
INFO COMCRUDESPAC
COMFLTACT YOKO
COMCORTRON 5
COMCORTRON 7
BT
DEFER ACTION PENDING SUBMISSION WEIGHT MOMENT COMPENSATION ACCORDANCE COMCRUDESPAC SER 9921 DTD 24 AUGUST 1951
BT

21 September 1951
Bureau of Ships
Washington, D.C.

LtrSer 1321P45
FM President, Board of Inspection and Survey
TO Chief of Naval Operations

1. Senior Member SubInSurv Japan Area reports repairs and alterations, which were not accomplished during subject vessel's recent overhaul.

2. It is considered that these items should be accomplished at the earliest practical date.

/s/ F. S. Hall

0830, September 29, 1951
Yokosuka Train Station
Yokosuka, Japan

This was their third week in Yokosuka. The ship has four more weeks of upkeep and modernization. Even so, SRF had put in for an additional three weeks because of the hard sea operations the Hoquiam had been in. About half the original crew was gone now, replaced by younger, regular Navy sailors.

The old crew had gone through two typhoons during the last Replenishment Group exercise. Everyone was beginning to relax and sleep better at night. No more pre-dawn General Quarters—at least until they put back to sea again.

ComFltActs Yokosuka had granted the ship's officers and men respite, in the form of four days of R and R in Kariazawa in the Japanese Alps. Barney and Stewart are now in the same duty section in the effort to balance the seasoned sailors and the newest members of the crew.

To their dismay, of the four R and R groups of 20 officers and men, they were in different groups. Pleading with the Personnel Officer, Lt. (jg) Trapp was reasonable and placed them in the last group, September 29 through October 2. That was okay with them.

Parks was the PO-in-Charge of their group. Standing on the platform waiting for their train, they looked at Parks and snickered quietly—but not quietly enough it. No question, he was pissed.

Parks began, "Fellows, we been together over a year now. So, if I say I do not want any shit out of you, don't let it dribble. You got that."

It was all Stewart could do to keep from laughing; he couldn't keep a straight face. Barney turned red trying to hold back, finally exploding into laughter.

"Aw shit!" Parks threw up his hands and stomped off, their laughter ringing in his ears. Almost three weeks had passed since the day of Charles Crosley and Kimiko Ansura's marriage and the night of his shame. He couldn't live it down.

They changed trains somewhere northwest of Tokyo to a narrow gauge huff and puffer. It was a coal-fed 2-6-2 engine with small drivers built for power, not speed. The train consisted of three Second Class passenger coaches.

With a peep of its tinny, peeper whistle, the train crept out of the station, slowly building up speed for the severe twisty 2.5 percent grade to Kariazawa.

Kariazawa, named for the palace, was the nearest village to the summer palace of the Empress Mother of Hirohito. The U.S. Occupation Forces had taken it over as a Rest Camp hotel.

The tiny train made three stops along the way for water. The engine worked hard, creeping up the canyon about five miles per hour, twisting and turning through torturous curves and steep grades. Arriving at Kariazawa, the sailors stepped off the train and shook coal soot from their clothes.

An olive drab bus took them to the R&R hotel. On the way along the hard-packed grit road, the passengers got the same welcoming speech Lee heard at Nara. The hotel beds were the same, too damn short for anyone over five feet ten inches tall. Their unlocked room was much closer to the toilets, basins, and showers this time.

"Hey Lee, I can sleep in this bed."

Lee dropped his gym bag on his own bunk, grabbed the pillow, and deliberately placed it on the floor with the blanket. Barney, knowing better, snickered, and got a dirty look for his troubles. They headed for the dining room, hungry travelers.

1715 September 29
Dining Room,
Empress Mother R&R Hotel
Kariazawa, Japan

Lee was again uncomfortable in his dungarees on liberty, even if it was Uniform of the Day, just not natural. Barney was happy as a clam. As they trotted downstairs, Lee noticed military dependents lined up at the dining room door with their husbands.

Holy Toledo, American women!

He whispered to Barney, "Get a load of the women," and walked directly to the line and stood as close as he could without being personal. He wanted to hear and smell an American woman again. He took deep breaths to smell the woman directly in front of them.

The two couples ahead of him, one with two small children, chattered away. Lee closed his eyes and absorbed the sound of their voices. They got quiet.

A hand tapped him on the shoulder.

"Hey buddy, move it. We can go in now."

Barney and Lee looked back at a large, smiling soldier.

Lee smiled back. "Sorry, I was smelling those women and forgot about the line."

"Yeah, those women don't smell like Jap cunt, do they? You just get here?"

"Yeah. Name's Lee Stewart. I'm on a ship in Yokosuka."

"Oh Yeah? Glad to meet you," he welcomed, sticking out his hand. I'm Standish, John, not related to the Indian lover, and this is my buddy, Albert. We're in the 187th RCT, back from the Korean Highlands for ten days.

"187th—John, isn't that the outfit that jumped in north of Pyongyang?"

"Yes, we did," he muttered, clearly was not in a mood to talk about it.

"John, you been here very long?"

"Long enough to find out it's going to be difficult finding pussy up here. There are a few working girls in the village down below. There's a catch, though."

"Okay, I'll bite. What's the catch?"

"The Nip police don't take kindly to working girls taking us guys into their rooms. They bust you and them."

"No shit?"

"No shit!"

They sat down at a table and looked around.

"All is not lost."

Hey, this is different. It has a menu.

"What do you mean all is not lost?"

"We know where to go but not until after it is dark. Wanna come along?"

Lee and Barney looked at each other and the two soldiers, and nodded.

The waiter came to the table to take their order. Lee grabbed the paper menu and checked it out.

"I'll have the meatloaf dinner."

The other guys looked at him in disgust.

"Lee, you can have meatloaf lots times at sea. Why here?" asked Barney.

"I like meatloaf. The steaks have to be smaller than breakfast steaks.

"Just the same, steak will be tastier."

"Maybe, but I went to Nara on R&R and saw what they served there. So far, this dining room with tables instead mess hall tables is the only thing different."

The woman server brought their plates. All of them were exactly the same except for steak or meatloaf. Lots of powdered mash potatoes, powdered brown gravy, and canned peas and diced carrots. Lee had also ordered a cottage cheese and pineapple salad, again.

Barney looked at his tiny steak, and then eyeballed Lee's much larger slice of meatloaf.

"Wonder if we can get seconds or thirds around here. This is an awfully small hunk of steak."

"Dunno, never tried," Lee replied. While he sampled his meatloaf, he studied his cottage cheese.

An ice cream scoop of cottage cheese and no pineapple.

He raised his cottage cheese for attention and the server anxiously hurried over to him.

"Where pineapple?" Lee made circular motions around his cottage cheese. The woman sucked in her breath, moaned a moment, and took it away. She came back with the Corporal in charge of the dining room.

"What seems to be your problem, sailor?"

"No problem, Mac. I asked for cottage cheese with a slice of pineapple. I asked her what happened to the pineapple."

"It is ground up into little bits and mixed in. Go ahead and taste it, you'll see."

Lee did as requested and was surprised at the amount of pineapple in the cottage cheese. He looked up at the Corporal and said, "Not bad at all. Thanks." The Corporal waved and went back to his desk by the dining room door.

8:30PM, September 29
Barroom
Empress Mother R&R Hotel
Kariazawa, Japan

The four guys were huddled close together along the bar. After several inexpensive but good booze drinks, they were ready for a walk in the woods.

"Okay, Swabbies." John was breathing heavily from all the bourbon he had stashed in his belly. "Here's the drill. We have to stay off the roads because that's where the local police patrol." He looked at Albert for confirmation, who nodded. "We need to walk through the woods to get to the house on the other side."

"What other side, John?" asked Barney.

"Well, we cut across the woods to the other road and sneak up to the house with Mama-san and four girls," said Albert. "And, we have to be quiet. Those cops have sharp ears."

John spoke up. "We will take off across country to the house where Albert and I went last night. Sneaking in the back way, the cops wouldn't know we were there."

Finally, they hoisted the last of their drinks, paid their bar bill, and headed for the door.

They weren't plastered. They were staggering under the influence of considerable liquor, however. Somehow, the friendly four managed to stagger into the wooded park and begin to crash through the brush and into trees. John stopped them.

"You sailors are making a racket. You need to walk stealthily through these woods like we're on patrol."

Barney looked at John indignantly. "You're the one who keeps crashing into the bushes, John. We're following you." "Yeah, well, keep quiet anyway."

Albert pulled out a laugh from deep in his belly. "John, you dumb sonofabitch, you always make noise on patrol. Let me lead. I know where we're going and this is not the right direction. Look at the stars."

John tipped his head back to get his bearings and promptly fell back on the ground with a crash and a groan.

Albert snickered and helped his buddy to his feet. Meanwhile, Lee, himself carrying quite a load, was beginning to wonder if this was such a good idea.

These guys have been in combat and they make this much noise? Wow!

Albert took the lead, guiding John who continued to stumble his way through the bushes, mumbling and cursing as he moved along.

"Hey, hold it guys," whispered Barney looking to his left. "I heard something over there."

Lee looked to where he was pointing. At first, he didn't see anything. Then, two Japanese cops with nightsticks and flashlights walked up to them.

"Sa rors—so jers, why yo walk in trees? Road hyar," he indicated pointing behind him.

Albert peered where the Jap cop pointed. They could see the road about fifteen yards away, parallel to their stumbling path.

"John, you dumb sonofabitch, you did it again. We're right along the road, not crossing the forest!"

Lee and Barney were amused and disgusted. This was going to be another pussyless night.

Mid-morning, September 30
Dining Room,
Empress Mother R&R Hotel
Kariazawa, Japan

Barney walked up to Lee's table and sat down, looking over Lee's breakfast. "Jeez, Lee, are those real eggs?"

"They sure taste like it. I don't know if these are local, or flown in from the states. Definitely better than powdered scrambled eggs on the ship." He said.

Lee speared a piece of sausage, dabbed it in egg yoke, and chewed it slowly, savoring the flavor. He looked at Barney studying the morning menu, and waited while Barney ordered the same thing.

"What took you so long, Barney?"

"I helped Albert drag John into the shower room. He looked awful. Musta barfed in their room, too. Albert was kinda pissed and carrying on about the dumb sonofabitch."

"Those guys been in some serious combat, Barney. I have a hunch they are some kind of fierce warriors we could follow, if we had to. That combat jump was last year, and they are still alive. They're just letting their hair down a little farther than we do."

"I wonder if John saved Albert's life in combat?" Barney asked.

"I'll tell you, Barney. They don't talk about those things to outsiders. We'll never find out—but it does have to be something like that, doesn't it?"

Barney's breakfast arrived and conversation stopped.

They were enjoying cigarettes and coffee when Albert joined them at their table. His face was full of storm clouds.

"Well, I think John is out of it for a few hours. He really hung on a load last night." He paused and looked at the two sailors watching him. "What are your plans for the day?"

"Well, I think pussy is o-u-t, so I'm game for about anything. You got something in mind?"

"Horses!" Leaped from Albert's mouth.

Barney looked up with a gleam in his eyes. "Riding or betting?"

"There is a pretty fair stable here. We get to check out horses for the bridal paths. Only problem is, we have to go in a group with a Jap guide leading us so we don't get into trouble. Whadaya think, you guys?"

Lee looked dubious with furrowed eyebrows.

Holy Toledo, I've never been on a horse before.

Barney was excited. "Man o man, just like home. I have a string back on Dad's ranch in Montana. Been more than a year since I slapped leather." He turned to Lee who was frowning. "Aw come on, Lee, it's great up on a horse."

What the hell, I can only break my neck!

"Okay, guys. I'm in. Let's go sign up."

While they looked at the Activities board for the map, Lee noticed that you could rent motor bicycles by the hour.

That ought to be fun—maybe this afternoon.

Locating the stables, they hurried out and signed up. They would go with the next group. Barney was a little doubtful.

"These are pretty beat up, guys. Don't expect much from them. I don't think they'd allow John up, he's so big."

The Jap stable boys motioned them in to mount their horses. Lee watched Barney stick his foot in the metal stirrup and jump up in the saddle, easily. The stable boy called out to another Jap who must be the guide and said something to him, pointing to Barney.

Albert got in the saddle with a little bit of trouble, but not much. Mostly, it was trying to jump up to swing his leg over.

Lee started to stick his foot in a stirrup. The stable boy started hollaring and Barney with a great sound of disgust said, "Dumb shit, you mount on the other side. Now that horse has you pegged for a tenderfoot."

Lee walked behind the horse to the other side and Barney exploded. "Dammit all to hell, Lee! Never, ever, walk that close behind a horse you don't know. It just might kick you into tomorrow land."

This only made Lee more nervous. The stable boy was there now to assist and watched him closely. With a great deal more casualness than he felt, Lee stuck his foot in the correct stirrup and mounted easily.

That wasn't so bad.

He heard the guide remonstrating with Barney and looked over to see what was going on. Barney had a look of disgust on his face.

"What's the matter, Barney?"

"These horses aren't trained to neck reining. Got to use one hand on each rein. Look at the way our guide is holding the reins. You pull on the side you want to go."

The stable boys cleared out of the area and opened the gate. The guide led out at a walk and stayed at a walk. As far as Lee was concerned, that was okay with him. Barney, however, mumbled nearly every step of the way. He wanted to try out his horse's various gaits. Albert just enjoyed the ride.

The guide stopped and waved all the troops up even with him. He pointed out to their front. "Disa Sunset Ridge. Yo come hyah for nica sunset." It was a great view of sharp mountains and valleys stretching into the distance.

"We go back now," the guide ordered, pointing back to the hotel. Lee was easing from one side of the saddle to the other. The bottoms of his hipbones were trying to cut through his flesh to the saddle. He tried standing in the stirrup and only made the inside of his knees sorer. Not only those, the bottom of his feet were getting sore, too.

"Barney, this is definitely not my cup of tea. I hurt."

Barney laughed. "Yeah, you're a tenderfoot, all right. You'll get over it. We'll go out again this afternoon and tomorrow, too. You'll almost be fit by the time we hit that train on the Second."

"My ass, we will. I'm going for the motor bicycles this afternoon, if the rest of me holds up."

Both Albert and Barney chimed together: "What motor bicycles?" Lee explained what he knew.

"I'm in," said Albert.

Barney, torn between wanting to stay with Lee and wanting to ride a horse some more, finally decided to go with more horses in the afternoon.

"I'm not all that happy with motorcycles and things like that. I'd rather ride another horse this afternoon, okay fellas?"

"Yeah, Barney, and I'm just not ready to set a horse for hours on end, either. So, guess we split after lunch and meet again for dinner, right?"

"Yeah."

1:25PM, September 30
Kariazawa Village, Japan

Albert and Lee were hot and sweaty after the walk down from the R&R hotel. They stopped in front of the motor bicycle shop and looked inside with interest.

"Lee, you ever ride anything like those?"

"Nooo, but it doesn't look too difficult. Watch how they start them."

A man who looked like a mechanic brought one of the machines out of the shop, and lifted the rear wheel onto its stand. Swinging over and settling on the seat, he pumped the bicycle pedals furiously while working two levers on the outer handlebars. A little bluish smoke began to trickle from the exhaust pipe as the engine caught and built up speed.

"Albert, the left lever is the clutch and the right one is the throttle. Where's the brakes?"

"Standard bicycle back pedal, I guess."

And that's exactly the way it worked. The mechanic had a small test track right along side the shop and ran the machine there. They saw that when he let out the clutch, he pedaled a little bit to get started.

Going in, they managed to get the price down to four hundred yen per hour because they wanted to ride until they could see the sunset on the ridge. The mechanic hastily checked to make sure the headlight was working on both machines. They paid twelve hundred yen each in advance and rode off to the anxious observation of the owner.

"Where we going, Pard?"

"Damned if I know. Shall we play it by sight and sound?" asked Albert.

"Let's do it."

All of the roads were hard-packed grit. They found a major road with asphalt going uphill to the west. Agreeing that would lead to the ridge, they putted along. A Jap bus, blaring its horn at them, swept by almost blowing them off the road.

Spotting some people in Army wash khakis, they stopped and got directions to Sunset Ridge. At the park, some distance from the bridal path, they discovered a little shop with food and drink. They carried their choice of eats and drinks up to the ridge and sat to watch the sunset.

The only sound was of the wind sighing through the treetops and different birds marking their territory. The silence was wonderful. Lee and Albert kept looking in different directions, watching as shadows formed, changing colors from green to purple and black, imagining they were still seeing green of the Japanese National Forest.

There was already snow on the Alps to the west, which the sun turned to burned silver, then pure white, fading to rose, gray, and black. It was as though they were watching a great concert in action, with God as the conductor.

The stars began to appear. Albert and Lee stirred, carrying their trash to a strange container.

As they were starting their bikes, Lee asked, "Albert, you think we can find our way out in the dark?"

"No sweat. All we have to do is go down hill to the east until we find that highway. Turning left, let's hope we don't overshoot the Kariazawa Village turnoff. Let's just hope we make last call for dinner."

Lee turned on his dim light and led off. Riding side by side, they discussed plans for the evening. Lee would like to pair up with Barney again and see what he had in mind, and Albert was of the same mind about John.

They rode slowly up to the shop where a worried and nervous owner was pacing back and forth. He was so relieved that the machines were okay, he forgot to be angry. He didn't forget to charge them for the overtime, though. The owner was nice enough to let them sit in the back of his motorcycle truck for a ride back to the R&R hotel.

The dining room was still open. They ordered dinner and explained they wanted to check their buddies in the rooms, since they were not here in the dining room.

Albert and Lee met at the top of the stairs. Neither of their buddies was in their rooms.

They settled for the special: Roast Beef, Mashed Potatoes, honeyed carrots, tossed salad, and milk, followed by cherry pie a la mode.

"I wonder where Barney is."

"Yeah, me too, on John. They could be together. Did you check the barroom?"

Lee noticed they were the last people in the dining room. "Let's go to the bar for a drink, and see what the movie is for tonight."

After the bourbon and water, Lee realized he was tired. He had seen the movie, anyway. Off to his bed on the floor he went.

OCTOBER

Early morning, October 1
Lee and Barney's room
Empress Mother R&R Hotel
Kariazawa, Japan

Lee woke to the sound of his door opening. A maid was standing there, giggling at him. He looked at his watch and discovered it was already 9:15AM. As he moved, his body shrieked in pain. His ass was a mess of hurt, and other places weren't too far behind. Junior was up in all its glory, not hurt but hurting for lack of action. He stuffed it back in his skivvies and stood up.

Boy, Barney's up early this morning. Must be out on the horses again.

"Yo fran, he no come hyah no sleep hyah. Whar yo fran?"

Holy shit! I wonder where he is."

Lee shrugged his shoulders and shooed the maid out.

She wouldn't have to make the beds, anyway.

Lee grabbed his toilet kit and a towel, and headed for the shower room. Albert was drying off when he came in. He looked behind Lee, then back at Lee.

"Where's Barney? Still asleep?"

"Fuck no, he didn't come back last night. How about John? He in any kind of shape now?"

"He didn't come back, either." He thought for a moment and scrunched up his face in anger. "You don't suppose those two assholes found some pussy, do you."

"If they did, I'm sure they will be back this morning and let us in on a good thing. Let's get dressed and go eat."

Lee stepped in the shower and adjusted the water until he could just stand the heat. He stood, turning this way and that, to pepper his muscles and loosen them.

Lee half-enjoyed his breakfast and probably would have enjoyed it more if he could have stood somewhere to eat. His bottom was really raw and sore from the horse. Drinking his second cup of coffee, he thought about what he'd like to do today. Tomorrow was back to the Hoquiam and back to traffic again. He decided to wander around the grounds, visit the library a little bit, and write some letters. There were several typewriters fastened to desks you could use. Paper, envelopes, and stamps were available at the desk.

"Albert, I'd just like to be alone and think, today. Have to go back to the ship tomorrow and want a little time to myself. That okay with you?"

"I understand, Lee. John and I have three more days here before we head back to our Regiment in Korea. Not looking forward to going up on the Line again, but that's the way it crumbles."

"Could you tell me about some of your combat experiences, Albert? We just don't know what goes on in close combat."

Albert looked at Lee and slowly shook his head. "No, Lee, because no matter how I painted it, you'd never understand about the smell, sheer terror of an artillery barrage, the hundreds of Chinks screaming their heads off as they charge you, going out on patrol, and praying you don't get it." He stared off into space and slowly shook his head some more. "Nah, you wouldn't—couldn't understand, Lee."

Disappointed, Lee nodded understanding. He got up and looked down at Albert. "I'll see you for chow, then."

Albert nodded. "Think I'll go looking for John. He's such a big guy, somebody might have seen him."

Later that afternoon, Lee returned to his room for some writing paper, and to drop off three paperbacks he had been able to take away. Barney was in his bed, dead to the world. A little pale, but otherwise looked okay.

If he isn't up before dinner, I'll hold reveille on him so he doesn't starve.

When Lee returned to his room just before dinner, Barney wasn't in his room. He checked the shower room and toilets. Then he checked the front desk for messages. There was no word.

He had dinner with Albert. John was still missing, and he was beginning to worry. After dinner, they retired to the barroom to play shuffleboard and wait for time for the movie.

9AM, October 2
Train Station
Kariazawa, Japan

Lee was pissed and disgusted with Barney. John and Barney had discovered a house with four girls and wore them out in a constant, non-stop screwing binge.

Barney finally had to stop and rest. He had come back to the hotel and was going to take Lee back with him but Lee was off doing something else. When he woke up and cleaned up, he headed right back to the house again.

He showed up at their room about 6:30 this morning, very pale and shaky.

"Hey, Lee. I'm really tired. Need to crash awhile," Barney pleaded, his voice shaky and face very pale.

"Where you been, shitbird? We were worried about you guys," screamed an angry Lee.

"We found these girls, see, and they took us to their house."

"You found girls and left us behind? Damn your ass. What a rotten friend you turned out to be." Lee paced back and forth in the tiny room, fuming.

Barney hung his head like a hurt dog. "I'm sorry, Lee. Pussy was there and we couldn't take a chance on losing it to someone else. There were only four girls and we really used them up."

Lee screamed again. "Son of a bitch! You had four girls and didn't think we wanted part of that? Damn you all to hell!"

"Don't scream, Lee. My head hurts."

After a little shouting on Lee's part and more hang doggy look on Barney's part, Lee left for the dining room to eat breakfast. He checked the menu and decided to have the same thing again this morning.

Barney showed up a little shamed-face and timid. Lee wasn't letting him off the hook.

"Hi good buddy, ole pal of mine, shipmate. Why don't you pull up that chair, sit on your thumb, and then eat shit for breakfast? While you're at it, keep your fuckin' mouth shut. I don't want any after action stories from you."

The Huff and Puffer engine glided by Lee and Barney's spots and came to a stop. Three passenger coaches and one freight car made up the train.

The whole R & R crew from the Hoquiam hopped aboard and found seats. Barney looked at Lee. "Mind if I sit with you, Lee?"

Lee glared at his best buddy and softened. "Yeah, Barney. Drag up a thumb and sit a while. So you found snatch, did you?"

Barney lit up and eagerly told of his and John's wild rides. The stories lasted until they arrived at

Yokosuka Junction where they caught the local back to Yokosuka.

1830, October 2, 1951
USS Hoquiam PF-5
Berth 7-B
SRF Yokosuka, Japan

There was something about the ship that was different. One of the new ensigns allowed them aboard.

"See you after a while, Barney. Gonna go hassle Hank about Kariazawa liberty."

"Yeah, I'm heading up to the Cubby."

Stewart walked into the radio shack and stopped in shock.

"What's the matter, Mr. Forsythe?" Lieutenant (jg) Forsythe sat on the deck in his wash khaki trousers and skivvy shirt. He and LeBerge were sealing a cardboard box marked "unclassified communication publications." LeBerge picked up the box and added it to a stack of others. Then Stewart noticed the two typewriters were gone from the Communications positions.

Lieutenant (jg) Forsythe stood up, brushing off his butt as he did. "Am I glad to see you, Stewart." He had a smile of relief on his face. I have something to tell you—

Stewart opened his mouth to say something.

—don't interrupt me. Wait until I tell you." Stewart frowned, dreading he knew not what.

"Stewart, you are the senior man in the radio gang now."

Stewart stared at his division officer without full comprehension.

"Griffin is on his way home to separation. He left on the 30th. Masters is on his way home on 30 days leave before reporting to his new command, the USS Perkins DDR-877. He left yesterday. The others, the newer men, have been transferred to other PF's that are in port right now." Stewart slowly sank into the Comm Two Chair position without a word.

"It's just the three of us now, and that's for just a few more days. On October 8, the Hoquiam is being decommissioned and turned over to the ROK Navy." Stewart patted his pockets looking for a cigarette. LeBerge held out his cigarettes and lighter, and Stewart accepted, nodding his head.

"Holy shit," he said softly. "Are there many people left on the ship?"

"About fifty officers and men. Just enough to close down American Navy operations. Everyone knows their next assignment already."

Stewart looked at Mr. Forsythe. "Oh, you are going to the USS Perkins DDR-877, too, in Long Beach, but not until after we're decommissioned."

Stewart nodded.

Hank and I will be shipmates again.

"You got all that so far?"

"Yes sir. It's so surprising. Now that we getting the Hocky Maru into shape, the Navy is giving up on her."

"Okay. Tomorrow morning after breakfast, gather all your personal effects and pack your sea bag. All enlisted men are moving into Barracks B next to the Receiving Station. As soon as the Hoquiam is decommissioned, you will be moved to the RecSta Annex at Oppama waiting for transportation to the States."

Stewart nodded and looked around the Shack.

Hey, who swiped our coffee mess?

Mr. Forsythe followed his eyes. "All private coffee messes from the ship were donated to the local Navy Relief Society."

Woulda been nice to have a cup of coffee.

"Finally, there are no more duty sections. We muster here at 0755 in time for morning colors; continue to close down the ship. Tomorrow morning, you eat your last meal here. Rivas has transferred all food stores to other ships.

Liberty commences at 1600 to expire on board at 0700 the next morning in Barracks B." He paused, searching his mind. "Oh, run down to disbursing now. They have your pay all made out. All you have to do is sign your pay chit and accept your money. Mr. Barris is ready to shut up shop as soon as you R and R pukes get back."

"Aye aye, sir." Still somewhat bewildered by this turn of events, Stewart swung down the ladder and back to Disbursing.

Either most of the other guys had already been paid, or he was ahead of them.

Lt.(jg) Barris looked up at the Stewart's fingernails rattling on the Dutch door. He smiled and nodded to Stewart. "Be right with you." Swinging around, he opened his safe and extracted a small box.

Thumbing through it, he found what he wanted. Stewart could see it was money and a pay chit. The box went back into the safe, which he closed. Standing, he came up to Stewart with a pen and the pay chit. "One hell of a shock, huh, Stewart?"

"Sir, I'm still trying to figure it out." He signed his pay chit and accepted his money. "Mr. Barris, what about changing MPC for real money. Where does that take place?"

"Just like when you arrived. It will be at the point of your embarkation. Stewart, enjoy your next duty station."

"Right, sir. Thank you."

Stewart moved aft, climbing the ladder by Sickbay and heading forward to the ladders to the Bridge. He wanted to see where Barney and Red were going.

It was dark on the Bridge. He walked all the way around without seeing any of the Signalmen.

Hell, that's a first. Oh wait. We don't have any more communications duty. Maybe it is the same for the Bridge crew.

He dashed back down to the Radio Shack to find Barney standing in the doorway talking with Mr. Forsythe.

The three of them stood staring at each other for a moment. LeBerge moved around nervously because he wasn't part of their thoughts.

"Well, Stew, can you believe this shit?"

"If Mr. Forsythe says it's true, you know it's gotta be true." Mr. Forsythe snapped his fingers. That's right, I didn't say Simon Says, did I?" Shaking his head, he looked at Stewart.

"Your final task is to clean out all drawers—everything. Put them in these cardboard boxes and label the boxes. Stack them in the middle of the deck. After someone removes the boxes, keep out of the way and listen to the 1MC."

"Aye aye, sir. Where will you be if I need you, Mr. Forsythe?"

"Try the Registered Pub locker and Crypto Room. Otherwise, across the passageway or in the Wardroom."

Lee nodded and turned to his buddy.

"Well, Barney."

"Shit, Lee. What orders did you draw?" I'm going to the Evansville PF-70 and start this shit all over again." Stewart shook his head.

"I drew a tincan. Going to the Perkins DDR-877 in Long Beach. Where is Red, up with Kimiko?"

"Oh, you don't know. The Captain put in a good word for Red, with ComNavFE. He got transferred to ComNavFE staff. He's a Signalman at the top of the tower on ComNavFE hill." Stewart thought about that.

"That means he ought to qualify for base housing for Kimiko and him. Oh, won't they like that?"

0930, October 8, 1951
USS Hoquiam PF-5
Piedmont Pier
SRF Yokosuka, Japan

Once again, a skeleton crew assembled around Secondary Conn aft of the stack of the U.S.S. Hoquiam (PF-5). This time, in Dress Blue Baker with ribbons. The Ship's Company bore an eerie resemblance to the Inaugural Crew of September 27, 1950 on Recommissioning Day.

Of the officers, only Commander Brown, Lt. Hansen, and Lt. Morgan remained. Lieutenant (jg) Roger Forsythe had said good-bye yesterday. He was returning to inactive duty status. Of the seven Washingtonians, only Stewart RMSN remained.

This was Decommissioning Day. Appropriate distinguished guests of the U.S. Navy, the American Embassy Tokyo, Military Advisory Group, Seoul, a South Korean Admiral, and Prospective Commanding Officer, Commander Soong, ROK Navy, were present.

In a few minutes, after several speeches extolling the heroic events and adventures of the last year, the U.S.S. Hoquiam PF-5 would lower her colors to become the ROKN Naktong PF65. The total officers and crew of the USS Hoquiam PF5, on board at this moment numbered 73.

The ship was bare of all personal effects. All personnel moved to the BOQ or the new Oppama Receiving Station across the bay. All classified material: returned to the Registered Publications office on the Naval Station. The boilers: cold iron.

Commander Maxfield J. Brown, Commanding Officer, stepped to the microphone:

"Ship's Company, Aaaa Tennn Shun!" He looked around at the last of his crew, and at the ship, briefly. "Radioman Seaman Stewart! Front and Center."

He cleared his throat.

Stewart stepped out of ranks, marched the few steps to his Commanding Officer, and saluted. "Aye, Captain?"

The Captain cleared his throat again. "You are the last Washingtonian in the crew. Haul down my Commission Pennant."

"Aye aye, Captain." Stewart, wearing three ribbons on his chest, the United Nations Medal, the Korean Service Medal with 4 battle stars, and the Victory Medal, saluted again, about faced, and stepped to the Mailmast truck halyard temporarily attached to the Foremast. He unfastened the halyard and looked up to the faded and frayed pennant. He lowered the pennant slowly, folded it once, twice, draped it on his left forearm, and secured the halyard. A Quartermaster blew his whistle.

"Shift Colors—Shift Colors."

The National Ensign came down from the fantail for the last time. At the bow, the Union Jack came down from the Jack Staff. Both flags, ceremoniously folded, came to the Captain.

Stewart, RMSN, about-faced and carried the pennant across to the Captain. Stewart lifted the pennant from his forearm and extended it to the Captain with both hands, who took it.

"Thank you, Stewart."

"You're welcome, Captain." They exchanged salutes and the Stewart returned to his place in the crew.

"Ship's Company, hand salute," commanded the Captain. "To." He paused and with a slightly different sound announced, "This vessel, the United States Ship Hoquiam, Patrol Frigate, hull number Five, is now decommissioned from United States Naval Service. My final order as Commanding Officer," he paused to clear his throat again, "Ship's Company, March Off!"

The Captain and crew exchanged a final salute. Department by department, the remaining crew headed to the gangway and ran off to the pier to reassemble and watch the South Korean Navy crew march on.

Two hundred fifty ROK officers, chiefs and men ran up the gangway and assembled where the American Navy crew had just departed, and raised their colors. After a few moments, which the Americans did not understand, the ROKN PF65 Naktong was commisioned in the South Korean Navy. The 1MC began to functionin the Korean language; only those on board the Naktong understood.

Four gray Navy buses pulled up next to the assembled Hoquiam crew.

Commander Brown had to shout to make him selfunderstood. "You all know there is a party at the Enlisted Men's Club beginning at Noon. I realize many of you will have already departed for your new stations or home. The best of luck to you all. These buses will take you to Oppama where you await transportation. Mr. Hansen and Mr. Morgan have your liberty cards. They are good until tomorrow morning. God Speed." He turned and got into a gray sedan. The Seaman driver drove slowly away from the ship.

Lieutenants Hansen and Morgan passed out the liberty cards to all the crew, kidding with them as they did. Stewart poked his in his jumper pocket as Mr. Morgan said, "Looks like we won't see you up on the Bridge anymore, Stewart. Where you heading?"

"A fast greyhound, Mr. Morgan: the Perkins DDR-877. She's in Long Beach waiting for me."

"Well, good luck."

"Thanks. You too, sir." They saluted and Stewart boarded one of the buses and sat down for the ride around the Inner Harbor to Oppama. He stared out to the derelict PF's still moored there.

Thank the good lord I don't have to go through that again. A fast, sleek destroyer. Now that will be the duty. Now how am I going to see both Kiki and Michko for the last time?

1140, October 8, 1951
B.O.Q.
U.S. Naval Station
Yokosuka, Japan

Commander Maxfield J. Brown, former Commanding Officer of the USS HOQUIAM PF-5, sat at his desk quietly, smoking a cigarette and sipping coffee. He opened his personal journal and stopped.

What to write? I'm going to a fast DD in the Carribean from this battered old ship. But she was quite a girl. I will truly miss her.

He thought for a moment more, uncapped his fountain pen, and leaned over the journal.

There being no further business, the USS Hoquiam PF5 is decommissioned from the

United States Navy, and transferred to the Republic of Korea Navy, as the NakTong PF65. Since recommissioning by the U.S. Navy, the HOQUIAM has earned the Navy Occupation Ribbon (Japan), the Korean Service Ribbon with four Stars, and the United Nations Medal.

MJB

Commander Brown capped his Parker fountain pen and slipped it in his shirt pocket. He closed his private journal.

A Chief Gunner's Mate stood waiting as the navy buses rolled to a stop in front of the new barracks. He waved them over to him.

"Okay sailors, listen up. This is the deal. I already have orders for seventeen of you. Immediately following noon chow, you will board a bus, which will take you to the U.S.N.S. General Mann, a very large transport. She is at the docks in Yokohama and is leaving for Seattle late this afternoon. Uniform of the Day will be undress blues."

There was a murmur of surprise from the seventy-three men. "I understand you all have been given overnight liberty cards. When I call your name, surrender your liberty card. You are on orders to the Mann. Stewart, Lee . . ."

Well, what a mixed piece of crap this is. I could almost look straight up the hill and say howdy to Kiki and Kimiko. Hey, I can see that white section of wall. I wonder if the Perkins will drop into Sasebo. Surely, she is coming back out here. Then again, would Michko even want to see me again?

Next time Barney was in Sasebo, Lee knew she would find out what happened. Stewart stepped up to the Chief and gave him his liberty card.

1330, October 8, 1951
Yokohama Piers,
USNS General Mann

The Mann was carrying members of all five services, government civilians, and military dependents. The seventeen ex-Hoquiam crewmembers' bus stopped about fifty feet from the enlisted troop gangway into the side of the ship. Stewart grabbed his sea bag and supported it in front of him with one hand while his other hand held his gym bag with records and orders in the other. They all shuffled toward the front of the bus and off. The driver was mumbling as they passed him. "Report to the troop gangway desk."

Stewart heaved his sea bag on his shoulder and walked the remaining distance to the short line at the desk with a big Navy blue and gold placard and a Marine red and gold placard.

"Orders, please."

Stewart opened his gym bag and pulled out the original and fourteen copies of his orders. As he shuffled along the line, Stewart learned they were stamping and scribbling on the original orders, keeping one of the copies, and handing back the rest. He would keep his records and personal gear.

His turn. He handed his original orders to the Marine Staff Sergeant at the desk. "Seaman Stewart, you are in a small troop compartment on the third deck with other non-rated sailors. You may be called upon for Mess Cooking duties—

Ah shit!

—if they run out of Doggies to do it. The Staff Sergeant looked at Stewart with amusement. "Don't hold your breath, Stewart. Combat veterans have preference, and the Doggies have a whole shitpot of people who never left Japan."

Oh ho!

"You're Regular Navy, right?"

"Yeah. I was only one of seven on the whole damn ship."

"So, enjoy the ride, Stewart." He stuck his hand out with a card for Stewart to take. "Go change your MPC to greenbacks just before the gangway."

Stewart looked around and spotted an Army Captain, guarded by army MP's, sitting at a small desk. Stewart stepped over and saluted the Captain, pulling out his billfold. He pulled out all his MPC bills without counting and handed them to the Captain. The Captain shook his head. "You ought to keep better track of your money, sailor."

"True, Captain, but it's only funny money and I will keep track of that beautiful green stuff."

The Captain smiled and handed him one hundred twenty eight dollars and seventy-five cents. Stewart saluted the Captain, who returned the salute. "Thanks, Captain."

Stuffing the money into his billfold and change in his jumper pocket, he heaved his seabag up, and strode up the gangway. A civilian, member of the Mann crew, glanced at his card, then at him.

"Take this Port passageway aft to the thwartships passageway. There is a stairway to the third deck. Your compartment is dead ahead and labeled navy non-rated men. Any bunk not already in use is yours. Got it?"

"Sure do." Stewart took off in this former civilian pleasure ship, found his compartment, and selected a middle of three bunks near the centerline. He opened his seabag long enough to jam the gym bag inside and lock his seabag onto the bunk chain.

Now, all the other non-rated guys know this is my bunk.

He decided to explore the ship and end up standing on deck watching the departure. Seemed like everywhere he went, there were 'Off Limits to Passengers' or "Crew Only, Keep Out' signs.

Just like the signs on the Chilton when we had troops aboard, except I'm on the other side now.

Stewart decided the best place to find a cup of coffee would be the Galley. He found the troop mess deck and pushed the door open looking for a coffee urn.

"Sailor, what are you doing in here?" came the harsh voice. Stewart ducked and twisted around with a smile.

"Oh please, sir," Cupping his hands in front of him, "I just want to steal a cup of coffee."

The civilian cook looked him up and down and laughed. "You sailors are all alike, Oliver. Just don't tell anyone where you got it." He handed Stewart a paper cup and pointed to the urn. "Help yourself and get out of here before your military types come in and draft you."

"Thanks Cookee," I won't forget it." Stewart responded with a grin.

"Yeah, you will. Get the hell outta here," he said, laughing.

Stewart wandered around deck until he found a place at the rail to watch people moving about on the pier and all the color. The Eighth Army Band played marches and popular tunes, including Glenn Miller arrangements.

A xylophone kind of thing played three notes up the scale, and a deep male voice announced,

"All visitors must depart the ship immediately. The Mann will withdraw the gangways in fifteen minutes to get underway."

Stewart leaned over the side and looked in both directions at the bollards.

Singled up, already. Oh dammit, this all happened so fast, I didn't get a card off to Ruth. Won't she be surprised!

0515, October 15, 1951
Straits of Juan de Fuca, Washington
USNS General Mann, Inbound to Seattle

This morning, Stewart woke a little earlier than usual. After showering and shaving, he joined the early breakfast line and filled up his tray. It would be a long day. Back in his compartment, he dug out his dress blues and peacoat and put them on. Stewart stood next to an Army Corporal wearing a khaki overcoat who was holding a portable radio. He had it tuned to Seattle radio station KIRO.

Stewart and several other people standing around the radio were hearing songs they had never heard before.

Holy Shit! A Commercial.

Commercials: they knew they were home now. AFRS, the Armed Forces Radio System, does not carry commercials.

The weather, full of surprises, was clear and very cold. Stars were fading as the Mann turned slightly, headed further down Puget Sound toward Seattle, then turned easterly into Elliot Bay.

Several fireboats and tugs were out in Elliot Bay to meet them. Huge fountains of water from the boats' fire guns arched up into the sky and fell, sirens whooped, rose and fell, many ships' whistles and horns bleated from all points of the compass. The men were silent as they watched the show just for them. A little of the spray fell on them, but who cared? The sun peeped over the Cascades and through the water arches.

Faintly, a band started playing, "Strike up the Band." As the ship turned more, pointing toward some piers now in sight, the Thirteenth Naval District band began playing all the military hymns, marches, and popular instrumentals. Two tugs came along side and tossed heaving lines up to the crew aboard. Hawsers went down to the tugs' bollards.

The xylophone, much better than a Bosun's Pipe, sounded its three-note song.

"Good morning," said the deep voice, "in case you were not aware of it, we are docking in Seattle, Washington, United States of America." A loud roar sounded all over the Mann.

"Mmm, yes!" There was a sound of approval in that word. "The order for disembarking will be as follows. All civilians will leave by the forward gangway. Once clear and inside the warehouse, military personnel will also disembark there. Meanwhile, all unaccompanied military personnel will disembark by the midships second deck hatch directly to the pier and walk toward their own service's buses. You will find the Red Cross has fresh hot coffee and donuts for you to eat on the bus."

"Trucks are parked at the head of your line of buses to take your duffle bags or seabag. The Coast Guardsmen will leave first. Their bus will take them to the Coast Guard Station, Elliot Bay. Depart by the second deck gangway directly to the dock. The Air Force is next. Your bus will take you to McCord Field near Tacoma. Navy and Marines leave next by the same exit. Your buses will take you to Receiving Station, Pier 91. Since the Army represents the largest group, you will depart by both gangways to your buses. You are going to Fort Lewis for processing. Good luck to all of you from the officers and crew of the General Mann."

As Stewart walked off the ship, he saw five Red Cross vans parked in a line stretching away from the trucks. He dumped his sea bag on the Navy truck after first being reassured this was going to the Receiving Station, Pier 91, and walked by the Red Cross vans.

There were all sorts of goodies. Americans who spoke American and smelled American, were pouring American drinks and serving them. Stewart grabbed an American donut and a cup of coffee and boarded a Navy bus.

He saw all seventeen of the ex-Hoquiam sailors on this bus and sat down with them. They looked at each other and grinned. No one spoke. Only one other sailor was on orders. The rest were for release to inactive duty or honorable discharges.

All the buses departed at the same time in a long line. At first, the buses speeded up for about three blocks, then slowed, turned onto another street, and really slowed down to walking speed.

“Hey, we’re in a parade!” someone yelled. Stewart looked closer around him and discovered people on both sides of the street. He could hear the sounds of two or more bands.

Wonder if these windows open?

Other sailors had the same thought.

Everyone lifted the windows open so the shouts and cheers of welcome were coming in. It was marvelous. High school and college cheerleaders lined the sides of the buses as they drove slowly by. A cheerleader hit Stewart and the guy behind him smack in the face with confetti. They watched the girl giggle in embarrassment and thought it was wonderful.

Then it was over. The buses all split into their specific routes and speeded up. There were still people on the sidewalks waving to them. Stewart thought he passed Ruth’s office as they drove downhill. Soon they were through the gate at Pier 91 and delivered to the Receiving Station. The truck with their gear was right there, waiting for them.

"All right, listen up. I have good news for you. We will get you processed, paid if you did not collect at your last command, and get you out of here before noon.

Wow, that's a surprise.

"Grab your gear and head in through that door. Take a seat on a bench and wait until they call your name. Bring your records and orders when you come up."

"Stewart, Lee H., Line 2."

Stewart picked up his gym bag and unzipped it as he headed to the desk and sat down. He looked at the Yeoman and laughed.

"What the fuck is so funny, Stewart?" the Yeoman said with a smile.

"You couldn't possibly remember me, but I was one pissed off sailor when you sent me by error to Tongue Point about eighteen months ago." The Yeoman scratched his head and looked carefully at Stewart.

"Yeah," he drawled, "I remember the incident. Hadn't you just shipped over and asked for some school, or something like that?"

"This is true. And I'm here to tell you, Tongue Point was the asshole of the Navy."

"Well, good to see you again. Let's see . . ." He scanned his orders, slipped one copy off the bottom, and inserted the original into his typewriter. Checking something on his desk, he rapidly typed something and stopped. "You eating noon chow aboard, or do you want to be on your way."

"On my way." The Yeoman nodded and smiled. He typed one more line and ripped his orders out of the mill. Grabbing his pen, he scribbled in some words and numbers, blotted it, and handed him his orders. Stewart carefully folded his orders and stuffed them in his wallet.

"You're set. On your way. Hey, were you the guy who asked for destroyers, anywhere?"

"Yeah."

"Well Stewart, looks like you finally lucked out. You are on four days travel time to San Diego, and thirty days annual leave. Today is October the fifteen. So, to avoid angering your new command, report in before midnight of November eighteenth."

"That's it?"

"Go!" he pointed to the door with a smile.

"Gone! Thanks."

Stewart walked back to his seabag and looked at his former shipmates. He walked over to them and shook hands down the line.

"Good luck, guys. See you around."

"Yeah, same to you, Stew."

He stuffed the gym bag back into his seabag and locked it. Heaving the seabag to his shoulder, he headed out the door to the payphone he saw around the corner. He already had a bunch of quarters, dimes and nickels for a long distance call.

"Number please."

"Long distance, Operator."

"Long Distance. What city?" she asked.

"Norfolk, Virginia, operator. I don't know the number, and I want to make a station to station call. How do we do this?" Lee asked.

What is the name and address in Norfolk, please?"

Lieutenant and Mrs. Ivan Stewart, 8350 Chesapeake Avenue."

"One moment, please."

Lee heard a series of clicks and tones.

"Norfolk information. What number do you want?" came a hollow voice.

"This is Seattle long distance, operator. We want Lieutenant and Mrs. Ivan Stewart, 8350 Chesapeake Avenue."

"Looking, one moment—that is, two, plus four one plus 6873309, operator."

"Thank you, operator. Please deposit three dollars and sixty-five cents."

Lee deposited fourteen quarters, a dime, and a nickel, then heard the phone ringing.

"Hello?" The coins crashed into the coin box.

"Hi Mom, it's Lee."

She screamed, "Where are you? Will you be home for dinner?"

Lee laughed. "No, Mom. I just arrived in Seattle on the USNS General Mann and cleared Pier Ninety-one Receiving Station. I'm on my way to Long Beach to report aboard the USS Perkins DDR877."

"Are you coming home—well, I mean, are you coming to visit us in Norfolk?"

Lee felt guilty as he replied, "No, fraid not. Want to get down and settled in my new duties on the Perkins."

"Oh, that's too bad. Ivan is up in Philly putting the finishing touches on decommissioning the Siboney. He's waiting for his new orders and is dreading another carrier."

Lee chuckled and said, "Well, it took me almost two years to get a tin can. And the Perkins is a new ship. Oh, hey. The Hoquiam recommended me for Radioman Third Class, so I will be taking the next Fleet Competitive Exam on the Perkins."

"Well, that is certainly good news. Your Dad will be pleased, too."

They continued to chat until the operator cut in and said Lee's three minutes were up.

"Bye Mom. I'll write as soon as I get settled down."

"We love you Lee. Take care of yourself." Her voice was a little choked.

Lee hung up the phone, picked up his sea bag and gym bag, turned and walked to the bus stop for down town.

Ruth, here I come. I hope you are there and glad to see me.

12:20PM
Abercrombie and Fitch
Seattle, Washington

Breathing deeply after walking up hill for two blocks from the bus stop, Lee paused to catch his breath and checked the name on the building.

Yep. This be the one.

He turned to the door, hesitated because the butterflies were roaring rampantly in his belly, then pressed down on the brass thumb latch and pushed in. He set his sea bag down, gym bag on top, removed his white hat, and set it on the gym bag.

Lee stepped to a young lady at the nearest desk who was staring at him with wide-open eyes.

"Excuse me, Miss . . .

"Ooooo, you're Lee, you're Lee Stewart," she gasped and gulped. A deep breath and whooped: "Ruth, Ruth, come quick," she shouted. The rest of the office staff, all ladies, looked up. All their voices rose in unison, chanting, "Ruth Ruth Ruth."

Stewart's eye popped as he looked one way, then another at all the women calling out her name. A curious Ruth and another woman peered around the corner to learn what the excitement was.

Ruth froze momentarily as she recognized Lee. She shrieked his name, dropping papers and folders, and ran across the office. Lee had only a second to brace himself as Ruth collided with him, and held him tight.

"Lee, oh Lee, you're home." She began crying in relief and happiness as she began to feel the warmth and hardness of his lean body. Ruth buried her head in his neck and kept crying and calling out his name. Lee, a little overwhelmed, kissed the top of her head, stroked her hair with one hand and her back with the other while he murmured in her ear.

Then she leaned back and looked into his grinning face.

"Hey baby, I'm here." Lee leaned down to give her a warm kiss. Ruth pulled his head down and began to kiss his face and lips. All the women in the office began clapping and cheering. Ruth and Lee burst apart and looked around in embarrassment. Ruth slipped her hand in Lee's and looked up into his face with shining eyes.

"Everybody, this is Lee Stewart, my friend."

Raucous laughter greeted that announcement.

"I mean," she stammered, "this is my boy friend."

That didn't help one bit. Bantering and teasing slipped into high gear with several suggestions hinting at what Lee was going to give Ruth. His erection was strong and quite evident against his left trouser leg. Lee watched the ladies teasing Ruth and realized she was very popular in her office.

Holy Toledo! I wonder if she passed my letters around the office. It's for sure my picture has made the rounds.

Ruth tugged on his hand and led him back to her office and shut the door.

There's the answer: my photo is on her desk in a silver frame.

"We've only got just a second, Lee. I want your hands all over me so I know it's true. You're back home again. Why didn't you let me know?"

"Ruth, the ship was decommissioned at 9AM, and I was on a bus to Yokohama for the General Mann at noon. I never had a chance to write. Besides, isn't this more fun?"

Lee wasted no time in sliding his hands over her breasts and rubbing them until he was sure her nipples stood out. Hands continued to slide down front and back, claiming her. She reached down and squeezed him. Grabbing his hands and pulling them to her shoulders, she moved in close against his throbbing hardness, and they kissed softly and tenderly, then broke apart.

"When can you get off, honey?" Her eyes flashed lavender fire as he said honey.

"I'll find out." She picked up the phone and began dialing, listened, and handed him the phone. "Talk to my mother," and she walked back into the front office.

"Hello?" The voice was very much like Ruth's.

"Hello, Mrs. Verlock. This is Lee Stewart on this fine day. How are you?"

"Lee? Where are you?"

"Sitting at Ruth's desk. Came in on the big transport this morning."

"That's wonderful. What are your immediate plans, Lee?" He hesitated, trying to read meaning.

"I mean, can you stay with us for a few days? Are you passing through?

Or what?

"We'd certainly like to sit around and hear some of your stories."

"Well, I guess it's up to Ruth. I think she'd like me to stay, but . . .

"Lee, you have the run of our house. Please come stay with us for a while." Moistness gathered in the corners of Lee's eyes.

"Mrs. Verlock, Ruth is finding out when she can leave, right now." Ruth reached over his head and took the phone.

"Mom, I'm off. We'll be home in about a half an hour. Bye," and hung up. "Come on, sailor boy. We have to make the grand departure through the front door. And I have a special request from the girls for you."

"What's that?" with a puzzled look on his face.

"The girls want to see you put your sea bag on your shoulder and walk out. They also got a good look at your butt and want another look to tide them over."

"You're kiddin'!" he protested with a wide grin.

"No. Your uniform is well tailored and shows off your muscles and certain bulges very well. Those ribbons are a nice touch, too. They want to get an eyeful of you." She laughed, "And that's all they get!"

These women are coo-coo. But, I'll play their game and do it up brown.

They walked into the outer office. Lee's hardon was beginning to soften but its outline was strong on his leg. He set his white hat properly and checked the ceiling for clearance. Lee reached down for the canvas strap handle in the middle of his white seabag, heaved it up onto his shoulder with ease of much practice, and squatted for the gym bag. He heard low moans from around the room and chuckled.

These women are just the same as men. Want to see it all.

Lee swung around to smile at everyone.

"Thanks for taking care of my girl, ladies. See you later." More friendly catcalls. Lee opened the door for Ruth and followed her out. As usual, he held the sea bag balanced by lightly touching the top end, stuck out in front of him.

"Okay Lee, how long before your next assignment?"

"I have four days travel time to San Diego, and thirty days annual leave. Sometime before midnight on November eighteenth, I report aboard the U.S.S. Perkins DDR-877, for duty."

"Uh huh! How long are you going to stay here with me—and my folks?"

"Luscious, I don't want to put your folks out. That's a hell of a burden your folks would have to carry." He paused shakily for a moment. "We getting into some serious stuff before we've even had a chance to shake hands or anything." It was starting to rain and they ducked into a doorway for a breather.

"Sweetie, you aren't going to have time to shake hands with me. So put that out of your mind." She gripped his hand tightly as they walked around the corner to her car.

"Won't your folks have something to say about that?" Lee could see an embarrassing encounter coming up.

"I'll bet Mom is cooking something special for you right now, buster. I am going to have a brief conversation with them this evening—much later." She frowned as she stuck her key in the trunk and opened it. Lee dropped his seabag in it and closed the lid. She handed him the keys. He refused them.

"No way, Ruth. I haven't driven in the States in a long time and can't handle it, yet. You gotta drive." She nodded, unlocked and opened her door, removed her coat to toss it in the back, and slid across the seat to open his door. Ruth moved back just far enough for Lee to get in and shut the door.

Then she crawled up into his lap and curled up. They held each other, petting and kissing for a little while until the windows were completely fogged up. Now she reached behind her shoulders, did something, and shrugged. She squirmed around until the front of her dress was open like a scoop, and leaned forward reaching inside.

Suddenly, both beautiful breasts were there for the tasting.

Oh Lawd a Mercy, Luscious!

She kept pressing his face in and back and forth. Finally, she leaned back and pushed him away.

"Lee Stewart, that is as close as you're going to get to shaking hands. Now help me reorganize my inners and outers so Mom won't notice anything except my lipstick all over your face."

Martha Verlock readily admitted to being 44 years old and weighed in the neighborhood of 130 pounds but she wasn't telling anyone. She had emerald green eyes and gray hair, and stood five feet, six inches tall. She refused to use hair coloring, saying it wasn't dignified. She was less serious than her husband.

Those around her were used to her mothering tactics and great culinary abilities. If she wasn't cleaning the house for her husband or attending many of her community and social activities during the day, you could find Martha in her roomy kitchen, baking something delicious or cooking dinner.

"That was a wonderful dinner, Mrs. Verlock." It's been a very long time since I ate anything as good as that." Ruth smiled at Lee and watched her mother blush with pleasure.

"Lee, we're all so happy that you're back. I just wanted to do something very special. You didn't give me too much warning, you know."

Benjamin and Martha had one child—Ruth, on whom they had doted on since she was born. Since her run-in with the bum who beat her horribly, they were more conscious of her free spirited behavior and were alarmed by it. While Ruth was a grown young woman, she was, after all, still their only daughter.

"Okay, Mrs. Verlock. I told Ruth I didn't have a chance to warn her. Everything moved so fast once the Hoquiam was decommissioned. Can I help clean up the table and kitchen?" Ruth laughed and Mr. Verlock growled as he stood up.

"Lee, let's go into the living room for a smoke. I have some interesting sherry decanted in there," he said with a pleased smile. He led the way into the other room.

"I don't believe I've ever had sherry, Mr. Verlock."

"That's fine, Lee. This wine is the sipping kind so you can savor the taste."

Benjamin Verlock at 46, stood five feet, ten inches tall, and weighed 163 pounds. He had blue eyes and a full head of black hair, cut in a bowl cut. At home, he generally wore a pair of worn out brown cord trousers, a Pendleton long sleeved shirt, covered by a disreputable green sweater. The sweater was special, given to him by his wife Martha many years ago.

Mr. Verlock walked directly to the sideboard without further talking. Glancing up at Lee, he selected two small crystal wineglasses and filled them from one of the crystal and silver decanters.

He picked up the glasses and carried them to Lee who was admiring the fire burning in the brick fireplace. Ben thrust a glass at Lee and motioned him to sit down in the overstuffed chair opposite him.

"Take a load off your feet, Lee, and enjoy the fire. Our womenfolk are busy in the kitchen and will leave us alone for awhile."

Our womenfolk?

"Thank you, Mr. Verlock . . ."

"That's another thing, Lee; my name is Benjamin. Call me Ben, please."

"Okay Ben. You know, sir, we talked all about the Hoquiam, the Korean War, Yokosuka, Sasebo, and me over dinner. What about you? What kind of work are you in?" While he talked, Lee was looking around the room, somewhat put off by its brownness. The room wasn't stuffy so much as gloomy.

Ben pulled a pipe out and began stuffing it with tobacco. "I work for Northern Pacific Railroad in the Classification Yard as a Dispatcher." Striking a match, he puffed and puffed as the flame alternately flared up and retreated.

Shaking the match out, he continued. "I set up the order of rolling stock that makes up the consist of a train. Always something different. Know anything about trains?"

"Only a little, Ben. Had the beginnings of a HO model railroad layout started when I joined the Navy. Guess the folks have stored my stuff somewhere."

"Ah ha! One of the other dispatchers set up a model of our classification yard to play with. He invited a bunch of people over for a potluck dinner. Really, he wanted his co-workers to see it and try out some switching games.

"The Division Superintendent heard about it and asked to see the layout. He was so impressed he talked the dispatcher into selling that layout to Northern Pacific Railroad. He had it installed in an unoccupied office at the Classification Yard as a training device."

"Yeah, I had heard that was happening in a lot of railroad companies. There was a story in the Model Railroader magazine about it. Sure would be nice to see." Lee had never tasted sherry before and sniffed it before he took a tiny sip of the smooth sherry.

That's pretty good stuff.

He reached for his cigarettes, then looked at Ben with a question in his eyes. Ben nodded. Lee pulled out a cigarette, lit up and took a deep drag. Then he settled back in the chair and relaxed.

"Ruth told us last year your home is in Bremerton. Are you going home in a couple of days? Would you like to call your folks?"

She didn't tell them all that much, I see.

"My home was in Bremerton. Dad was ordered to another ship in Norfolk, Virginia. Once they moved, I didn't have a home base anymore." Ben's eyebrows shot up in surprise. "Nowadays, my home is where I hang my white hat aboard ship. Anyhow, I called Mom from Pier 91 before I came out to Ruth's office."

"Want to talk with you a bit, Lee. You up to some serious conversation?" Lee looked up, a little startled.

"Well, I suppose so. What about?" he answered apprehensively.

Ben laughed out loud. Stopped, then chuckled for a few seconds. "I suppose that did come across a little strong. No, Lee, I'm not asking your intentions about my daughter. I'm just wondering if you've thought about what you want to do when you get out of the Navy, that sort of thing. For example, are you interested in railroading as a career?"

"Well, that might be a good way to go later. The Navy is my career. I've got about seventeen years to go before I consider retiring from the Navy—four and a half years on this hitch yet."

Lee laughed under his breath. He didn't see the surprised look on Ben's face. "The Reservists aboard the Hoquiam thought it was horrible and called me a Lifer." Ben took his pipe out of his mouth and pointed it at Lee.

"You really mean you plan on staying in the Navy for twenty years?"

"Yes sir. Maybe more. I hope to become a commissioned officer, but even if I don't, I'll have no problem making Chief one of these days."

Ben shrugged, slightly bowed his head, and looked up at Lee through his eyebrows. "So, then, is Ruth just a passing fancy? A port in any storm?"

Wow! Now we get to it!

Lee shifted around and sat closer to the edge of his chair, so he was looking squarely at Ben. "Ben, I'm going to lay it on the line. However, let me put this first. In one sense, that isn't any of your business."

Ben clearly frowned and sat deeper in his overstuffed dark brown chair, puffing furiously.

"But on the other hand, protection of your family, that is your business. I take it this is a private conversation between us?"

Ben shook his head. "Martha really wants to know and I will tell her after we go to bed tonight." Lee nodded.

"I do hope you know I have pretty deep feelings for Ruth, Ben. I get the very strong impression Ruth feels the same. The main question seems to be: are we on a positive collision course, or are we passing in the night. I don't have an answer for you right now." Ben's frown deepened.

"But, get this, Ben. I'm only twenty and cannot even sign a contract for another three months. Did you know that in the state of Washington, I can't get married without my parents written permission until I reach my majority at twenty-one?" Ben shook his head in surprise. "Also, I'm only a Seaman, an E-3, making ninety-five dollars a month with sea pay and clothing allowance. That is not enough to support a family." Ben agreed, nodding his head.

"In a few months, I take the exam for Radioman, Petty Officer Third Class, and I am confident I will make it. That brings me up to about one twenty-five a month.

"The Navy stipulates that if a sailor marries before he is a Second Class, the Navy will not grant a marriage subsistence allotment." He felt someone sit down on the overstuffed arm of his chair. He knew it was Ruth.

"However, upon making Second Class Petty Officer, and being married, the Navy will take part of my pay and add $77.10 to it for my wife. When there are two or more children, that subsistence increases to $96.90.

I cannot make Second Class before late 1953. Have to have so much time in grade to advance, and not only that, be recommended by my command to take and pass a Navy-wide competitive written examination."

Lee felt Ruth's trembling hand slide across and rest lightly on the back of his neck. He heard Mrs. Verlock walk in and stop just at the edge of his sight.

"Having said all that Ben, it still doesn't really answer what you didn't ask out loud. For what it is worth, Ruth is the best thing that has happened to me in my life. She's worth more than Rice Crispies to me." Ruth's fingernails dug into the back of his neck. "And that, Ben, is as far as I want to go now. Is that enough?"

Martha interjected, "It most certainly is. More than enough. Ben Verlock, what on earth did you ask Lee? Did you ask his intentions?"

Ben looked uncomfortable. "We were just talking, Martha, and somehow it came down to whether he could afford to keep our daughter."

Not exactly, but close enough!

Ruth stirred restlessly, not saying a word, but walked stiffly to the fireplace and poked at the fire. She stayed quiet as her mother glared at her father.

"Mom and Dad, let's go into the Parlor to the two sofas. You two take one and we'll sit in the other. Then, ask what you will. Cause when you finish, I'll have something to say.

Oh man, can her eyes flash fire when she is angry.

Ruth strode out of the room, disappearing.

"Lee, I think it best if you begin to call me Martha right now. Will you do that?"

"Yes Ma'am, ahh Martha," said a slightly tense Lee.

She took his arm, lifting and tossing her head at Ben in anger. She patted his arm as they walked out of the Living Room.

The Parlor was a formal room with two sofas opposite each other, and two stuffed chairs at each end, forming a box. Little tables with table lamps were located at each corner of the chairs and sofas.

Ruth was already sitting on one of the sofas and reached out for Lee. Martha went around turning on a few low-level wall lamps and sat down exactly opposite Ruth. Ben came in and sat down rigidly next to Martha. He knew he was in trouble with two women, maybe Lee, too.

The room was stuffy without airflow. It took a little while for Lee to realize this formal room was from another era, and seldom used, except for very formal occasions.

"Well Mother—Dad, shall we continue the inquisition?"

Oh, she is pissed!

"Ruth, we are only interested in your happiness and welfare. I think we have a right to know more about this man," said Martha plaintively.

At least, she's calling me a man, not a boy.

"I think Lee handled himself very well trying to respond to some of my tough questions, Ruth. He's a good boy—

Really!

—who has been in battle and came out a man. He is certainly not the same fellow we met at Seaside over a year ago."

Thank you, Ben.

Ruth's breast heaved as she took a deep breath. "Have you two any idea that Lee has written over one hundred letters to me?" They both shook their heads in surprise. "In all those letters, we talked out a lot of ideas about the future. I'll be glad to show you the stack if you don't believe me." They shook their heads rapidly. "Right answer. Right up there with I believe you, Ruth."

"Ruth, we just . . ."

"You're not getting off the hook that easily. How come you never asked my intentions about Lee?"

"Well, Ruth . . ."

"Don't you dare ask me that question. I'm almost twenty-three, Mom. I can and have been making my own decisions since I started working at Abercrombie. Lee's the best thing that has happened to me, too. Better than Oatmeal with raisins." Lee snickered at the play on Rice Crispies. She looked over at Lee and took his hand.

"Right now, as Lee is home, we're the best thing we have. Neither one of us know if this is going to be a lasting thing. And neither one of us is ready to force the issue. Lee has thirty days leave he can spend here with us, or Lee and I can go to San Diego until he has to report in." Lee's heart thudded hard.

Did she just imply what I think she said? Oh man, she can be fierce!

"The shoe is on the other foot, my parents that I so dearly love. Are you going to let us enjoy a honeymoon here, or do I pack now?" Ben sank low on the sofa.

Martha, who had been sitting quietly with her hands folded on her lap, looked across at her daughter. "Ruth dear, if you will check the basement bedroom, you will find I made the bed with two pillows." Then she turned to Lee.

"I do hope we haven't spoiled your celebration and homecoming, Lee. We enjoyed your letters to us. You have done a lot to boost Ruth's ego when she was down." She looked at Ben who was looking at her with a stunned look on his face.

"Oh, for crying out loud, Ben, think back to 1929, and in the Depression, and our own decisions," she snapped in exasperation. Ruth stared at her mother in surprise and counted, obviously, on her fingers, then slowly nodded her head and smiled back at her mother.

"Sometimes, Ruth, we slept in fields or under trees. The most money we had at one time in 1932 was one whole dollar in brass tokens from picking crops. Mostly, our money was pennies, nickels, and dimes. Seeing a quarter was big money. Better things began when Ben landed a job with Northern Pacific as a gandy dancer." She paused, looking at her daughter Ruth and Ruth's man, Lee. "Good night."

She stood up and smoothed her dress. "Come, Ben, its time for us to go to bed."

Ruth and Lee sat still, looking at each other, not touching.

"Lee, you go downstairs. I want you to shave before I get there. I have some things I need from my room. Then, why don't we take a shower and start out fresh?"

KNOCK OFF SHIP'S WORK

0904, 26 August 1968
U.S.S. Northampton (CC-1)
Pier 7, Naval Operating Base
Norfolk, Virginia

Ship's Current Operational Status:
Officer of the Deck at Forward Quarterdeck
National Emergency Command Post Afloat: Staff aboard.
Special Sea Detail: Manned and ready
Four boilers on line
Ship-Shore connections removed
After gangway removed
Forward gangway present
All lines singled up, starboard side to
Two navy tugs standing by, Port side amidships

Lee Harrison Stewart, ramrod straight, exactly six feet tall in his stocking feet, stood in front of the mirror in his small stateroom. He critically examined his appearance for any kind of blemish. He was in the Uniform of the Day for officers and chiefs: khaki trousers and short-sleeved khaki shirt without black tie.

Gold and silver Senior Chief Petty Officer devices gleamed at the tips of his Dacron shirt collar. Three rows of service ribbons adorned his chest just above the left shirt pocket. Sharply creased gabardine trousers fitted with a khaki web belt and brass buckle hung from his waist. Highly polished brown shoes and a combination hat with khaki cover completed his uniform. Stewart, a Radioman in the United States Navy, attained the rank of Senior Chief Petty Officer four years ago.

He picked up his brand new, gray ID card, serial number 0001961. This ID card would become effective as soon as he stepped across the brow, leaving the ship this morning. Senior Chief Stewart had felt his pucker string draw tight when he gave up his green ID card a few minutes ago. Since he had a moment, he took the time to study every entry on the new ID card.

His photograph was less than an hour old. Expiration Date: Indefinite.

Until I die, that is.

Weight: 183. Grinning, he recalled the day he graduated from Boot Camp back in May 1949. At that time, he weighed 149-1/2 pounds: a half-pound lighter than the day he joined.

Holy Toledo, it must be the good life!

Chuckling, he reached for his wallet and stuffed the ID card in it. His phone rang.

"Senior Chief Stewart speaking, sir."

"This is the Captain. I thought I would catch you there, Senior Chief. Just wanted to pass along my best wishes, and that of the command, to your new life as a civilian. Good luck, Mr. Stewart."

Stewart chuckled appreciatively. "Thank you, Captain. It has been a good life but it is time to move along. Have a good career, Captain, and catch some stars." He listened as the Captain hung up, clamped his own phone in its holder, and smiled broadly, just glad the Captain had taken time to call him from the Bridge. After 7,131 days and 19 hours, his active duty career in the United States Navy was ending.

Senior Chief Stewart picked up his combination hat by the top and glanced around his stateroom. This had been his home away from home for the past two years. Looking in the washbasin mirror one last time, he donned his hat, flicked the lights off, and pounded up the ladder two flights to the Second Deck Port Passageway.

Sailors in their dungarees or undress blues smiled and waved at him as he made his way aft to the Chiefs' Mess. Their comments rang in his ears as he struggled with his composure.

"Good luck, Senior Chief."

"See ya round, Chief."

"Not going to make a career out of it, huh, Chief?"

Another chief punched Stewart's shoulder as he hurried to his Special Sea and Anchor Detail duties. The news of his retirement had been in this morning's Snortin' Nort'n newspaper.

He, Ruth, his wife of 15 years, and their four kids had come aboard this morning from their beach campsite for breakfast. This was the last time they would enjoy a meal in the Chiefs' Mess. Though they had been aboard for dinner and ridden the Northampton motor launch several times, the kids knew this was very special.

The four blond, blue-eyed kids, Anne Joyce, Ronald Herbert, John Stuart, and Charles Jimmy, sat solemnly, eyes darting everywhere, eating their scrambled eggs, bacon, pancake, and orange juice breakfast without a word. They listened to other Chiefs kidding their Dad as he ate his breakfast. His wife kept reaching under the table to give his hand or thigh a squeeze of love, happiness, and reassurance. She knew this had been an agonizing decision for him.

Senior Chief Stewart excused himself for a moment and walked over to the senior compartment cleaner. "Jonesy, take this for you and someone else," he said handing him two bills. "Go to my stateroom, grab my gear, and take it out to my red Rambler station wagon, please. The tailgate is unlocked."

Jones nodded, looking at the two Five-Dollar bills in his hand. "No sweat, Senior Chief. We'll have everything out there in a couple of minutes." He motioned to another Compartment Cleaner and they hurried up the ladder.

The Chief Master-At-Arms moved restlessly by the ladder, glancing at the Stewart family.

"Come on, Stew. Gotta hustle. The Captain is already on the Bridge waiting for your departure."

Stewart nodded to the few shipmates remaining in the Chiefs' Mess and ushered his family in front of him. Master Chief Boatswain's Mate Henley, the Chief Master-At-Arms, hurried the Stewart's forward to the Executive Officer's Stateroom and knocked on the door.

"Come."

Master Chief Henley opened the door and stood aside to let the Stewart family enter first. Commander Earles looked up at Senior Chief Stewart and his family, placed his pen in its stand, stood, and smiled.

"Good morning, Commander. May I present my wife, Ruth Stewart and our children, Anne, Ronald, John, and Charles?" Commander Earles shook Mrs. Stewarts's hand and patted Charles on the head.

"It'll be good to spend more time with these great looking kids, Senior Chief. Any nibbles to those resumes you mailed out?"

"Yes sir, Commander. Got three negatives and two possibles. I'm going to look them over in a week or so."

"Well, good luck out there. It's a cruel world."

"And the same to you, Commander. I understand it's a cruel world in here," he grinned.

Commander Earles laughed, and picked up an envelope and plaque from his desk. Stewart accepted his Fleet Reserve sheepskin and a plaque of the Northampton and shook hands with the Commander.

The Chief Master-At-Arms herded the Stewarts out, guiding the family onto the Port Main Deck and forward across to the Officers' Starboard Quarterdeck. Seventeen Communications Department junior officers stood at attention in one rank, waiting to say good-bye to Senior Chief Stewart.

He stepped along, smiling stiffly, shaking hands, and mumbling small words of good-bye. He heard, rather than saw, Master Chief Henley escort his family onto the gangway landing where they would have a good view. His throat was beginning to tighten and ache, his pulse quickened, his belly began thumping, and water trickled from his armpits.

The Assistant Communications Officer, Lieutenant Finster, an old Mustang and good friend, nudged him with a thumb behind his elbow and whispered, "Turn around and look up, Stew."

Lee looked up at the Captain on the Bridge who was watching and waiting. He nodded to Stewart. Nearly twenty years of conditioning dictated Stewart's next move. He snapped to attention, saluted and held until the Captain returned his salute. Lee smiled and nodded back.

Lee dropped his gaze to the Cigarette Deck just above. Most of his 137 chiefs and sailors stood watching him.

No, that's not true. They're not mine anymore. Must be getting windy. My eyes are blurring.

He quickly straightened and saluted them casually, certainly no less respectfully, not daring to speak.

I'll miss them.

He tried to clear his throat as he turned to the Officer of the Deck, but it was too tight and dry. It hurt to swallow.

Senior Chief Lee Harrison Stewart saluted smartly, hand and forearm stiff and straight, touching the glossy bill of his combination hat, and asked with a somewhat choked voice: "I have been relieved of my Naval duties. Permission to leave the ship, sir?"

With the traditional long glass tucked under his left arm, the Officer of the Deck, just as smartly, returned Senior Chief Stewart's salute and gave him the standard response: "Permission granted, Senior Chief," and softly added, "Bon Voyage."

Senior Chief Douglas turned toward the gangway. A Boson's Pipe pipped shrilly four times. Eight Chiefs stepped forward as Honorary Side Boys.

Oh Lordy, here we go.

He kept his wet eyes focused on the gangway and began walking toward it. Again, this time long and sweet, the Boson's Pipe sang its three-note song. His belly began pounding; his armpits and sides were already wet.

The Chiefs, Officer of the Deck, and seventeen officers raised their hands in salute.

The Bos'uns pipe sounded attention over the 1MC:

"Senior Chief Radioman Stewart departing."

Stupid tears in full flow now; no place for damage control.

Stewart returned their salute, pivoted and saluted the Colors on the Fantail. Then he turned again and stepped off the ship onto the brow's landing.

It's over!

Lee herded his family down the stairway from the ship.

The Quartermaster of the Watch wrote the event into the Rough Log.

> **0921 SENIOR CHIEF RADIOMAN LEE H. STEWART 392-51-44 USN, PIPED OVER THE SIDE INTO THE U.S. NAVAL FLEET RESERVE.**

As the Stewarts descended, Douglas heard another call and voice announcement over the 1MC, for the last time.

"Now hear this, the Officer of the Deck is shifting his watch to the Bridge."

The Stewarts began to settle in their car while a civilian crane operator lifted the gangway from the forward brow. They sat in the car and watched as the Northampton pulled in her lines.

The Captain looked at his Sea Detail Officer of the Deck. He cleared his throat and asked, "How was that ceremony, Mr. Ebons?"

Lieutenant Ebons looked at the Captain pensively. "I do not believe Senior Chief Stewart really wanted to leave, Captain. The water works were on strong."

He cleared his throat and said, "Wish I had known the Chief. Obviously, the Comm Department J.O.'s were fond—yes, fond of him. As well as his department personnel." He thought for a minute. "I am puzzled why Lieutenant Commander Bowman wasn't there to see him off," shaking his head.

The Captain looked at Ebons in amusement. "You didn't know there was bad blood between the two? The Chief showed up Bowman at least twice that I know of. Mr. Bowman is not a forgiving man. He refused to recommend Stewart for Master Chief. Rather petty, I thought. You did not hear that, understand?" Lieutenant Ebons nodded.

The Captain looked around, saw the brow was cleared. "Mr. Ebons, let's get the show on the road. Time for us to take National Emergency Command Post, Afloat (NECPA) duty for the next six weeks."

"Aye aye, Captain." He turned and addressed the required Pilot. "Take us out, Andy."

Andy nodded and walked to the far side of the Open Bridge, raised his portable radio and gave instructions to the two tugs.

Senior Chief Stewart's emotions were as colors of the rainbow. Panicky, he wanted to call out: wait, wait for me. Never before had he seen his ship get underway without being on her.

"Shift colors—Shift colors."

Three loud blasts roared harshly from the ship's horn as the U.S.S. Northampton (CC-1), began backing into the James River for another six-week patrol.

"Mommy, Daddy's crying!" called Anne.

Ruth's face wrinkled in a frown. This was a side of her husband she had never seen before. "Shhh. This is a sad and important day for Daddy. He's saying good-bye to the Navy and he is going to miss his ship."

Senior Chief Radioman Lee Harrison Stewart, watching his ship back into the James River, had just become a member of the United States Navy Fleet Reserve at the age of 37. He would draw half pay of a Senior Chief every month for the rest of his life, beginning at $273.00 per month. His final DD-214-N showed he had accumulated 19 years, 6 months, and 12 days of active service, with credit for 15 additional days. Stewart had served seven tours of duty aboard ships, six tours ashore on various stations, including four years in a joint command, and attended two schools.

Stewart collected a Good Conduct Medal with four stars, the Navy Occupation Service Medal (Japan), the China Service Ribbon, the National Defense Service Medal with one star, the Korean Service Medal with six stars representing amphibious landings, battles, and campaigns along the Northeast Coast of Korea, the United Nations Medal with Korean Bar, and the South Korean Presidential Unit Citation.

There were several Letters of Commendation for Meritorious Service in his Service Record. The Navy was never big on medals. When you are a part of the whole, fighting in a ship, it is difficult for an individual to stand so far above the rest to receive special recognition.

Lee served on the USS HOQUIAM PF-5 and USS PERKINS DDR-877 in the Korean War. Both ships exchanged gunfire with North Korean and Chinese Communist army batteries. Everyone aboard helped fire those salvos blasting the Communist batteries. On the flip side, everyone sweat out the Communist gunfire trying to hit and sink the ships.

It didn't matter that the Communist shells hit one of those ships and machine gun bullets hit the other ship. His ships won those encounters and the Communists lost. You just did your duty where and when it counted.

A short time after Stewart transferred to the Fleet Reserve, the Department of Defense issued the Vietnam freeze. DoD canceled all Honorable Discharges, transfers to the Navy Fleet Reserve, and Retirements. By the blindass luck of the draw, his timing to retire was perfect.

On October 16, 1968, Congress's new pay raise for U. S. Military service personnel went into effect. It was by far the best pay raise in American Military history.

The Stewarts, happily singing in their red '67 American Motors Rambler station wagon, raced madly back to their bright yellow double sidewall Sears tent at Hampton Roads Beach State Park. They were camping and sightseeing for a week on a well-earned family vacation. Senior Chief Stewart slipped out of his uniform and folded it for the last time.

Hurrying, Lee shoved his legs into an outrageous pair of blue and green shorts his wife had picked out for him, grabbed his binoculars, and ran across the dunes to his family on the beach.

Lee Stewart came to an abrupt halt, staring at the gray silhouette of the Northampton in Hampton Roads, outbound. Picking up speed, she gradually lost definition in the mist. Just for a fleeting second through wet eyes, the distant ship seemed to change shape to the old Hocky Maru from the Korean War.

He gazed rigidly for a moment as the Northampton faded completely, and then stared off into the sea. Lee shook his head and blinked rapidly. He sank to the sand by his wife and looked at her.

"You know Hon, if I had to do it all over, I would."

Ruth reached over, nuzzled his neck and kissed him, all the while secretly smiling with relief. Lee stared out at the ocean and thought back with amazement:

Was it really eighteen years since he left Tongue Point for the USS Hoquiam PF-5—the old Hocky Maru? You know, someone ought to write a story about those Patrol Frigates.

This is the end of the story. You may join Stewart at the beginning of the story as he joins the Navy in,

"Of Sea Stories and Fairy Tales, The Time Before Hoquiam."

Author's Note. This last section is indeed my final hours in the Navy.

The events that take place in the other volumes are true to the best of my recollection, except no comment about the romance here and there. The people I worked with and for are not named or portrayed within these historical novels about life in the Navy below decks in 1949 through 1952.

One correction: The meeting between the Hoquiam and the Soviet task group never took place. There was scuttlebutt that a destroyer did meet up with a Soviet task group up there.

My Dad, Ivan Herbert Douglas, retired as a Commander in 1964. My introduction to the Navy began on Thanksgiving 1938 aboard his ship, the USS SARATOGA CV-3.

See my website, "hoquiampf5.com" for other information and period photographs.

Mark Douglas
Gardnerville, Nevada markdgls@me.com
September 2012